PEG AND ROSE PLAY THE PONIES

Books by Laurien Berenson

Melanie Travis Mysteries

A PEDIGREE TO DIE FOR
UNDERDOG
DOG EAT DOG
HAIR OF THE DOG
WATCHDOG
HUSH PUPPY
UNLEASHED
ONCE BITTEN
HOT DOG
BEST IN SHOW
JINGLE BELL BARK
RAINING CATS AND DOGS
CHOW DOWN
HOUNDED TO DEATH
DOGGIE DAY CARE MURDER
GONE WITH THE WOOF
DEATH OF A DOG WHISPERER
THE BARK BEFORE CHRISTMAS
LIVE AND LET GROWL
MURDER AT THE PUPPY FEST
WAGGING THROUGH THE SNOW
RUFF JUSTICE
BITE CLUB
HERE COMES SANTA PAWS
GAME OF DOG BONES
HOWLOWEEN MURDER
PUP FICTION
SHOW ME THE BUNNY
KILLER CUPID

A Senior Sleuths Mystery

PEG AND ROSE SOLVE A MURDER
PEG AND ROSE STIR UP TROUBLE
PEG AND ROSE PLAY THE PONIES

Published by Kensington Publishing Corp.

PEG AND ROSE PLAY THE PONIES

LAURIEN BERENSON

Kensington Publishing Corp.
www.kensingtonbooks.com

KENSINGTON BOOKS are published by

Kensington Publishing Corp.
900 Third Avenue
New York, NY 10022

All Kensington titles, imprints and distributed lines are available at special quantity discounts for bulk purchases for sales promotion, premiums, fund-raising, educational or institutional use. Special book excerpts or customized printings can also be created to fit specific needs. For details, write or phone the office of the Kensington Special Sales Manager: Kensington Publishing Corp., 900 Third Ave., New York, NY 10022. Attn. Special Sales Department. Phone: 1-800-221-2647.

KENSINGTON and the KENSINGTON COZIES teapot logo Reg. US Pat. & TM Off.

Library of Congress Control Number: 2024932362

ISBN: 978-1-4967-4668-9

First Kensington Hardcover Edition: July 2024

ISBN: 978-1-4967-4670-2 (ebook)

10 9 8 7 6 5 4 3 2 1

Printed in the United States of America

PEG AND ROSE PLAY THE PONIES

Chapter 1

"Have I ever mentioned that I own a horse?" Peg Turnbull asked.

She'd arrived at the Gallagher House to visit her sister-in-law, Rose Donovan, and had been directed around the back of the narrow, three-story building in downtown Stamford, Connecticut. Originally a home, the house now served as a women's shelter that was owned and operated by Rose and her husband, Peter.

"No, you haven't." Rose looked up as Peg walked around the side of the building and used the question to announce her presence. Trust Peg to make an unusual entrance.

Rose was a slender woman in her late sixties, with angular features and short gray hair that she wore tucked behind her ears. At the moment, she was holding a rake in her hands. Peg had no idea why.

The tiny yard behind the shelter consisted mostly of hard packed dirt with a few scraggly tufts of grass. The only spot of color was a row of tomato plants growing near the tall fence that separated the property from its neighbor. Peg couldn't see anything in the area that called for the implementation of a rake.

Then again, she'd just arrived. Perhaps enlightenment would be forthcoming.

"And now that you are mentioning it," Rose continued, "I'm not sure I believe you. I've been to your house on numerous occasions. If you had a horse there, I'm quite certain I would have noticed."

"Lucky Luna doesn't live with me," Peg replied. "In fact, she doesn't even live in Connecticut."

"Good." Rose nodded. "At your age, you shouldn't be galloping around anyway."

Peg was in her seventies, a few years older than Rose. Apart from that, the two women had few similarities. Peg was taller in stature and broad through the shoulders. Not only did she possess a bigger build, Peg also had the forceful personality to match.

"No one is galloping anywhere on Luna," Peg said. "She's a Thoroughbred broodmare, boarding at a farm in Kentucky. Every year or so, she produces a foal."

"That sounds like more than one horse," Rose commented. "Years add up, you know."

Peg's lips flattened. They were both well aware of that.

"Are your foals adding up too?"

"No, and that's actually why I'm here."

"So there's a reason for your visit." Rose smiled to soften the words, which had come out sounding sharper than she'd intended. Then she abruptly went still. "Please tell me you're not offering me a horse."

"Would you accept it if I were?"

"Of course not." Rose was half-afraid Peg might be serious. When she was around, you never knew what might happen next.

Though they'd been related for more than fifty years, Rose and Peg had spent the majority of that time pointedly not speaking to each other. A few months earlier, they'd finally managed to rectify that situation. Even so, their relationship wasn't all smooth sailing. Dealing with Peg, Rose often felt like she was rocketing down the slope of a rather steep learning curve.

"Not even a cute foal?" Peg prodded. "Maybe an equine companion for Marmalade?"

Marmalade was Rose's kitten. What Peg thought Marmie might do with a baby horse, Rose had no idea. And certainly no desire to find out.

"Marmie gets plenty of companionship from me and Peter. Not to mention the women who come through the shelter," she said. "Now stop teasing and tell me why you're really here."

Two plastic lawn chairs had been placed side by side in the middle of the yard. Peg took one and gestured toward the other. "Put down your rake and let's sit for a minute."

Rose looked down at the tool as if she'd forgotten she was holding it. She leaned it against the fence, then walked over to join Peg.

"What were you doing with that thing anyway?" Peg asked, as Rose swished her lightweight cotton skirt to one side and sat down too.

"Raking leaves."

Peg frowned. She let her gaze travel slowly around the enclosed space. There were no leaves on the ground. It was much too early for that. "What leaves?"

"You know." Rose flapped a hand in the air. "In the yard. I'm tidying up."

"First of all, it's barely September. And second"—did Peg really have to point this out?—"you don't have a tree."

"Well, no. But our neighbor does."

Both women glanced at the large maple next door. Its spreading branches crossed over the wall between the two properties to shade a portion of the shelter's yard. Rose nodded as if she'd scored a major point.

Peg wasn't having it. "Yes, I see a tree. I can also see perfectly well that its leaves are still attached."

"You know me. I like to be proactive."

Peg stared. "I believe that's the dumbest thing you've

ever said. What's the real reason you're out here brandish-
ing a garden tool?"

Rose sighed and rolled her shoulders. "Peter's holding a
group counseling session in the living room this afternoon.
This one's about managing stress and conflict resolution.
As you might imagine, sometimes things get a little in-
tense. To stay out of the way, I decided to come out here
and make myself useful."

Useful. Peg eyed the rake again. She didn't think so.

"Also, I love my husband dearly, but sometimes I just
need a little space," Rose admitted. "You know?"

A nod seemed called for, so Peg obliged. But she didn't
know. Not really.

Her decades-long marriage to Rose's older brother, Max,
had been an utterly blissful period in her life. She and Max
were soulmates, content to share everything with each other.
They'd lived, loved, and worked as a team. At least that
was how Peg—who'd lost her husband to a heart attack
ten years earlier—remembered that time now.

"Space," she said briskly. "I can help with that."

"How?"

"I have an upcoming judging assignment at the Bluegrass Cluster in Lexington, Kentucky. That's four back-to-
back dog shows over Labor Day weekend."

"Three days from now?"

"Indeed." Peg nodded. "I'll be judging the Non-Sporting
Group on Saturday, then the Toy Group plus several Herding breeds on Sunday."

Not long ago, that explanation would have sounded
like gibberish to Rose. Now, sadly, she understood most of
it. But that still didn't offer a clue where she fit in.

"And?" she prompted.

"Remember Lucky Luna?"

"Of course I remember Lucky Luna. We were just talking about her two minutes ago."

"The foal she produced last year is now a yearling."

"As if I couldn't do the math," Rose muttered.

Peg ignored that and kept talking. "There are plenty of people who breed racehorses but have no interest in actually racing them. Those breeders sell their horses—usually when they're yearlings—to people who don't want to breed but do want to race."

Rose peered over at her. "That sounds like the beginning of a riddle. Or maybe a joke. Is there a punchline coming?"

"No, but what *is* coming is the Keeneland September Yearling Sale. It's the biggest sale of its kind in the world. And Lucky Luna's yearling is entered."

"To sell?" Rose guessed. She hoped she had that right.

"That's the plan," Peg confirmed. "In the time I've owned her, Luna has had two previous offspring go through the sale. The farm where she boards arranged everything for me and I watched the proceedings from afar on the Keeneland website. This time, with a judging assignment taking me to Lexington just a few days earlier, I intend to be on hand to observe the process in person. I thought you might want to go with me."

Rose blinked slowly. "To Kentucky."

"Right."

"In three days," she added.

"Actually one day," Peg corrected. "I'm going to drive rather than fly, which means it will take us a day to get there. Plus, I'd like to arrive a day early so I can visit Six Oaks, the farm where Lucky Luna lives."

One day!

Rose gulped. "Let me think about it."

"Oh pish. As you just pointed out, there's no time for that. Just say yes and pack your bags."

"No," Rose said firmly. "You can't just spring something on me like that and expect me to agree right away."

"Of course I can. I just did. Besides, you said yourself that you wouldn't mind getting away for a bit."

"I did not."

"You did." Peg sounded complacent, as if she was sure she'd already won. "I heard you. You said you needed some space."

"Yes, space—like thirty feet. Not a thousand miles."

"Actually, it's closer to seven hundred and fifty."

As if that was the point. Were Rose's teeth clamped together? It felt like they might be. Interacting with Peg often had that effect on her.

"What about your Poodles?" she asked, stalling for time. "Who will look after them?"

Peg blithely waved away that objection. "Hope will come with us, of course."

At the age of eleven, Hope was Peg's oldest Standard Poodle. She was also the one who was almost constantly at her side. At one time, Peg and Max's kennel had been filled with black Standard Poodles. Their Cedar Crest dogs had been known worldwide for their excellent quality and superb temperaments. They'd successfully exhibited their Poodles at numerous dog shows nearly every week of the year.

Now the kennel was gone and Peg was too busy with her judging career to breed more than the occasional litter. In addition to Hope, there were just two other Standard Poodles in her house. Coral and Joker were both young dogs. Coral had recently finished her championship, and Joker, who'd just turned a year old, was awaiting his turn to get back into the show ring.

"What about the other ones?" Rose asked.

Of course she remembered their names. Peg spoke about her Poodles often enough. She even made them sound like they were members of the family. Which irked Rose more than it should have—enough to make her want to annoy Peg by pretending ignorance.

"Coral and Joker," Peg supplied, rising to the jab as Rose had known she would. "They'll stay home with my dog sitter, Colleen. The Poodles adore her, which is a good thing considering how often I need to travel to shows. So everything's taken care of except you. I'm still waiting for an answer. Are you coming with me or not?"

Rose was running out of excuses, and they both knew it.

"I'll have to talk to Peter," she said. "And check my calendar. You know I often have other commitments . . ."

Trust Rose to want to arrange the fun out of everything, Peg thought. The woman was entirely too methodical. Maybe even a bit of a plodder. Peg, by comparison, was a free spirit, happy to be always on the go.

"What you really mean is that you need time to think of another reason to say no."

"Don't put words in my mouth." Rose frowned. "That's not what I said."

"Said about what?" Peter asked. He closed the shelter's door behind him and started down the back stairs. A thoughtful and deliberate man who wore his years well, he was stepping carefully to avoid the ginger-and-white kitten that was bouncing around his feet. Peter's warm brown eyes twinkled behind tortoiseshell glasses as he looked over at the two women. "Am I interrupting something?"

"Not at all," Peg said. "Please join us. I have a question for you."

Peter unfolded a third lawn chair that was leaning against the back of the building. He carried it over and put it beside theirs. As he sat down, Marmalade reared up to grab Peter's pant leg and use it as a scratching post. He gently disentangled the kitten's tiny claws, then turned to Peg. "I'm all ears."

Rose quickly jumped in before Peg had a chance to

speak. "Peg's going on a road trip to Kentucky. It sounds as though she'll be gone for at least a week. She thinks I should go with her, but I told her I have responsibilities here."

"You do," Peter replied carefully. "But there's nothing that can't be set aside long enough for you to take a small trip. I think you should go."

"You do?" Rose was surprised.

A few weeks earlier, she'd been involved in a serious accident. A glancing blow from a speeding car had sent her careening onto the hard pavement outside the shelter. Rose's injuries were mostly healed now, but Peter still continued to hover over her as though she were made of glass. She knew he meant well, but his solicitousness was beginning to drive her a little crazy. Under the circumstances, she'd just assumed he'd take her side.

"When are you leaving?" he asked Peg.

"The day after tomorrow. Up and out at the crack of dawn. I've made the trip before and it can be done in a single day as long as we don't dawdle."

Rose snorted under her breath. Peg drove like a speed fiend. Dawdling wasn't an option when she was behind the wheel.

Peter turned back to his wife. "This sounds like a wonderful idea to me. A nice, relaxing vacation is just what you need."

"Relaxing?" Rose said skeptically. "With Peg?"

"I can be relaxing," Peg said.

Nobody even bothered to reply to that.

Instead Peter changed the subject. "What's the purpose of your trip?"

"Dogs and horses," Peg said. "I'll be judging at two dog shows, then attending a Thoroughbred sale."

"It turns out Peg owns several racehorses," Rose added.

Peter had seen a great number of things in his life. He'd first been a priest, then a college professor, a missionary, and now the proprietor of a women's shelter. Not much surprised him anymore. This did. It was also a topic he knew almost nothing about.

"Racehorses?" he echoed faintly. "How unusual."

"The first one came to me as an unexpected bequest," Peg told him. "As you might imagine, I could hardly refuse."

"No, of course not." He pondered that, then added, "Are you selling a horse at the sale?"

"I am. It's the first time I'll have the opportunity to attend in person, and I'm looking forward to observing the process. I think Rose might enjoy it too."

"Except that I'm too busy to go," Rose said.

"Doing what, exactly?" Peg inquired.

"Cooking, cleaning, keeping the books . . ."

"Maura can handle everything but the accounting," Peter said. Their live-in housekeeper, Maura Nettles, was a whiz at keeping things running smoothly. "And that can wait until you get back."

"What about painting the third-floor hallway and arranging to have the gutters cleaned?"

"I'm sure Jason is on top of both those things." Hiring Jason Abercrombie as the shelter's new handyman had been an excellent decision. Among other things, it meant that Peter now had more free time to devote to his counseling sessions.

Rose blew out a breath. "So what you're saying is that I'm superfluous?"

"No." Peter's tone was gentle. "What I'm saying is that everyone here cares about you. And that we're ready to support you in any way you need. Your body may be almost recovered, but mental trauma can linger too. It might be good for you to get away and enjoy a change of scenery."

"Now you're just ganging up on me," Rose said irritably.

Peter shook his head. "We just want what's best for you. That's all."

When he put it like that, there wasn't much else Rose could say. She looked at Peg and nodded.

"I'm glad that's settled." Peg quickly stood up before Rose could change her mind. "You'll see," she told her. "This trip is going to be epic."

Chapter 2

"I've never been to the middle of the country before," Rose said.

Earlier she'd been the one driving. Now it was Peg's turn. That afforded Rose the opportunity to gaze avidly out the minivan's side window as they sped through central Kentucky. She marveled at the wide expanse of blue sky above them. Though it was late in the day, the sun was still high. It shined down on vast acres of open land, mostly green fields and gently rolling hills.

"I visited here several years ago, just after I inherited Lucky Luna," Peg said. "Kentucky is a beautiful state."

She paused to peek at the back seat where Hope was asleep with her muzzle nestled between her front paws. Now that she was older, her muzzle had turned gray and her eyesight wasn't as sharp as it had once been. Even so, the big Poodle was content. As long as she and Peg were together, Hope knew she would always be all right.

"I discovered that. Though the pictures online didn't do justice to the reality." Rose was still gazing from side to side. "Of course you only gave me one day's notice to research the state, so I might have missed something."

"I doubt it." Peg glanced over. When Rose had a task to do, she was nothing if not thorough. "You're probably better informed than I am. Tell me three fun facts about Kentucky."

"Number one, it's the horse capital of the world."

"That doesn't count." Peg scoffed. "Everybody knows that."

"I didn't," Rose said, then tried again. "There are more barrels of bourbon in the state than people."

Peg laughed. "Really?"

"Really. And actually, Kentucky isn't a state, it's a commonwealth. It's also the only commonwealth that isn't one of the thirteen original colonies."

"Meaning there are others?"

"Massachusetts, Pennsylvania, and Virginia," Rose told her.

"This is all very interesting." Peg loved learning new things. "Tell me more."

"The world's longest cave system is here. It's called Mammoth Cave and there are four hundred miles of interconnected caves."

"I'd love to see that." Peg turned on her signal and changed lanes. They were reaching the outskirts of Fayette County, where Lexington was located, and she didn't want to miss a turn. "Is it near Lexington?"

Rose didn't know. She got out her phone and looked it up. "Unfortunately, no. It's several hours away, heading in the other direction."

"That's a shame. We'll have to add it to our itinerary next time."

"Next time?" Rose looked up. "There's going to be a next time?"

"I should think so. After all, why not? As you're so aptly illustrating, Kentucky has a lot to commend it."

When the minivan slowed for the exit, Hope lifted her head. She blinked several times, then sat up and looked around as though she was trying to orient herself.

"I'm right here," Peg said gently. She reached a hand back between the front seats, running her fingers through the dense dark curls on Hope's shoulder. "I know it's been a long day. You've been very patient and we're almost there."

"Eyes on the road," Rose snapped. Her gaze went to the speedometer and she winced. "Hands on the wheel."

"Don't be ridiculous." Peg turned back to face forward. "I know what I'm doing. I've been driving for nearly six decades."

"Somehow I don't find that nearly as reassuring as you might think."

"It's not my fault you didn't get a driver's license until you were in your fifties. Those of us with years of experience on the road know how to do two things at once."

Rose sighed. It wasn't the first time Peg had lectured her about her shortcomings. Most were due to the fact that Rose had spent the majority of her adult life as a Sister of Divine Mercy. She refused to dwell on the things she'd missed during her years in the convent. After all, that time had produced benefits and blessings too. Nevertheless, it sometimes felt as though Rose was being forced to play catch-up now.

She hardly needed Peg to point that out for her, however.

"It's past time for you to get over the fact that I used to be a nun," she said firmly.

"I don't think so," Peg retorted. "You're still too prim and proper for your own good. 'Hands on the wheel' indeed."

"There's nothing wrong with taking a cautious approach—"

"Oh please. You need to learn how to cut loose and live a little."

Rose swiveled in Peg's direction. "I left the convent. I

married Peter. I've even managed to come to terms with all your years of rude behavior. To use your terminology, I *am* cutting loose."

"Oh." Peg considered that. Belatedly it occurred to her that she might have sounded like a bit of a bully. Which hadn't been her intention at all.

What she really wanted was for Rose to take a break from following every single rule in creation. Was that too much to ask? Maybe so. Because it suddenly felt as though the tenuous détente that had allowed them to reshape their former relationship into something more agreeable was more fragile than she'd thought. Peg wasn't pleased by that realization.

"Okay," she said. "Good for you."

"What's good for me?" Rose's eyes narrowed. Peg's abrupt capitulation had made her suspicious.

"What you said."

"I didn't say anything." Now Rose was baffled. "You started it."

"And I'm ending it," Peg said. "I apologize."

"For what?"

Peg had hoped Rose wouldn't ask. Because, truthfully, she wasn't entirely sure. She tossed out the first thing that came to mind. "For being wrong."

Rose didn't look convinced. "I thought you were never wrong."

"I do my best," said Peg.

"So do I," Rose shot back.

"Then we're in agreement. Right?"

Rose nodded—grudgingly—and hoped that was good enough to appease Peg. She still had no idea what they were talking about.

On the seat behind them, Hope stood up. She pressed her nose against the window and began to wag her pom-ponned tail. They were driving past a field that held a small herd of mares and foals.

Peg smiled at the sight. A moment later, Rose did too. *Welcome to Kentucky*, Peg thought.

Peg had made reservations at a hotel that was less than a mile from the Kentucky Horse Park, site of the upcoming dog shows. The location was also an easy drive to Midway, the tiny and utterly charming town where Lucky Luna boarded at Six Oaks Farm. With multiple dog shows in town, the clerk at the front desk didn't even blink when she saw Hope. Instead, she simply handed Peg and Rose their key cards and directed them around the corner to their adjoining rooms on the first floor.

While Peg took Hope outside for a walk, Rose called Peter to check in and tell him they'd arrived safely. He assured her that everything was under control at home, then deftly dodged Rose's questions about specifics. "Don't worry about us," Peter said firmly. "Just relax and enjoy your vacation. You deserve it."

When the call ended, Peg and Hope still hadn't returned. Rose tucked her phone back in her pocket and went outside to unpack the minivan. She lugged their suitcases and Hope's supplies into their two rooms. As she placed a stack of stainless steel dog bowls on the dresser in Peg's room, Rose found herself wondering how relaxing her "vacation" would turn out to be.

After twelve hours on the road together, she and Peg were already sniping at each other. Again. Not only that, but a trip devoted entirely to horse-and-dog events was so far outside Rose's wheelhouse that she couldn't imagine being able to contribute anything useful to the proceedings. Her time in the convent had instilled a strong work ethic. Rose liked to keep busy. She hated the idea that she might merely be a spectator on this trip, while Peg was the person who was actually accomplishing things.

With that in mind, Rose picked up one of the dog bowls, filled it with cold water, then set it down on the bathroom floor, in case Hope was thirsty when she returned. Peg's other supplies—a medium-sized bag of kibble and a cooler—were still sitting by the door. When Rose found a minifridge tucked inside a cabinet, she hauled the cooler over beside it.

She hoped Peg had brought along some snacks. Their stop for lunch had taken place hours earlier. Rose suddenly realized she was starving.

She lifted the cooler's lid and looked inside. The first thing she saw was a stack of clear food-storage bags. They were medium in size and filled with what looked like beef stew. Rose had been hoping to find some fruit. Even protein bars would have sufficed. Now she wondered if Peg had dietary restrictions she hadn't previously been aware of.

Behind her, the door to the room opened. Hope came bounding across the carpeted floor. Despite how long she and Peg been gone, the big Poodle was still full of energy. She trotted over to greet Rose, then saw the open cooler. Hope leaned down and stuck her nose inside. Without thinking, Rose slammed the lid shut.

Just in time, Hope snatched her head back. She looked at Rose reproachfully. Rose knew she deserved that. Even though it was an accident, she'd come close to injuring the Poodle. How was she supposed to apologize to a dog? Rose didn't have a clue.

She reached her hand out tentatively and patted the top of Hope's head. The poufy topknot felt soft beneath Rose's fingers. Hope's tail began to wag. Rose hoped that meant all was forgiven.

Peg was still standing in the doorway to the room. Busy balling up Hope's six-foot leather leash, she'd missed the interaction entirely. Rose didn't know whether she ought to be relieved—or immediately confess what she'd done. Then Hope leaned in, pressing her solid body against

Rose's leg. Rose decided to take that as another gesture of support.

"I see you've found Hope's food," Peg said. "It needs to last until we go home, so let's get it unpacked and into the refrigerator."

"*Hope's* food?"

"Yes, I cooked it and bagged it before we left. What did you think . . . ?" Peg had started across the room. She stopped and began to chuckle.

"It looks like beef stew," Rose said in her own defense. "And I unloaded that bag of kibble . . ."

Peg was still amused. "It *is* beef stew, more or less. And the kibble gets mixed in too."

Now Rose just felt silly. "Next you'll be telling me you brought dessert for her too," she grumbled.

"No, but I did bring along a bag of treats."

"Cookies?" Rose asked hopefully. She was well acquainted with Peg's sweet tooth.

"Peanut butter biscuits. And a couple of rawhide bones."

"You're no help." Rose walked over and sat down on the edge of the bed. From the sound of things, dinner was still a long time away.

"Of course I am," Peg replied. "I've already made us a reservation at Carson's in downtown Lexington. As soon as I get Hope fed and settled in, you and I can be on our way."

The next morning, Peg and Rose were up and out of the hotel early. Peg had an appointment at Six Oaks Farm at nine A.M. and she couldn't wait to get started. Even Hope, who'd spent most of the previous day in the minivan, hopped back inside the vehicle with a smile on her face.

Several years had passed since Peg's first visit to Six Oaks, but she still recalled how to get there. The farm was a full-service Thoroughbred facility set on a thousand acres of land just outside Midway. In addition to boarding broodmares and their offspring, Six Oaks also offered consignment services at the various Thoroughbred sales. One section of the property had a training center with a racetrack where young Thoroughbreds could begin their early education.

As she approached the stone gateposts that marked the end of the farm's driveway, Peg was pleased to see that little had changed since the last time she was here. On either side of the entrance were acres of grass pastures, each enclosed by dark four-board fencing and occupied by small herds of sleek mares and playful foals. When the minivan drew near, an ornate double gate swung open to admit them.

Once they were inside, a long driveway bordered by low stone walls unfurled before them. There were more pastures, and a row of tall barns was visible in the distance. Everything around them was lush and green, and all of it was beautifully maintained. There wasn't a leaf, or rock, or even a piece of hay out of place.

"Wow." Rose exhaled slowly. "This place is amazing."

"I know." Peg's first visit had had that effect on her too. Even Hope hopped to her feet to take a look.

Rose's head swung from side to side as she tried to take in everything at once. "All this is really just for horses?"

Peg smiled. "You know there are people on this farm, too. Right?"

"I should hope so," Rose replied. "Otherwise I'm not getting out of the car."

"Wait a minute." Peg suddenly remembered Rose's introduction to her rambunctious trio of Standard Poodles. Rose had been all but frozen in place. Apparently everyone except Rose knew that Peg's dogs were harmless. Peg pictured the look of horror she'd seen on Rose's face at the time. "You're not afraid of horses, are you?"

Rose's lips pursed, as if she wasn't sure how to answer what should have been an easy question. "I don't know," she said finally.

"What does that mean?"

"It means I know that they're big. And that they don't look very friendly. But I've never met a live horse before."

"Never?" Peg was astounded.

"Never," Rose repeated. Now she sounded huffy. "It's not my fault I don't have your full range of life experiences."

Peg processed that. It took a minute. Then she reached over and patted Rose's arm.

"Brace yourself," she said. "Because life as you know it is about to change."

Chapter 3

The first building they came to had a sign identifying it as the farm office. Peg scanned the parking area out front and chose a spot deep in the shade. Before turning off the engine, she opened each of the minivan's windows halfway.

Rose noted that move and knew what it meant. "If Hope is going to wait here, maybe I should too."

"Don't be silly. Of course you're coming with me." Peg hopped out, walked around the front of the van, and opened Rose's door. "It's different for Hope. Kentuckians don't like unfamiliar dogs on their property. I was thoroughly schooled about that the last time I was here."

"That's not very friendly of them," Rose said as she stepped out.

Peg just shrugged. "When you consider how much these Thoroughbreds are worth, you can appreciate why their caretakers want to take every precaution to keep them safe." She opened the glove box and got out a rawhide bone. "Luckily it's not too warm out. Hope will be perfectly content here until we return."

The office reception area was a small room paneled in dark wood and furnished with a leather sofa and matching chairs. Glass-fronted shelves filled with gleaming silver trophies lined the back wall. A trio of oil paintings caught

Rose's eye. The racehorses they featured reminded her of those Degas had painted. She stepped in for a closer look while Peg went to talk to the receptionist.

There was barely time for Peg to mention her name before a nearby door opened and a young woman entered the room. She was in her mid-twenties and had a cheerful expression on her face. Her long dark hair was pulled back in a ponytail that hung halfway down her back. Dressed in the farm uniform of khaki pants, sturdy boots, and a navy blue polo shirt with the Six Oaks logo, she looked strong enough to toss around a few hay bales should the need arise.

The woman's hand was already outstretched as she approached Peg. "You must be Mrs. Turnbull. I'm Lucia Alvarez. Your account manager, Ben Burrell, thought you might enjoy seeing your horses first, before you sit down with him in his office. If you approve, he wants you to know that he'll be ready to see you when we get back."

"That sounds like a fine idea," Peg agreed as they shook hands. She'd take animals over office work any day.

"Lucky Luna and the foal she produced in April are in one of our broodmare barns," Lucia told her. "As you know, her yearling colt is entered in next week's Keeneland sale. He and the other yearlings in our consignment are in the barns near the training center where we do sales prep. I'm ready to go if you are."

"Of course." Peg beckoned Rose over and introduced her. "This is my sister-in-law, Rose Donovan. She doesn't know much about Thoroughbreds, but she's looking forward to learning."

"I'm pleased to meet you," Lucia said as she led the way to the door. "If you're interested in knowing more about Thoroughbreds, you've come to the right place."

"The right place being Kentucky or Six Oaks Farm?" Rose asked.

"Both." Lucia looked at her and smiled. "I've been here

at Six Oaks for seven years. I can assure you it's one of the premier Thoroughbred facilities in the country."

"Seven years?" Peg was surprised. "You must have started when you were a baby."

"I suppose I did," Lucia said. She was striding across the small lot toward a navy blue pickup truck with the farm logo on the door. "From the time I was a small child, I always knew I wanted to make a living around horses. My father was a jockey in Mexico. My younger brother is an exercise rider in Southern California. My horse dreams brought me to Kentucky, and I'm lucky to have landed here."

Lucia paused beside the truck's passenger door. "If you don't mind, it'll be easier if I drive. And of course, I'll bring you back here when we're finished." She glanced at Peg's minivan, then did a quick double take.

Hope was standing up on the back seat. Her muzzle was poking out through the window opening as she watched them get ready to leave.

"Is that a Poodle?" Lucia asked. "I've never seen one that big before."

"She's a Standard Poodle. That's the largest variety that Poodles come in." Peg could never resist a teaching opportunity. She stepped over to the minivan to offer the bitch a few reassuring words. "Her name is Hope."

"Hope," Lucia repeated. "I like that. She's a pretty dog."

The Poodle wagged her tail in acknowledgment.

"Hope is quite an accomplished Poodle." Rose had only ever heard of one racehorse. Trying the sound knowledgeable, she added, "If she were a Thoroughbred, she'd be Secretariat."

"Really?" Lucia regarded the bitch with fresh appreciation. "She must be an amazing dog."

"Not quite Secretariat's caliber," Peg corrected with a chuckle. "But she's amazing nonetheless."

When Hope lay back down with the rawhide bone between her paws, the three women returned to the farm truck. Rose was hoping to sit up front, but Peg quickly nabbed shotgun for herself. Instead, Rose ended up on the bench seat in the back.

She leaned forward so she could watch where they were going through the windshield. Everything about this experience felt new to her. She didn't want to miss a single moment.

The ride to their destination went by quickly. Along the way, they passed a very large tractor, two stone bridges, more fields filled with young Thoroughbreds, and a muscular colt being loaded into the side of a horse van. Peg and Lucia were busy chatting up front, but Rose had no desire to join the conversation. She was enthralled by the behind-the-scenes look at the inner workings of a Kentucky horse farm.

"We'll start here," Lucia said. She parked the truck outside a tall, center aisle barn. There was a second, matching, barn beside it. Rows of small, fenced paddocks fanned out around both buildings. "This is where we do our sales prep. Colts in this barn"—she gestured toward the building in front of them—"and fillies in the other." She laughed, then added, "And never the twain shall meet."

"Even at this young age?" Peg asked as she got out of the truck.

"Absolutely." Lucia nodded. "It happens all the time in the wild. So we're very careful to keep them separated."

Off in the distance, Rose could see a racetrack. The three-quarter mile oval had a dirt surface and was enclosed by a pristine white rail. As she watched, a pair of horses went galloping past. Their coats gleamed in the early morning light and the cadence of their movement was surprisingly graceful. To Rose, it looked like they were flying along.

Unexpectedly she felt her heart lift in response to the

horses' performance. For a moment, it was as though she was flying with them. She imagined it must be wonderful to actually be able to do that.

"*Rose?*" Peg's voice broke into her reverie. "Are you coming?"

"Yes, of course." Rose tore her gaze away from the track and scrambled out of the back seat. "I was just enjoying the view. Actual racehorses doing racehorse things!"

"Galloping," Peg supplied. She'd learned a few things on her previous visit. Compared to most horse people, Peg was still a novice. But next to Rose, she felt like an expert. "They're working on building up their stamina before they leave here to ship to a real racetrack."

While they were talking, Lucia had walked on ahead. She was just outside the entrance to the barn when a man stepped out of a side door and into the aisle. He was six feet tall and solidly built. When he planted his feet and crossed his arms over his chest, he deliberately blocked her path. The man's features were shaded by a Six Oaks ball cap that was pulled low over his eyes. Despite that, Peg could see that he was scowling.

"What are you doing here?" he said in a hostile tone.

Lucia stopped walking. "My job. I'm escorting a couple of clients around the farm. The staff is expecting us. We're here to see Lucky Luna's colt."

"Those are Ben's clients. Not yours." He didn't step out of her way.

"Yes, but—"

It only took several quick steps for Peg to reach the young woman's side. "Lucia's with us. We're lucky to have her helping with the first part of our visit. She's doing a wonderful job." Peg paused and held out her hand. "I'm Peg Turnbull, Lucky Luna's owner. And you are?"

The man stared for a moment. Then he reached out and loosely grasped her fingers with a callused grip. "Jim

Grable. I'm the yearling manager. I'm supposed to be kept apprised of all visitors to the barns."

Rose also moved up to stand beside Lucia. She saw the woman roll her eyes. Rose didn't blame her. Hadn't she just told Grable that the staff was expecting them?

"The yearling manager." Peg smiled sweetly. "Excellent. That makes you the man in charge of making sure my colt will look perfect for the sale. Perhaps we could take a look at him now?"

"Sure." Grable dipped his head in a short nod. "Why don't you step over to the show ring? I'll have him brought out to you momentarily."

The show ring turned out to be not a ring at all, but rather a level spot in the grass yard where a six-foot-wide path had been cleared and covered in peastone.

"I apologize for that," Lucia said under her breath as the three women made their way there. "I should have realized we might run into Jim."

"You have nothing to be sorry for," Peg told her. "If anything, Mr. Grable appeared to be in the wrong."

"He was. But that never stops him from trying to put the blame on someone else. He can get pretty testy about what goes on around here."

" 'Testy' is putting it mildly," Rose said. "That was more like territorial."

"Jim likes to think that he's in control of everybody and everything—" Lucia gasped and abruptly stopped speaking. She clapped a hand over her mouth. "Please forget I said anything. I really shouldn't be gossiping about other employees."

"Don't worry," Peg said. "Rose and I will pretend we didn't hear a thing. Won't we?"

When Rose nodded, she was happy to see Lucia's shoulders relax.

"Let's talk about something else," Peg said. "While we

wait for my colt to come out, why don't you tell us what 'sales prep' entails? I've seen the notation on my bills and I'm sure I have a rough idea. But if you wouldn't mind giving me specifics, I'd be grateful to learn more."

"Of course." Lucia smiled. "And please feel free to ask any other questions you have. As I'm sure you know, Thoroughbred sales are a big business. The Keeneland September Yearling Sale, for example, grosses more than four hundred million dollars annually."

Rose made a strangled sound deep in her throat. The Donovans' most recent missionary trip had taken them to Honduras, where she and Peter had witnessed poverty and deprivation beyond anything she'd previously imagined. It was difficult to reconcile what she'd seen there with the notion that people were spending such outrageous sums *every year* on a luxury item like racehorses.

"Pardon me?" Lucia said.

"Nothing," Rose told her. "Please continue."

"In the olden days . . ." Lucia began again.

This time, Peg was the one who swallowed a snort. She suspected that the "olden days" Lucia was referencing fell well within her lifespan.

". . . breeders used to simply pull their yearlings out of the pasture and send them off to a sale. Soon it became clear, however, that fit, shiny, bright-eyed babies brought higher prices than the ones who were presented in a more natural state. That's when the idea of sales prep came into being."

"That makes sense," Peg said.

"It does," Lucia agreed. "Everyone wants to maximize their returns, and here at Six Oaks, we know how to help you do just that. Several months before a sale, all our yearlings are put into prep. Rather than going out during the day when the sun will burn their coats and make them look dull, they're put on night turnout instead. Colts, who can be quite rambunctious, are separated in single-horse paddocks so they don't end up covered with dings and scrapes."

Rose nodded. That explained the rows of small enclosures she'd seen beside the barns.

"In addition," Lucia continued, "the yearlings are exercised daily to build muscle. In most cases, that means they're either hand walked, or they swim, or they spend time on a walker. Their feed is adjusted to account for the extra activity, and the farrier trims their feet more often to make sure their limbs stay straight. They're bathed and thoroughly groomed every day. And, of course, they're also trained how to stand and pose in a way that shows them to maximum advantage."

The long explanation was beginning to bore Rose. It centered around a topic she had little interest in learning more about. Peg, however, was listening avidly to everything Lucia had to say.

"What about X-rays?" she asked. "I've been billed for those too."

"Usually there are two sets," Lucia told her. "The first is done early in the year to see if there are any skeletal issues that need to be corrected presale. The second set happens in the days just before the sale. It's important for a yearling to have current X-rays in the repository so potential buyers can have their vets examine them before they bid."

Peg nodded thoughtfully. "All this time, I had no idea there was so much was involved in getting a horse ready for a sale."

"That's because you didn't need to know," Lucia replied. "Six Oaks takes care of all those details for you so you don't have to worry about a thing."

"Look!" Rose cried. She was delighted to have a reason to change the subject. "Here comes a little horse now. This must be Lucky Luna's baby."

Chapter 4

"Yearling," Peg corrected as a striking chestnut colt came striding toward them. Her judge's eye was more attuned to dogs than horses, but she still recognized quality when she saw it. "Foals are the babies. This colt is a year old. And what a handsome fellow he is."

The handler was a wiry Hispanic man, dressed in jeans and a Six Oaks shirt. Young, like Lucia, he controlled the colt handily with a gentle touch on the lead shank. The man slipped Lucia a quick wink as he stopped the chestnut in front of them. He then rocked the colt back and forth slightly until his legs were positioned the way he wanted. When the man loosened his hold on the shank, the colt lifted his head and pricked his ears.

"Thank you, Manny," Lucia cast a glance back toward the barn. "Everything okay in there?"

"Sure." He shrugged. "No problem. Jim's just a little edgy this morning. You know."

She nodded, then said under her breath, "If he can't take it out on me, he'll find someone else."

Manny shrugged again. He wasn't worried about that.

Lucia turned to Peg. "What do you think?"

"Oh my," Peg said on an exhale. Delighted with what she saw, she hardly knew where to begin. "He's gorgeous, isn't he?"

The colt's fiery coat, the color of a new penny, glowed in the sunlight. His neck was arched and muscles rippled over his shoulders and across his hindquarters. The colt's eyes were dark and intelligent. There was a large star in the shape of a diamond on his forehead, and his mane and tail were as smooth as silk.

"We think so." Lucia was pleased by Peg's response. "I'm glad you do too. How about you, Mrs. Donovan? What's your opinion?"

"Umm . . ." Rose waffled. "He's very shiny." Whatever attributes Peg was rhapsodizing about were invisible to her. As far as Rose was concerned, the colt looked like any other horse. Then, with relief, she thought of a question she could ask. "What's his name?"

"His name?" Lucia sounded surprised. "As far I know, he doesn't have one." She turned to Peg. "Unless you've registered a name with the Jockey Club? In which case we should know that so we can update his sales information."

"I haven't," Peg said. "I assumed his new owners would do that after the sale."

"Surely you must call him something," Rose said.

"Lucky Luna." Manny spoke up. "All the young horses here are referred to by their dams' names until they either sell or go into training. This guy, I call him Lucky." He reached up and patted the colt's neck. "Because he's gonna be good luck for you at the sale."

"I certainly hope so," Peg said.

"Take my word for it." Manny grinned. "This colt is all class."

He moved the young Thoroughbred up and down the peastone walkway several times so Peg could assess his movement. She scrutinized each step with a discerning eye, and once again was pleased. When the colt went back to his stall, Peg was sorry to see him leave.

Next on the agenda was a visit to Lucky Luna and her foal. This time, when the three women returned to the truck,

Rose managed to nab the front seat. Peg grumbled about being both taller and older than Rose, but Rose refused to budge. Eventually, Peg gave in and wedged herself in back so they could move on.

"I'd like to apologize again for Jim's rudeness," Lucia said once they were underway. "I'm sorry you had to witness our conversation. I'd hate for you to think Six Oaks considers behavior like that acceptable."

"Don't give it another thought," Rose said. "Anyone can have a bad day."

"Thank you." Lucia was chewing on her lower lip. "If you don't mind, it would be better if you didn't mention what you saw back there to Ben Burrell."

Peg and Rose shared a look.

"It's just that it would make my life easier." She rushed on. "If the incident was reported, it could make me look bad. Like I don't know how to do my job. And I like working here. I like it a lot."

"I see," Peg said from the back.

Rose wondered what Peg meant. Somehow the conversation seemed to have taken a turn that she didn't quite understand. Maybe she shouldn't have been so quick to grab the front seat.

"You know," Peg mused, "based on the small amount of exposure I've had, I gather that the horseracing industry is mostly run by men. Good old boys who take care to look out for each other."

Lucia's gaze was focused on the road ahead of them. Her fingers curled tightly around the steering wheel. "You're right about that," she muttered.

Comprehension finally dawned for Rose. Having spent the majority of her life surrounded by women, she was often clueless when it came to male/female dynamics. She'd been a step behind, but at least she now knew what they were talking about.

"Ben won't hear a word from me," Peg promised.

"Nor from me." Rose added her support.

"Thank you." Lucia looked relieved. "Now let's go see Luna and her baby."

Lucky Luna lived in a cream-colored, U-shaped barn with lots of windows. The staff there must have been waiting for their arrival because as soon as Lucia parked the truck, a man exited a stall at the far end of the shedrow. Leading a tall bay mare, he headed for a sunny spot in the center of the wide courtyard. A woman followed closely behind him. She had her arms looped around the front end of a prancing bay foal.

Rose jumped out of the truck with a smile on her face. Peg quickly followed. Lucia laughed as they took off toward the barn.

"The foals always have that effect on people," she said, hurrying to catch up. "Everybody wants to see the babies."

"Hi, Nico," Peg said, recognizing the groom she'd met on her previous visit. "How's my mare doing?"

"Everything's perfect." Nico nodded. He had an athletic physique and a wide smile that lit up his whole face. "This mare, she does everything right."

"I'm glad to hear that," Peg said.

Rose hung back, leaving plenty of space between her and the two horses. Not Peg. She quickly went forward, approaching the mare and running a gentle hand down her neck. Luna flicked an ear in Peg's direction and blew out a soft breath. She had kind eyes and a star that matched the one they'd seen on her yearling colt.

"She looks wonderful," Peg enthused. "You take great care of her."

"That's our job," Lucia said. She glanced back at Rose.

"Luna's a very gentle mare. She won't mind if you want to come and say hello to her."

"Thank you, but no." Rose held up both hands in front of her and took a step back. She was keeping a wary eye on the energetic foal who was now bouncing up and down in place. "I'm fine over here."

"Suit yourself," Peg said. She moved around the other side of the mare and approached the foal.

This colt was a bay like his dam. He had a black mane and tail, a narrow blaze down the center of his face, and two white socks behind. His wispy forelock was standing straight up in the air, giving him a comical appearance.

"Careful," the woman holding him cautioned as Peg drew near. The colt was wearing a halter with a lead rope attached to it, but the woman continued to guide him using her hands and arms. "At this age, foals don't understand the concept of personal space. Also, they have no idea how fragile we humans are compared to them."

"Ladies, please meet Tammy Radnor," Lucia said. "Tammy is one of the longest-serving employees here at Six Oaks. What she doesn't know about young Thoroughbreds isn't even worth discussing. Tammy, this is Peg Turnbull and Rose Donovan."

Tammy nodded in their direction. She was closer in age to Peg and Rose than anyone else they'd met on the farm, probably nearing sixty. Her gray hair was in a long braid that was flipped forward over her shoulder. She had a gravelly voice and forearms that were ropey with muscle. One of her fingers had an odd bend, as if it had been broken at one point and never correctly healed.

"I'd offer to shake your hands," she said, "but I'm otherwise engaged at the moment."

"I can see that." Peg laughed. "He looks like a frisky fellow."

"Frisky is good," Tammy told her. "It's the quiet ones you have to worry about."

"Are you pleased with how he's coming along?"

"Very much so," Tammy replied. "He eats, he poops, he runs around the pasture like a little demon. No complaints at all."

"Speaking of running around," said Lucia. "Now that you've had a chance to see these two up close, we'll turn them out with the other mares and foals in the big field so you can watch them in action."

"But we'll still be outside the fence?" Rose asked. "Right?"

Curiosity had prompted her to inch a bit closer to Lucky Luna. The mare stood and regarded her calmly, making no attempt to bite or kick. Rose thought Thoroughbreds were supposed to be wild and hard to control, but the ones she'd seen so far were nothing like that.

"Of course," Lucia assured her. "No one has any desire to put you in harm's way."

Nico and Lucky Luna led the way to a pasture that was at least twenty acres in size. The area around the gate was empty, but a small band of mares and foals was visible in the distance. Peg and Rose walked over to stand beside the four-board fence.

As Lucia unlatched the gate and pushed it open, Lucky Luna lifted her head. Her lips quivered with a soft whinny. Her colt also knew what was about to happen. He squealed and kicked up his heels. Rose gasped, but Tammy just dodged nimbly to one side, then laughed at the youngster's antics.

Nico unclipped the lead rope attached to Lucky Luna's halter. Tammy released the foal and stepped back. Luna looked around to check on her colt, then she took off at a gallop in the direction of the herd. The colt went racing after her, keeping up with his dam easily.

"That was great," Peg said, turning away after a minute. "We should definitely do this more often."

Lucia drove Peg and Rose back to the office and dropped them off in the parking lot. "Is it all right if I leave you here?" she asked, looking at a message on her phone. "Ben's expecting you, so you can go right in."

"It's fine," Peg replied, and Rose nodded. "Thank you for the tour. We enjoyed all of it."

"I'm glad to hear that." Lucia gave them a quick smile before casting a worried glance down at the screen. "It was my pleasure."

"Go on," Rose said, shutting the door as soon as Peg was out of the truck. It was clear that Lucia was needed elsewhere.

Lucia sketched a small wave and quickly drove away. When Rose turned around, she saw that Peg was already back at her minivan. As soon as Peg slid the door open, Hope jumped out into her arms.

Rose would have been bowled over by fifty pounds of flying Poodle, but Peg caught her dog with surprising ease. Hope wrapped her front legs around Peg's neck. The Poodle's tail whipped back and forth. Rose was sure if Peg had a tail, it would be wagging too.

"Ben Burrell is waiting for you," Rose reminded her.

"I'm on my way." Peg dropped the big Poodle lightly to the ground.

"You don't sound thrilled by the prospect."

"Honestly, I'm not." Peg sighed. "Seeing Lucky Luna and her offspring was the fun part of the day. Now comes the boring stuff. There'll be decisions to make, papers to sign, and possibly even a check to write. I'd imagine I'll also have to listen to another lecture from Ben about why it would make sense to hold Luna's yearling back from this sale and offer him at a two-year-old sale next year instead, after the farm has put him into training."

"I take it you don't like that idea?"

"Not particularly. The reward for doing so is potentially higher, but so's the risk. That's something I'd prefer to mitigate. It's a cleaner transaction if I sell the colt now and let his next owner worry about training him."

"The owner who will get to choose his name." Rose remembered that part. "If the risk is higher, why does Ben Burrell think it's a good idea?"

"Because he works for the farm, of course." Peg didn't look pleased. "The longer the colt stays here, the more board bills I pay. Then when he starts training in a few months, there will be bills for that too. And if he sells for a higher price next spring, the commission Six Oaks makes for consigning him will also increase."

Rose considered that. "What if something goes wrong in the meantime and the colt is worth less next year than he is now?"

"Then I'm the one who loses money on the deal."

"That doesn't sound right," Rose said. "It seems like you're absorbing all the risk, and they're the ones reaping the reward."

"Only if I agree," Peg pointed out. "Which I have no intention of doing."

Hope was sniffing the base of a tree nearby. Peg snapped her fingers to call her back. Then she hopped the Poodle back into the minivan. Hope obeyed, but when she sat down on the seat, her ears were flattened against her head. She looked at Peg unhappily.

Rose looked at the Poodle and made a quick decision. "Move over," she said. When Hope obliged, Rose climbed into the back of the minivan beside her. "She and I will wait together."

"You'll be more comfortable inside," Peg told her.

Rose shrugged.

"I might be half an hour, maybe longer."

"That's all right. In the meantime, Hope and I will have

a lovely chat." Rose looped an arm around the Poodle's neck, and Hope parted her lips in a doggy smile.

Peg stared at the two of them. "You always insist you don't understand a word my dogs are saying."

"And you always insist that they're scintillating conversationalists," Rose shot back. "I guess we're about to find out which one of us is right."

Chapter 5

Peg emerged from the office forty minutes later to find Hope and Rose still together in the back of the minivan. Rose was reading aloud from a book she'd downloaded onto her phone. Hope was beside her, listening to the rise and fall of Rose's voice with her head tipped to one side. Peg was quite certain that didn't qualify as a conversation, but since Hope looked pleased with the arrangement, she decided not to quibble.

Instead, Peg opened the front door and slid behind the wheel. "I'm finished with work for the day," she said. "Let's go exploring."

Lexington and the surrounding area had plenty of interesting things to see and do. They visited Henry Clay's Ashland estate, then had pizza for lunch and honey bourbon ice cream for dessert in the city's newly revitalized distillery district. After that, they toured Rupp Arena, followed by Mary Todd Lincoln's House. Then they returned to farm country to finish their explorations at Woodford Reserve, Kentucky's oldest bourbon distillery, where Peg and Rose both sampled the wares liberally.

Despite all the running around they'd done, once again Peg was up shortly after dawn the following morning. That day she'd be judging all the breeds in the Non-Sporting Group, plus the group itself. Peg knew there would be lots of good dogs on hand. She'd been looking forward to the assignment for weeks.

Rose was just getting out of bed when Peg returned from taking Hope for a long walk. They'd left the adjoining doors between their two rooms unlocked. Now Peg stood in the doorway and looked pointedly at her watch. "Chop chop," she said. "We're out the door in half an hour. And not a minute more."

Rose frowned. "Perhaps when you were extolling the virtues of this trip, you should have also mentioned that you act like a drill sergeant in the morning."

"I'm on the clock," Peg informed her. "I need to be in my ring by eight A.M. sharp. And I refuse to be late. I'll make Hope's breakfast and brew some tea while you shower and dress."

"Hope's breakfast," Rose said. "What about our breakfast?"

"If you wanted a meal, you should have gotten up earlier. I'm sure you'll be able to grab something at the Alltech Arena. While I'm judging, you and Hope will have plenty of time to wander around and see what's what."

Almost to the bathroom, Rose stopped abruptly. "Wait a minute. Repeat that part about me and Hope."

"You'll be spending the day together."

"We will?"

"Of course you will. I can't take her into the show ring with me, and I'm certainly not going to leave her in the van all day. What did you think we were going to do?"

Truth be told, Rose hadn't thought about it. Having never owned a dog, she'd never previously needed to take a dog's requirements into account. Yesterday had been one thing. Then, all she'd had to do was sit with Hope and wait for Peg to return. Rose had no intention of confessing this to Peg, but she'd actually spent most of the time playing Wordle on her phone.

"But . . ." she sputtered. "That's a long time for me to look after her. What will we do all day?"

"I'm sure you'll figure it out." Peg glanced down at Hope adoringly. "Won't she?"

The Poodle wagged her tail in reply. She agreed with everything Peg said.

Rose eyed the two of them. The bond between Peg and her Poodle was undeniable. And Rose had to admit that the pair did seem to possess some form of subliminal communication. But despite what she'd said to Peg the day before, Rose still had no idea how to understand what dogs said. Or thought. Or really much of anything about them.

"See?" Peg said happily. She and Hope were still sharing a moment. "Hope's on board with this plan. Trust me. The two of you will have a great time."

The Kentucky Horse Park was one of the premier tourist attractions in the state. In addition to hosting numerous and diverse equestrian competitions, it was also a working horse farm, open year-round to the public. Equine museums offered education on various breeds. There were trail rides and interactive tours, and a large campground was available for visitors who preferred to stay on-site.

The Alltech Arena where the Bluegrass Cluster was being held was the largest indoor competition venue on the horse park grounds. Though usually reserved for horse events of various kinds, on Labor Day weekend the facility devoted itself to the dogs.

Peg didn't need to have worried. They arrived at the arena in plenty of time for her assignment. Ample parking was available just outside the venue. Mindful of the requirements of her job, Peg had dressed in loose clothing that allowed extra room for reaching and bending. Since she'd be spending most of the day on her feet, she'd opted for shoes that offered good arch support. Peg also had a sweater draped over her arm in case the facility proved to be cooler indoors than it was outside.

In short, she was ready for pretty much anything. Except, apparently, for Rose, who was taking her time about getting out of the minivan.

Peg stood on the tarmac and tapped her foot impatiently. Hope was eager to head inside too. A show dog in her youth, she recognized all the signs: rows of vans and trailers in the lot, exhibitors unloading their crates and equipment onto dollies, and dogs of all shapes and sizes visible everywhere she looked.

"Are you coming?" Peg asked. "Or shall I leave you and Hope out here?"

Rose finally emerged. She looked around the hectic parking area, which was overrun with dogs. Peg was obviously in her element, relaxed and confident about everything that was to come. Rose, however, was already nervous. At least the canines inside the building would be leashed and under the control of their handlers. She wouldn't have to interact with any of them.

Except, of course, for Hope. Who was going to be her responsibility.

Rose cast a glance downward. The big black Poodle was glued to Peg's side. It figured. It looked as though Rose wasn't the only one who was worried about her ability to act as Hope's caretaker.

The main entrance to the building deposited them on an upper-seating level, from which the arena was visible below. The center of its floor was filled with a double row of back-to-back show rings, each bordered by a low retractable fence. Rubber mats provided slip-proof footing for dogs and handlers alike. Chairs were available for spectators who wanted to sit and watch. The perimeter of the arena floor offered an array of concessions that sold everything from dog supplies to books, to canine artwork and jewelry.

Though it was early, the venue was already bustling with activity. Grooming space for exhibitors was available in a large room beside the main arena. The area was crowded with handlers' setups: numerous rows of stacked crates, grooming tables, and exercise pens. The whine of dozens of blow dryers filled the air. With the show due to start soon, everyone was hard at work.

"I need to go check in," Peg told Rose. She handed her Hope's leash, then stooped down and cupped the Poodle's muzzle between her palms. "Even though you're with Rose today, I'll be *right here* if you need anything. Understand?"

Hope swished her tail from side to side to indicate that she did.

"You take good care of Rose, okay?"

The Poodle's dark eyes flickered in Rose's direction. She didn't look happy about the way the conversation was going.

"Yes," Peg said firmly. "Rose is in charge."

That directive didn't merit an acknowledgment from Hope. The Poodle was as dubious about the arrangement as Rose was.

"Good. That's settled." Peg stood up. "And now I have to go. Have fun, you two!"

Peg strode away without looking back. Hope and Rose both watched until she'd disappeared from the arena floor. Then Rose glanced down at Hope, only to discover that the Poodle was gazing up at her. Hope looked as though she was waiting for an indication about what was going to happen next. Funny thing, Rose was wondering about that too.

"I guess we're on our own." She paused in case Hope wanted to weigh in, but the Poodle made no sign that she was even listening to Rose. Now she was looking wistfully in the direction Peg had gone.

"I'm sorry," Rose said with a sigh. "Unfortunately, you're

stuck with me whether you like it or not. We might as well take a walk around and see what there is to see."

Rose hadn't been to many previous dog shows, but it turned out that whether they were held in Connecticut or Kentucky, all the events were pretty much the same. The experience consisted of a cornucopia of dog-related things, the sights and sounds of which left Rose mostly baffled and Hope eager to look in all directions at once. At least Hope's enthusiasm kept things interesting. The Poodle escorted Rose from one curious scene to the next.

Together, they checked out show rings that held dogs with straight hair, dogs with curly hair, and dogs with no hair at all. At least that was how Rose categorized the canines. No doubt Hope had a different system, probably one that was better informed.

Without Peg there to explain the details of the judging, or at least tell her the names of the breeds they were watching, Rose found the entire exercise monotonous. As far as she was concerned, all the classes looked alike—just dogs, and then more dogs, running around a ring. By late morning, Rose was out of ideas for how to keep Hope entertained.

There was a concession stand nearby that sold dog toys. In desperation, Rose steered the Poodle that way. The stand appeared to offer just about anything a dog might want. There were bones and balls, snakes and stuffed animals. And all of them either squeaked, or squawked, or jingled.

"Go ahead," Rose offered. "Take your pick."

Hope walked over to a display of life-sized stuffed animals. She delicately sniffed a squirrel with a long fluffy tail.

"That one?" Rose asked. It looked like a good choice to her.

Not surprisingly, Hope didn't reply. Nevertheless, Rose unclipped the toy from its hanger and paid for it, then de-

clined the offer of a shopping bag. Instead, she held the
squirrel up in the air and jiggled it back and forth. When
she squeezed its furry body, the toy issued a loud squeak.

Hope's head popped up. Her tail did too. When Rose
squeaked the toy a second time, the Poodle leapt up and
snatched it from her fingers. Hope pranced away from the
concession stand, shaking her head from side to side. She
appeared to be delighted when the squirrel's tail smacked
her in the face.

Finally Rose had managed to get something right.

Buoyed by the small victory, Rose led Hope over to the
ring where Peg was judging. Maybe Peg would glance over
and see what a great job Rose was doing. The ring was
filled with dogs that were easy to recognize. Thanks to
Disney, and the breed's distinctive spotted coats, even
Rose knew what Dalmatians looked like. She and Hope
moved into an open space beside the enclosure's low bar-
rier to watch.

Peg was standing in the middle of the ring, staring at the
line of dogs with a frown of concentration on her face.
After a moment, she plucked a dog from the back of the
line and sent it all the way to the front. Rose heard a small
gasp from someone in the ringside audience. The handler
holding the dog who'd advanced managed to look both
shocked and pleased.

Peg studied the order of her new line briefly, then sent
the Dalmatians gaiting around the ring. Rose knew what
that meant. Peg was about to pin the class.

"Best of Breed and Best of Winners," Peg said, pointing
to the Dalmatian at the front. Then she gestured to the dog
that was second in line. "Best of Opposite Sex."

A woman was sitting near Rose with a catalog open in
her lap. She stared at the outcome for a moment, then
began to chuckle. "Trust Peg to do something unexpected,"
she said.

"Excuse me." Rose turned her way. "Are you talking to me?"

The woman looked up. She had bright blue eyes and a ready smile. "Not really. I was just making a general comment about the judging."

There was an empty chair nearby. Rose pulled it over and sat down. "It sounds like you're pretty knowledgeable about these things."

"You mean dogs?" She laughed again. Her dangling earrings chimed softly as they swung back and forth. "You might say that. I've been coming to shows for thirty years."

"I'm impressed. Altogether, this is my fifth dog show. I'm Rose Donovan."

"Lois Bilby," the woman replied. "Five shows make you a newbie. Welcome to the sport."

"Thank you." Rose carefully maneuvered Hope into the space between their two chairs. Out of the flow of traffic, the Poodle could sit down and relax.

Hope dropped the stuffed squirrel in Rose's lap, then turned to face the ring. Three Standard Poodle puppies had just entered, but Hope ignored them. She only had eyes for Peg.

"That's a pretty Standard Poodle," Lois commented. Her gaze went to the puppies in the ring, then returned to Hope.

"Thank you," Rose said. "She isn't actually mine."

"No?"

"Hope belongs to Peg." Rose nodded toward the ring. "I'm just taking care of her for the day. And probably not doing a very good job. This is the happiest I've seen her since we arrived this morning."

"Peg's Hope?" Lois took a closer look. She reached out and used her fingers to gently turn Hope's head in her direction. "Is that Champion Cedar Crest Hope Springs?"

"Ummm." Rose honestly didn't know. She'd never heard

Peg refer to her Standard Poodle as anything other than Hope. "Maybe?"

"One of Peg's, indeed." Lois looked amused. "Of course you're a lovely bitch." Lois slipped her hand beneath Hope's chin and began to rub the spot just in front of her ear. Hope huffed out a pleased sigh and leaned into the caress.

Perplexed, Rose watched the interaction between them. How did everyone but her make it look so easy to connect with Peg's Poodles?

"What's your connection to Peg?" Lois asked. "I know you must have one. Peg never would have trusted Hope with a stranger."

"She's my sister-in-law."

"And this is only your fifth dog show?" Lois looked surprised. "You must be the family outlier."

"Something like that." Rose wasn't about to mention her years of estrangement from Peg. "We came to Kentucky for these dog shows and a horse sale next week."

"The Keeneland September sale?"

Rose glanced over. "You know about that?"

"Everyone in Lexington knows about it. It's a big deal."

"Oh." Maybe Rose should have realized that.

"I guess you could say the Keeneland sale is as important to the Thoroughbred industry as Peg is to the dog world."

Rose heard Lois's words, but somehow her brain refused to process them. "I'm sorry," she said. "Peg is what?"

"She's revered in dog show circles. Surely you're aware of that. Most of us admire her like crazy. That's why her entries are so big today. She's going to be on her feet for hours because everyone wants her opinion about their dogs."

Rose blinked several times, as if doing so might bring the meaning of Lois's comments into sharper focus. It still didn't work. Was Peg revered by the people around them?

Were her classes bigger than everyone else's? How would Rose have been expected to know those things?

"I thought Peg just really liked dogs," she said weakly.

"She does," Lois replied. "As do the rest of us. But Peg has made the Poodle breed her life's work. The important families, the practical purpose for their conformation, that famous Poodley temperament? Peg has done more than anyone in the history of the breed to promote and protect those things."

A comment seemed called for. "Good for her?" Rose tried.

Lois nodded. "And good for the dog world too. We're lucky to have someone with her dedication in our midst. You really didn't know?"

"No." Rose was beginning to feel like an idiot. How was it possible that she didn't even know Peg as well as some random woman at a dog show?

Lois turned her eyes back to the ring where Peg was finishing her examination of the three Standard puppies. "You must not be a dog person."

"No, but I have a kitten."

That didn't earn Rose even a glance. Then it occurred to her that she did know one thing about Peg that was exceptional.

"Peg talks to dogs," she said brightly. "And they answer back. They have whole conversations. That's pretty great."

"Sure," Lois agreed easily. She swiveled in her seat to face Rose. "But just in case you didn't know? We all do that."

Chapter 6

Peg had just finished judging her Dalmatians when she saw Rose and Hope approach her ring. She was glad they'd stopped by. She'd been wondering how they were getting along.

Hope's ears pricked and her step quickened at the sight of Peg, who mouthed a greeting in her Poodle's direction. But what was that awful thing Hope was carrying in her mouth? It looked like some sort of dead animal. Surely Rose wouldn't have let Hope pick up something objectionable. At least not if she'd been paying attention.

Peg frowned at the pair. Apparently that wasn't a given. Peg noted the lack of tension in Hope's leash. With the way it was simply hanging between them, either Rose or the Poodle could have easily tripped over it. Indeed, Rose barely seemed to be focused on Hope at all.

Nor did she look interested in any of the other entertaining things going on around the busy arena floor. Rose certainly didn't have a poker face. Every emotion she felt was telegraphed across her features. And what Peg saw wasn't good. Rose looked as though she'd rather be just about anywhere else.

Ah, well, Peg thought. Dog shows really weren't Rose's thing. She probably should have anticipated that.

It was too late for her to do anything about Rose's feel-

ings now, however. Peg's steward was calling the first of
her Standard Poodle classes into the ring. She enjoyed all
the different breeds she was approved to judge, but her
Standard entry was always the highlight of her day.

Peg snuck one last glance back at Rose and Hope.
Thankfully the two of them were now settled in at ringside, where she could keep an eye on them. That would
give Rose the opportunity to watch Peg do her job. Surely
she'd find some enjoyment in that.

And Peg would just have to worry about that dead animal later.

The Puppy Dog class consisted of two cute babies
who'd probably been entered for experience and one typey
older puppy with real potential. By the time she'd run her
eye down the line for the first time, Peg already knew how
she was going to place the three dogs. Assuming there
weren't any unfortunate surprises found beneath the hair
when she put her hands on them—which, thankfully, there
were not.

Peg's Bred-by-Exhibitor dog was a big stallion of a Standard Poodle. Perhaps a little coarser than she might have
preferred, but otherwise correct in every way, and he covered the ground beautifully. The fact that he was the only
entrant in his class earned him an easy blue ribbon.

After that, the entry in the Open Dog class was under-
whelming. Four dogs in front of her, and the best that
could be said for them was that they all had a copious
amount of hair. Nicely trimmed hair, but still. There were
light eyes, flat feet, a low tail set, and a dog who'd clearly
considered taking a nip out of her hand. Peg was tempted
to roll her eyes at the dismal group, but she was afraid
someone sitting ringside might notice. These days, all sorts
of things seemed to end up online, and she wasn't about to
take the chance.

Winners Dog and the day's major points were awarded
to the Bred-by dog whose owner/handler was effusive in

his thanks. The puppy with potential was Reserve Winners.

Peg's Standard Poodle bitches entered the ring next. Overall they were a lovely group. Peg could have awarded the points to any of three different Poodles—each of whom would have been a deserving winner. The choice between Winners Bitch and Reserve Winners was the most difficult decision she'd make all day. Peg wondered if the following day's Poodle judge would reverse their order when he made his decision.

She awarded Best of Variety to a handsome specials dog who, though young, was already making a name for himself in the Midwest. This was the first time Peg had the opportunity to put her hands on him. She was delighted to discover that the body beneath his huge mane coat was just as correct as she'd hoped it would be.

Best of all, from Peg's point of view, the dog's very competent professional handler knew better than to fuss. He simply stood back at the end of his lead and let the Poodle show himself. The dog was more than capable of turning in a stellar performance on his own. When Peg pointed to him as the winner, the popular decision prompted a spontaneous burst of applause from ringside.

Even Rose got into the spirit of things. She was clapping along with everyone else as the day's winners lined up beside the award markers.

"Congratulations," Peg said as she handed the dog's handler the purple-and-gold Best of Variety rosette. "It was a pleasure to judge your dog. He's one of the nicest Standards I've had my hands on recently."

"Thank you." The man smiled at the compliment as his Poodle frolicked on his toes between them. The dog was pleased with himself too. "Coming from you, that means a great deal."

Peg nodded, accepting the praise as her due. "I'll look forward to seeing him in the group."

She quickly handed out the remainder of the ribbons, hoping to have a spare moment to cross the ring and say hello to Hope. Unfortunately, the entrants in her next breed, Löwchen, were already gathering at the gate. Her steward was about to start bringing them in. Peg had no choice but to get back to work.

The next several hours went by in a flash. Peg judged a dozen more non-sporting breeds, sorting through each of them with the deft efficiency of a woman who knew what she wanted to see in a dog and had every intention of finding it.

Peg was well aware that she was considered to be a tough judge. Though some exhibitors felt that her exacting standards were too high, she adamantly refused to lower her expectations. Today's winners would play a role in determining the direction a breed would take in the future, which meant that Peg couldn't afford to compromise. Not on breed type, soundness, temperament, or good health. Those four attributes were the foundation upon which superior dogs were bred. They formed the cornerstones of the job she'd been hired to do.

When Peg finished her breed assignment, she had an hour's break until she was due back in the ring to judge the Non-Sporting Group. Peg would have preferred to spend the time sitting down and sipping a hot beverage, preferably with her feet up and her shoes off.

Rose and Hope had other ideas, however. Before Peg had even finished packing up her things, the pair was already waiting for her outside the gate. When Rose let go of the end of Hope's leash, the Poodle dashed into the now-empty ring and launched herself at Peg.

"Hello, you." Peg crooned happily as Hope danced happily around her legs. She leaned over to give the Poodle a hug. "What a good girl you are. I've missed you too. I hope you took good care of Rose."

Standing two feet away, Rose cleared her throat loudly.
"What?" Peg looked up.

"I hope you're joking."

"Not entirely," Peg said, straightening. She picked up Hope's leash and wound it around her hand. "I'd like to think that the two of you have been taking care of each other. You've been watching out for Hope's welfare and she's been keeping you company."

When Peg put it like that, Rose supposed she'd sound churlish if she complained. Even though she *had* been dog-sitting all day.

Peg checked her watch, then headed out of the ring. "I'm sure we could all use a chance to stretch our legs. Let's take Hope outside. I assume she's had fresh water and a potty break recently?"

"Of course." Rose tried not to sound snippy. She might not be an expert in dog care, but she knew enough not to neglect the basics. "I took care of both those things no more than an hour ago."

"Perfect." Hope trotted on ahead as Peg went marching toward the nearest exit. Rose was left to bring up the rear. "Should I even ask what that ugly thing is that's dangling from your purse?"

"It's a squirrel." When Hope had left the toy on the floor, Rose picked it up and stuck it in the top of her bag.

Peg glanced back. "Dead, I hope?"

"Stuffed. I bought it for Hope at a concession stand."

"It looks hideous," Peg said as they all left the building together. "It's no wonder she doesn't want to carry it."

"Hope picked it out," Rose retorted.

"I very much doubt that." Peg sniffed. "Maybe she was humoring you."

"Maybe she'd been wishing for years that you would buy her an ugly squirrel—but instead she had to wait for me to come along and do it."

Peg declined to dignify that comment with a response. On the other side of the parking lot was a large, grassy field. She led everyone in that direction.

In midafternoon, the day's temperature was still in the eighties. At home in Connecticut, that would have felt too warm. Here, it was perfect. Peg paused and turned her face up to the sun. After spending so many hours in the artificially lit arena, it felt wonderful to be outside again.

"I thought you wanted to walk," said Rose. Hope looked impatient to be moving along too.

"Pish," said Peg. "I'm just taking a moment to enjoy the lovely weather. While I do that, tell me what you learned today."

"Learned?" Rose was surprised by the question. "What would I learn at a dog show?"

"I wasn't necessarily talking about the show. What I want to know is, did you enjoy spending time with Hope?"

The Poodle heard her name and tipped her head upward to listen. She didn't want to miss anything important.

Rose considered briefly before replying. "Yes, and no."

Peg frowned. She'd clearly been expecting a different response. "Explain."

"Hope's a dog."

"A Poodle," Peg corrected.

Rose bit back the first reply that came to mind. Instead, she said, "She was a reasonably undemanding companion, which was good. However, she was also a responsibility. Had I been on my own, I probably would have sat down in a quiet corner and read a book."

"Quiet corner, indeed." Peg snorted. "Hope's company wasn't a burden, it was a benefit. She makes a very endearing companion. I thought you would enjoy being with her."

"I see what you're doing here," Rose said.

"Oh? What's that?"

"You seem to think you can turn me into a dog person through the sheer force of your will."

Peg decided it was a good time to start walking again. Hope agreed. The two of them set out together.

"I have no intention of turning you into anything," she said, when Rose had caught up. "I simply thought that given a decent amount of exposure to Hope's captivating qualities, you might decide to moderate your antidog stance."

Rose growled under her breath. She'd been right. Peg always thought she knew better than anyone else. Apparently that justified manipulating Rose to achieve her own ends.

"A little louder, please," Peg said. "If you want me to take your complaints seriously, you need to make sure I can hear them."

"I have nothing against dogs."

"I disagree," Peg replied. "So that's one vote on your side, and one opposed. Shall we ask Hope to break the tie?"

In spite of herself, Rose laughed. "You know that's not fair. Especially since you're the only one who'll understand what she's saying."

"There is that," Peg allowed.

"I like dogs perfectly fine. As long as they belong to someone else."

"And therein lies the problem."

"Not for me," Rose said firmly. Then she was struck by a sudden thought. "Actually, I did learn something today."

"Oh?" Peg turned to her with interest. "What was that?"

"Apparently you're sort of famous."

Rose thought Peg might deny the claim, but she didn't. Instead she said, "Only in certain circles."

"I met a woman who recognized Hope and knew who you were. She said you were a big deal."

"I *am* a big deal," Peg agreed.

Rose stopped walking and turned to face her. "How come you never told me that?"

"I guess I just assumed you knew. How could you *not* know? What did you think I've been doing all these years?"

Rose shrugged. "I suppose I just thought you were keeping busy. And besides, I didn't even know someone *could* be famous because of a dog."

"Not one dog," Peg corrected. "Many."

As if that made a quantifiable difference.

"Plus, to be perfectly honest, you spend so much time talking about dogs that I don't always listen to what you're saying. Some of it just goes in one ear and out the other."

"Perhaps I should stop talking," Peg said archly.

"Like that's ever going to happen."

Peg readied a retort. Then she realized Rose was right. So instead, she gathered up Hope's leash.

"Come on," she said. "We need to be getting back inside. I have a group to judge."

In the time they'd been outside, the individual breed judging had finished. Then the grounds crew had opened up several smaller rings to form one large one. The Sporting Group was currently being judged. Rose paused to watch a majestic Irish Setter gait around the perimeter with its handler. The big red dog appeared to float around the ring.

"They're lovely, aren't they?" Peg said. She was a connoisseur of canine beauty, no matter what breed.

"Gorgeous," Rose agreed. "Why don't you have Setters?"

"Because I have Standard Poodles," Peg replied, as if the answer was perfectly obvious. Which, perhaps, it was.

Peg went off to do judge things, and Hope and Rose were once again left on their own. By now, the crowd of spectators in the arena had thinned. Rose had no problem finding a place for the two of them beside the ring. As she sat down, then got Hope settled next to her, a Clumber Spaniel was awarded the blue ribbon. The Irish Setter placed third.

Rose retrieved the toy squirrel from her purse and held it out to Hope. The Poodle looked at it disdainfully. Even when Rose wiggled the squirrel's fuzzy tail, Hope made no move to take it.

"Really?" Rose asked. "Don't you want to chew on it or something?"

Hope turned back to the ring. The non-sporting dogs, lined up in size and speed order, were beginning to file in. The Standard Poodle was first, followed by the Dalmatian. The little Boston Terrier was last.

"You liked this toy before Peg told you it was hideous," Rose mentioned.

Hope didn't respond. Not that Rose expected her to. Now the Poodle was staring at Peg, who'd moved into the center of the ring to take a look at the entire group for the first time.

Peg had judged all these dogs earlier in the day. She'd found each of them to be the best representative of their individual breeds. Now it was time for her to compare their merits to the rest of the competition and see how they stacked up.

"Fine." Rose sighed. "Have it your way."

She stuffed the squirrel back in her purse and took out her phone. Hope might be enthralled, but Rose had already had her fill of watching Peg judge. She placed a call to Peter and was delighted when he picked up.

Unfortunately, the call turned out to be brief. Peter informed her that he was holding the bottom of the tall extension ladder while Jason cleaned out the shelter's gutters. Once again, he assured Rose everything was proceeding smoothly and that she was not to worry about a thing.

"It sounds as though you hardly even miss me," she said.

"Oh Rose." Peter's voice dropped. "Never doubt that for a moment. You are the light of my life and always will be."

Rose's heart squeezed. "Even when I'm a thousand miles away?"

"Even then," he replied. "But I'm afraid I have to go. Jason is glaring at me from two stories up. If I don't hang up soon, he's going to drop gutter gunk on my head."

"Be careful," Rose told him.

"Always," Peter said. Then the connection ended.

Still holding her phone, Rose lifted her gaze and looked around. Peg was busy in the ring. Hope was lying quietly on the floor beside her chair. For the moment, no one needed anything from her. That was a pleasant change. She decided to look up Lexington restaurants. Maybe when Peg was finished for the day, Rose could make a recommendation.

She was scrolling through a list of local eateries when a news bulletin popped up on her screen. A familiar name caught Rose's eye. Abruptly her fingers stopped moving.

MAN KILLED IN FARM ACCIDENT, the headline said in bold lettering. Below that was a slightly smaller line of print: JIM GRABLE PRONOUNCED DEAD AT THE SCENE.

Rose sucked in a shocked breath. Jim Grable was the yearling manager she and Peg had met the day before at Six Oaks. She clicked on the link, then skimmed quickly through the remainder of the article. It offered some details, but also left many questions unanswered.

Jim Grable, 42, a longtime resident of Woodford County, was found dead yesterday afternoon in a barn at a prominent Midway Thoroughbred facility. A groom went to investigate when a loose yearling came running out of a barn. He found Grable lying in the aisle beside an open stall door. Grable, an experienced horseman, was unconscious and had sustained a serious head injury. The authorities quickly responded, but Grable was pronounced dead at the scene. The police are looking into what might have caused the accident.

"No," Rose said in a stunned whisper.

Hope lifted her head and looked at her in concern.

Still processing what she'd read, Rose reached over and absently gave the Poodle a pat. "Don't worry. Everything's going to be fine."

Hope didn't look convinced by the reassurance. Rose couldn't blame her. She wasn't convinced either.

Chapter 7

"I enjoyed that," Peg told her ring steward when she finished judging her group. She'd wasted no time in putting the Standard Poodle on top. In fact, she wouldn't be surprised if the dog went all the way to Best in Show.

Peg was equally pleased with the rest of her placements. The French Bulldog, always a ringside favorite, had been second. The Coton de Tulear was third. A deserving Tibetan Spaniel had strutted its way to fourth. There was nothing more rewarding than having a group of quality breed winners to choose from, and this one had been first-rate.

Peg exited the ring in high spirits, congratulating herself on a job well done. She hoped she'd be able to convince Rose to remain at the Alltech Arena long enough to watch the last group and Best in Show. She wanted to see if her prediction about the Standard Poodle was correct. Hopefully the handsome dog would cap off the day with another triumph.

Peg skirted around the big ring to reach the far side where Hope and Rose were waiting for her. As soon as she was near enough to see the expression on Rose's face, however, Peg's buoyant mood faded. Something was wrong.

Her stride quickened. Peg's gaze immediately went to Hope. The Poodle appeared to be fine. She'd risen to her feet and was wagging her tail in anticipation of Peg's arrival. That caused Peg to relax a bit. Maybe nothing too awful had happened.

Except that Rose—normally a stickler for good posture—was slumped in her chair. She was bent over her phone with an unhappy grimace on her face. Rose didn't even notice Peg's approach. That was very odd.

Peg swooped in beside the pair and reached for Hope's leash. Rose finally looked up when the narrow strip of leather was tugged from her hands.

"What's the matter?" Peg asked. "You look like someone died."

Rose swallowed heavily. "Someone did."

The news hit Peg like a punch. She hadn't expected that. There was a free chair on Hope's other side. Peg sank down into it.

"Who?"

"Jim Grable."

Fresh from her triumphant turn in the group, Peg's head was still filled with dogs. She couldn't immediately place the name.

"Who?" she asked again.

"We met him yesterday morning, at Six Oaks Farm. He was the yearling manager."

"Right." Peg nodded. "The man who was so rude to Lucia."

"Precisely."

"Dead?" Peg found that hard to believe. "He seemed fine when we were there. Are you sure?"

Rose passed over her phone. The story was still on the screen. Peg could read it for herself.

Peg's first thought was the same that Rose's had been. There wasn't nearly enough information in the short article. "A serious head injury," she mused. "What do you suppose that means?"

Rose didn't know either. "A skull fracture maybe?"

"And the loose yearling? Is that important? Do you suppose Jim got kicked?"

"Rather than asking questions I can't answer," Rose said, "you might as well say what you're really thinking."

"All right." Peg handed back the phone "What am I thinking?"

"The same thing I'm thinking. Since no one appears to have witnessed what happened, why are the police so sure it was an accident?"

"Another question we can't answer," Peg said. "Maybe it's because on a farm like Six Oaks—one with lots of big, strong, animals—accidents *do* happen." She'd witnessed that for herself on her previous trip to Kentucky. "Or maybe it has something to do with the nature of the wound."

"Which isn't specified," Rose pointed out with a frown. "A few more details might help us make sense of this."

"You mean gory details." Peg didn't sound displeased.

Rose just shrugged. "Gory details can be enormously helpful. The months Peter and I spent working in the slums of Honduras taught us that. With doctors in short supply, we always carried a medical kit. There's no point in being squeamish when having the right information can make all the difference. Presented with a wound that needed care, one of the first things we learned was to ask for specific details about how it happened."

"I doubt that anyone's going to offer us details about what happened here," Peg said. Then suddenly she uttered an oath under her breath. "Unless . . ."

"Now what?" Rose was beginning to feel as though she'd already dealt with enough turmoil for one day.

"In a barn full of yearlings, what are the chances that the one that got loose and caused trouble was mine?"

The Standard Poodle won Best in Show.

That should have brightened Peg's mood. Instead, she

barely noticed. She was still thinking about Jim Grable's death when the BIS judge pointed to the glamorous Poodle as his winner.

"That's done." Rose stood up. She'd spent much of the day sitting down, so why did her feet ache? "We can go home now, right?"

Hope's head lifted at the mention of *home*. Like Rose, the Poodle had had a very long day. Peg was the only one who looked as though she wouldn't mind starting the dog show over again.

"Sorry, girl." Peg reached over to scratch beneath Hope's chin. "Rose misspoke. We're a long way from home. But we'll take you back to the hotel where you can have a good dinner and then fall asleep on my bed. How does that sound?"

"Like heaven," said Rose. "Can I do the same thing?"

"If you wish. Although unless you intend to make do with Hope's kibble and stew, we'll have to come up with some dinner."

"Whatever," Rose grumbled. She was almost too tired to care.

Rose let Peg drive. She and Hope curled up together on the back seat and closed their eyes. Neither one stirred when Peg detoured to a popular barbecue place on the way to the hotel. But when she returned to the minivan with two boxed dinners, the aroma coming from the bags made Rose and Hope both sit up.

"Yum," said Rose. "What's that?"

"Brisket, pulled pork, baked beans, potato salad, and corn pudding. I only asked for two platters, but it looks like enough to feed an army."

"Perfect." Rose was suddenly starving. "I feel like I could eat a whole iguana if I had to."

Peg glanced back over her shoulder. "Please tell me you're not speaking from experience."

"When in Rome . . ." Rose shrugged and left it at that.

Back at the hotel, all three made quick work of their dinners. While they ate, Rose searched through the local news channels for more information on Jim Grable's death. None was forthcoming.

Eventually they gave up and streamed a movie, a romantic comedy that made Rose laugh and Peg snort in disbelief. She was due back at the Alltech Arena at eight A.M. on Sunday for her next assignment, so Hope had one last walk when the movie ended. Then they all turned in.

By the time Peg was ready to go the next morning, Rose had come up with a new plan. She and Hope were opting out of the day's dog show.

"What do you mean?" Peg asked as if the idea was unfathomable.

"We're not going with you," Rose said firmly.

Peg was standing in the doorway between their two rooms. Rose was seated in an armchair near her window. Hope was lying on her bed. Neither one looked as though they were about to budge.

"Why not?"

"Because dog shows are your thing, not ours."

Peg gave Hope—her finished champion and obedience winner—a meaningful look. Which Rose intercepted. She spoke up on the Poodle's behalf.

"It was different when Hope was younger and competing in the show ring herself. Then she had a reason for being there, like you did yesterday. But face it, Peg. Hope and I were superfluous. It was too long a day for an old dog." Rose paused then added, "And for this old lady."

Peg wanted to argue. She really did. Except that she could see the merit in what Rose was saying. "But if you stay here, what will you do all day?"

"We don't know." Rose glanced at Hope. "I'm sure we'll come up with something fun to occupy our time, won't we?"

Hope's tail flapped up and down on the duvet that covered the bed. She was always happy to be included in a conversation, even when she didn't know what it was about.

Rose stood up and headed for the door. As if everything was already settled. Which, in her mind, it was.

"Come on, it's getting late. We'll take you to the Horse Park and drop you off. You can call me later when you're ready to be picked up."

"Hmmph," Peg grumbled. She'd enjoyed seeing Rose and Hope sitting outside her ring the day before. Well, apparently that wasn't going to happen again. And Rose was right; time was passing. She needed to be on her way.

"Never mind about me," she said. "Half the judges from the show are staying at this hotel. Surely someone can give me a lift. While you and Hope are planning your exciting day, I'll just go stand in the parking lot and stick out my thumb."

Rose turned around. "I didn't mean to hurt your feelings."

"Don't be silly." Peg headed back to her room where she swept a cable knit sweater off the foot of her bed. The arena had been pleasantly cool the day before. "My feelings have nothing to do with it. If you'd rather spend your time gallivanting, that's certainly your prerogative."

"Gallivanting," Rose repeated, liking the sound of the word. She'd followed Peg into her room. "That's exactly what we'll do. Besides, you know perfectly well that you'll be too busy to miss us."

Peg was determined to have the final word.

"Speak for yourself," she said haughtily. "I shall see you later." She opened the door, exited the room, then let the door slam shut behind her.

Rose turned back to see Hope standing in the doorway between the two rooms. The big Poodle looked at Rose uncertainly. She wasn't accustomed to Peg leaving without saying goodbye. Or to slamming doors.

For a moment, Rose hesitated. Some sort of action on her part seemed called for. Maybe a comforting hug. Not that Rose had ever hugged a dog before.

She tried to think what Peg would do in this situation. Probably she'd just snap her fingers and suddenly everything would be right again. Well, that wasn't going to work for Rose. Lord only knew why it worked for Peg.

Rose walked over to Hope and knelt down so that she and the Poodle were face-to-face. Hope's eyes were dark and expressive. They truly did look like windows to her soul. And right now, her soul looked unhappy.

That was interesting, Rose mused. She'd never thought about dogs having souls before. She opened her arms and beckoned gently.

Hope took a tentative step forward. That was all Rose needed. She slid her hands, and then her arms, around the Poodle's neck. Slowly she gathered the big dog close. Hope's body felt warm and solid next to Rose's. The silky hair on Hope's ears tickled her nose. Briefly the two of them breathed in unison. *In and out. In and out.*

"You have nothing to worry about," Rose said gently. "You're with me now. And we're going to be great together."

She'd barely finished speaking before Hope drew her head away. For a moment, Rose worried that she'd done the wrong thing. But then the Poodle's pink tongue emerged from her mouth, and she licked the side of Rose's face. Two months earlier, Rose would have been repulsed by the gesture.

Now it felt just right.

An hour later, they still hadn't left the hotel room. Rose was sitting by the window reading a book. Hope was content to snooze on the bed. They both lifted their heads when a knock sounded on the door.

"It's probably housekeeping," Rose told Hope. She stood up and went to answer it. "You and I can go to the other room while they clean this one."

Rose opened the door, expecting to see a maid with a housekeeping cart. Instead, a young woman dressed in khakis, boots, and a blue polo shirt was standing in the hallway. Lucia Alvarez.

Two days earlier, when Lucia had taken Rose and Peg on their tour of Six Oaks, she'd looked pulled together and professional. Now, her shirt was untucked, her dark hair was disheveled, and her eyes were rimmed in red, as though she might have been crying.

Caught by surprise, Rose was momentarily lost for words.

"Mrs. Donovan, I'm sorry to disturb you." Lucia spoke quickly, as if she half expected the door to close in her face. Her fingers were clasped together in front of her chest in what looked like a gesture of prayer. Or perhaps supplication. "But I had no choice. I'm in trouble, and I need your help."

There was only one thing Rose could do. She drew the door open wide and stepped back out of the way. "You'd better come inside," she said.

Chapter 8

Lucia stepped across the threshold and stopped. She gazed around the room, looking at its stock hotel bureau and chairs, then the unmade bed and the big black dog. Hope was now standing on top of the rumpled covers.

"That's Hope," Rose reminded her. "You saw her the other day."

"Yes." Lucia still didn't move. "She looks even bigger when she's not locked inside your minivan."

Rose understood that reaction. "The first time I met Hope, she and Peg's other two Standard Poodles had me surrounded. All I could see were three sets of big white teeth. I thought I was going to die."

The story prompted a small smile from Lucia. "I'm glad you survived."

"Me too. Hope is very friendly. You can trust me on that." Rose nodded toward the upholstered chair beside the window. "Come and sit down and we can talk about what's troubling you. Would you like something to drink? There's bottled water in the refrigerator."

"Water would be great. Thank you."

Lucia left plenty of room between herself and the bed as she made her way to the chair. Rose had left her book sitting open on the seat. Lucia carefully marked her page, then set the book on the small table nearby.

Meanwhile, Rose got out a bottle of water. She handed it over, then took a seat on the edge of the bed. When Hope lay down beside her, Rose draped her arm over the Poodle's shoulders.

She waited for Lucia to speak first. Peter had a degree in counseling. Occasionally Rose had the opportunity to watch him in action. She knew there was nothing to be gained by trying to hasten things along.

Lucia sat down and twisted off the bottle cap with a quick flick of her wrist. Her first swallow drained nearly half the bottle. She set it aside, then dug in her pocket for a hairband. With practiced movements, she wove her hair into a long braid and tied it off. When Lucia finally looked up, Rose and Hope were both staring at her.

"I'm afraid I have some unpleasant news to share," she said. "One of the men who worked with Mrs. Turnbull's colt has died. Jim Grable. You met him briefly the other day."

"We're aware of that," Rose told her. "Peg and I learned about the accident on the news."

"Yes, but what the news didn't say is that his death wasn't an accident."

Rose closed her eyes briefly. She and Peg had harbored suspicions. Even so, it was a shock to have them confirmed. Rose was happy to have Hope's supportive presence beside her. "Are you sure?"

Lucia nodded. "There's no doubt. That's what the police said."

"The report mentioned a loose horse. We thought perhaps . . . ?"

"It wasn't the yearling's fault." Lucia's voice was flat, as if she was making an effort to hold her emotions in check. "Someone hit Jim on the back of his head with a hammer. The police found the tool lying nearby."

No, Rose thought. *That didn't sound like an accident.*

"Do they know who did it?" she asked.

"No, nobody saw a thing. The barn is usually pretty

empty at that time of day. There were no witnesses aside from the horses. That's why I have a problem."

"Go on," Rose said.

"Ricky, one of the grooms at the farm, told the police that Jim and I didn't get along. He also said that he'd seen me and Jim fighting earlier in the day."

"That's not good." Rose grimaced. "Was he referring to the interaction that took place when we stopped by to see Peg's yearling?"

"He must have been," Lucia said unhappily. "It's the only time I've been near that barn in weeks. But you and Mrs. Turnbull were there too. You saw what happened. Jim and I weren't fighting. He was just being his usual jackass self. I didn't do anything to set him off."

"No, you didn't," Rose agreed. "He was already upset before you'd even said a thing."

"Exactly. So there's no way his death could be my fault."

"Wait a minute." Rose held up a hand. Maybe she should have seen that coming. But the notion was so outlandish, she hadn't even considered it. "Do the police think you had something to do with it?"

"Yes—all because of what Ricky told them. That's why I need your help." Lucia looked at Rose imploringly. "The police will listen to you and Mrs. Turnbull. You have to tell them there was nothing going on between me and Jim. That I had no reason to want him dead."

Lucia reached for her water bottle and took another long swallow. Her cheeks were red with indignation. Her fingernails were bitten down to the quick. All at once, she looked very young. And possibly afraid that Rose wouldn't believe her.

There was no chance of that. Before Lucia had even finished drinking, Rose knew she was going to try to help. But first she needed more information.

"That doesn't make sense," she mused. "Despite what

Ricky told them. All the police have is the report of a spat that was barely incidental to the crime. That's a flimsy premise on which to hang a suspicion of murder."

"Not if they don't have any better ideas," Lucia grumbled. "Because the police are under pressure to wrap things up quickly and quietly. Not only do they have a murder with no witnesses and no suspects, they also have Six Oaks telling them to make the problem go away. All the farm cares about is protecting the business."

"Quietly?" Rose repeated. "Is that why Grable's death was reported as an accident rather than a murder?"

"I'm sure it was. Somebody at the top must have taken care of it. The big Thoroughbred farms are like major corporations. They wield a great deal of power in the small towns around here. Maintaining their clients' trust means everything. It's bad enough having to admit to an accident taking place on the farm. A murder would be much worse."

Rose mulled over what Lucia had said. "If your only connection to Grable's death is someone pointing a finger at you, I don't see how the police will be able to build a case against you."

"They won't have to," Lucia said bitterly. "Just naming me a suspect will be enough to get me fired from a job I worked damn hard to get. Even worse, it would put an end to my hopes of working anywhere in the Thoroughbred industry."

Rose started to interrupt, but Lucia wasn't finished.

"You don't understand. People look at me and see a young Hispanic woman all on her own. No family to protect her, no big brothers to ease her way onto the farms where they hold jobs themselves. Half the people I meet probably assume I'm not even legal."

Lucia scowled at that. "I started at the bottom at Six

Oaks, mucking stalls six days a week. And I busted my butt to work my way up. I showed up when it was a hundred degrees outside, and when there was a foot of snow on the ground. Along the way, I've broken two bones and knocked out a tooth. Working with young horses is hard, but it's the only thing I've wanted to do. And even after all that, you know what?"

Rose remained silent and shook her head.

"The higher-ups at Six Oaks still consider me expendable. They know they could fire me today and find another girl to take my place tomorrow. And if there was even the slightest chance that I posed a PR threat to the farm, no one there would hesitate to make that happen."

Lucia's chest was heaving. A tear had welled up in the corner of her eye. She lifted a hand and dashed it away angrily. Rose went to get another bottle of water out of the refrigerator. Lucia accepted it from her and immediately took a drink.

"I'm sorry I lost my temper," she said when she'd caught her breath. She was already starting to rise. "After you had to listen to that, I guess it's stupid for me to think you might still want to help me."

"Quite the opposite." Rose reached out a hand to stop her. "Now I'm even more determined to help you find justice. And I'm sure Peg will feel the same way."

Rose was aware that Hope had been observing the interaction between her and Lucia. It almost felt as though the Poodle was listening to what they were saying. Sitting with her arm looped over Hope's body, Rose could feel when the dog's scrutiny shifted from her to Lucia as each of them spoke. *How interesting was that?*

When Rose left to get the water, Hope hopped off the bed and pressed herself against Lucia's leg. Initially, the woman recoiled at her touch, but Hope persevered. Moments later, Lucia's hand dropped down to rest on Hope's back. Her fingers began to comb through the thick curls. Lucia's shoulders began to relax. "Thank you," she said. She appeared to be speaking to both Hope and Rose.

"Don't thank me yet." Rose reclaimed her seat on the bed. "It sounds as though we have a lot of work to do."

Lucia looked hopeful. "Does that mean you and Mrs. Turnbull will talk to the police? You'll tell them what you saw?"

"If it comes to that." Rose was already considering other options. "But first things first. There's no need to call me Mrs. Donovan. My name is Rose. And Mrs. Turnbull is Peg. If we're going to be friends, we should be on a first name basis."

"Are we"—Lucia paused—"going to be friends?"

"I should hope so," Rose replied. "It sounds as though you could use some good people on your side. Do you mind if I ask you a few questions?"

"No. Of course not."

Rose settled in and got comfortable. "Then let's go back to the beginning. You said that a groom . . . Ricky . . . ?"

Lucia nodded.

". . . told the police about the conversation you'd had with Jim Grable that morning. Did the police also speak with you directly about it?"

"Yes," Lucia said. "Although that happened later. First they interviewed everyone who was in the vicinity of the yearling barn when Jim's body was discovered."

"Which you were not?" Rose guessed.

"No. For the past several months, I've worked in various positions all around the farm. Some days I'm in the office. Other times, I'm filling in at a barn or the training center. I didn't find out about Jim's death until at least an hour later. If I'd been in the office, I'd have already known there was an accident and that police and an ambulance were responding."

"Are accidents a frequent occurrence on the farm?"

Lucia shrugged. "Horses. You know. But usually it's not a big deal. We either patch the guy up and send him home for the day, or worst case, someone drives the injured person over to Urgent Care. As far as I know, this is the first time the police have been called to the farm."

"Good to know," Rose murmured.

"Friday afternoon I was assisting at one of the broodmare barns. I had no idea what was going on when a patrol car pulled up outside, and an officer came to find me."

"Did you get the officer's name?" Rose asked. She wasn't nearly as good at asking questions as Peg was. But she knew this was the kind of information Peg would want to have later.

"Officer Sherlock."

Rose snorted out a laugh. "Really?"

"I know," Lucia said. "What are the chances?"

"And when Sherlock came to speak with you, that was the first time you heard that Jim Grable was dead?"

"Yes."

"Were you shocked by the news?"

"Of course." Lucia frowned. "Who wouldn't be?"

Rose sat back, putting some extra space between Lucia and herself. She'd seen Peter make a similar move when he wanted to lower the pressure on someone he was counseling. "Quick answer without stopping to think. What was the first thing that crossed your mind when you heard that Jim was dead?"

"I was relieved," Lucia said, then immediately looked mortified. "Wait! That's not what I meant."

Rose smiled at the contradictory response. "It *is* what you meant," she said. "And that's okay too."

"No, it's not. It makes me sound like a horrible person."

"It makes you sound like someone who told the truth.

Which is exactly what I wanted you to do." When Rose sat up, the rumpled bed covers shifted with her. Her pillow rolled off the edge of the bed and landed onto the floor.

Lucia leaned down and picked it up. "Do you want me to make that bed for you?"

"No." Rose was surprised. "Why would you do that?"

"My first job when I came to this country at seventeen was as a hotel maid. I'm good at it."

"Seventeen?"

Lucia nodded. "My brother and I came together. He's two years older than me."

"Still." Rose tried not to sound shocked. "You were just a couple of kids."

"We had an opportunity and we took it," Lucia said practically. "Both of us were willing to work hard to get ahead, and this is where the jobs are."

Rose took a minute to process that. It occurred to her that she hadn't been much older than that when she'd entered the convent.

"My first job—if you want to call it that—was as a Sister of Divine Mercy," she said.

Lucia's eyes widened. "You were a nun?"

"I was. We got up early every morning and made our own beds." Rose was enjoying Lucia's reaction. "Heaven forbid our corners weren't perfect. Mother Superior didn't tolerate sloppiness. So I'm good at bed-making too."

"A nun," Lucia said again, as if she couldn't quite believe it. "Does that mean you always have to tell the truth?"

"Well, I'm not a member of the order anymore," Rose pointed out. "But I do still try to lead a principled life."

"I see." Lucia's gaze skittered away.

Rose sighed. "Is there something you want to tell me?"

"No. Everything's fine." Lucia didn't look like everything was fine. "I would never lie to a nun."

A former nun, Rose thought, but she didn't voice the

thought aloud. Despite her current, non-secular status, she hoped Lucia's statement still applied.

"Let's backtrack for a moment," she said instead. "So Officer Sherlock came to find you. He told you that Jim Grable was dead. Was that when he asked you about what Ricky said?"

"Yes," Lucia confirmed. "I immediately told him that none of what he'd heard was true. Ricky was blowing things way out of proportion. Jim and I weren't fighting. I was just . . ."

"Dealing with a jackass?" Rose supplied.

"Something like that."

"Did Sherlock believe you?"

"No. At least I don't think so. I got the impression that he was happy to have a lead to pursue. It felt to me like, since I'd already been labeled a suspicious person, nothing I could say was going to change that."

"That's ridiculous," Rose snorted.

"I agree. And it's why I came to see you. I hoped that your voice, and Peg's, would carry more weight than mine."

Lucia glanced at her watch. Then she nudged Hope to one side and rose gracefully to her feet. "I have to go. I should already be at work. I'd told them I'd be late this morning, but now I'm pushing my luck. Will you think about what I said?" Her voice held a note of entreaty. "*Please?*"

"I doubt I'll think about anything else," Rose said as they walked to the door. "But I still have two more questions. I'll try to be quick."

Lucia's hand was already reaching for the doorknob. She paused and waited.

"You said the Thoroughbred farms are like major corporations. Do they have security cameras in the barns at Six Oaks?"

"No. Lots of racetracks have them, but we don't. There's never been a need before."

"Okay. Second question: who would have had a motive for killing Jim Grable?"

Lucia turned back to face her. "Everyone."

"Excuse me?"

"I mean, the entire staff at Six Oaks anyway. I guess I can only speak for the farm. Jim was a terrible boss. He made everyone's lives miserable. Ask anyone who had to work with him. Everybody hated him."

Chapter 9

Peg was in a good mood when she returned to the hotel late that afternoon.

Not only had the Affenpinscher from her Toy Group won Best in Show, but she'd also plucked a sable smooth Collie out of the Bred-by-Exhibitor Class, awarded her Best of Variety, then watched the bitch place third in a very competitive Herding Group. All in all, she was feeling rather pleased with what she'd accomplished that day.

Now she couldn't wait to get back to her room to rescue Hope. Without Peg there to provide entertainment, the poor Poodle had probably been stuck inside for most of the day. Rose was likely to have buried herself in a book and totally lost track of time. Peg hoped she had had at least remembered to take Hope outside for a bit of exercise every so often.

Peg fit her key in the lock and threw open the door to her room with a smile on her face. No doubt hearing what she'd been up to would be the highlight of Rose and Hope's day. She couldn't wait to tell them all about it.

Except . . . nobody was there to greet her. The room was empty. The bed was made, the drapes were partially closed, and a pair of Peg's shoes was tucked neatly beneath the bureau. Other than that, there was nothing to see.

Peg went to the adjoining door and checked Rose's room

next door. That was empty too. What a disappointment. Peg had been so ready to share the news of her judging triumphs. She could hardly celebrate without an appreciative audience to applaud her success.

Peg took out her phone and pulled up Rose's number. Before she could make the connection, however, the door opened and Hope came bounding into the room. Rose followed close behind.

She was dressed in leggings, sneakers, and an oversized T-shirt. Her cheeks were flushed from exertion. Her short gray hair was standing up on end as though she'd been raking her fingers through it. Rose tossed a balled-up leash onto the bureau, then turned to Peg.

"Good, you're back!" she said, as Hope trotted into the bathroom and took a drink of cold water from the bowl on the floor. "Hope and I have had a very interesting day. I have so much to tell you."

"I do too," Peg started to reply, then she paused and frowned. "Wait . . . what's going on around here? Where have you two been?"

"We were exploring the Legacy Trail. I read about it online. It's a twelve-mile hiking trail that goes all the way from the Horse Park to downtown Lexington. It's pretty cool." Rose swooped down and nabbed a bottle of water from the mini-fridge.

Peg looked at Rose incredulously. "You just got back from *hiking twelve miles?*"

"No, of course not." Rose laughed. "You don't have to do the whole thing. We went maybe two miles. Just enough to get our blood pumping. Right, Hope?"

Hope had finished drinking and gone to say hello to Peg. Now she was standing on her hind legs with her front paws braced against Peg's chest. Peg was stroking both sides of the Poodle's body with her hands. Hearing her name, Hope glanced back at Rose and woofed softly.

Perplexed, Peg looked back and forth between them.

This wasn't anything like the homecoming she'd envisioned. When had Hope and Rose learned to communicate? And what other curious things had they gotten up to while she was away?

"You go first," Rose said. She flopped down on the bed. "How was your dog show?"

"Fine." Peg was suddenly beginning to suspect her day might not have been the most stimulating one.

"Just fine? I don't think I've ever heard you describe a show in such a tepid manner before. Who won Best in Show?" The question seemed like a safe bet to Rose. Peg always got excited about things like that.

"The Affenpinscher."

"Oh." Rose's face fell. She had no idea what that meant. Truthfully it sounded as though Peg had just sneezed. "Well then, good for him."

"Indeed," Peg agreed. "He was a lovely dog, and it was a well-deserved win. Now, perhaps you'd better tell me what's been going on around here."

Peg pulled out the desk chair and sat down, prepared to listen to whatever outlandish tale Rose was going to tell. Hope lay down on the floor between the two women. She lowered her head to rest between her paws and promptly went to sleep. Clearly she hadn't been sitting around waiting for Peg to return. Peg supposed she should have been gratified by that. Instead, she felt slightly miffed.

"Hope and I had a visitor this morning," Rose said. "Lucia Alvarez showed up not long after you left."

"Oh?" Peg's brow rose. That *was* interesting. And unexpected. "Was she looking for me? Were there papers relating to the sale that I neglected to sign the other day?"

"No, she was looking for both of us and she wanted our help. Apparently Lucia has become a suspect in Jim Grable's murder."

"Suspect?" Peg echoed faintly. Then her eyes widened and her voice rose. "*Murder?*"

"That's right."

"The news report said it was an accident."

"According to Lucia, Six Oaks squelched the true story."

Peg didn't look surprised. "I guess I can see that. The big farms around here wield plenty of influence in local affairs. And you can understand why they wouldn't want the news to get out. Being associated with a murder is bad for business."

"Lucia said the same thing."

Rose scooted up the bed so she could lie with her back against the wall and her legs extended out in front of her. She figured she might as well get comfortable. This conversation was going to take a while.

"What else did she say?" Peg asked with interest. "I thought the dog show was going to be our hot topic of conversation, but it appears I was wrong."

Rose snorted under her breath. Peg was *always* wrong about that.

"How did Lucia become a suspect in Jim Grable's death? And—not that I'm displeased by this turn of events, mind you, but I *am* curious—why did she come to us for help?"

Rose spent the next ten minutes outlining everything Lucia had told her. She thought she'd gleaned a great deal of information from her conversation with the young woman. Even so, when she finished her explanation, Peg was still impatient to know more.

"Of course you and I are going to help her," she said firmly. "Did you tell Lucia that?"

"I did." Rose nodded. "But I need you to clarify something for me. Do you mean we'll help, as in we'll contact Officer Sherlock and refute what Ricky told him? Or as in we'll lend our assistance in solving the crime?"

"That remains to be seen," Peg said briskly. "It occurs to me that there are several important questions you neglected to ask."

Of course there were. That was nothing new. The only time things were done to Peg's satisfaction was when she was doing them herself.

"Did Lucia tell you when, specifically, Jim Grable died?"

"It was in the afternoon."

"More specific than that," Peg said. "As I understand it, everything about the sales yearlings' schedule is regulated. Whether it's feeding, grooming, exercise, or turnout, it happens at the same time each day. What I'm wondering is, which farm employees would have been in the barn at that particular time?"

"Apparently none of them," Rose told her. "Lucia said it happened at a time when the barn is usually empty. That's why there were no witnesses."

Peg gazed at her across the short distance between them. "That makes sense except for one thing."

"What?"

"If the barn was supposed to be empty, what was Jim Grable doing there?"

Rose frowned. That was a good question. Obviously she should have thought to ask it herself.

"I'd imagine we'll be able to find out more about the timetable from Lucia," she said. "Although it's less likely that she'll be able to account for Grable's activities or whereabouts."

Peg's fingers were drumming lightly on the desk behind her. "Once we pin down the time of death, I'd like to know where Lucia was when it happened. I don't suppose she mentioned that either?"

"Unfortunately, no." Once again, Rose had been caught short. It was demoralizing how easily Peg was able to expose the inadequacies of her interrogation technique. "She said she's been doing a variety of jobs around the farm recently. When Officer Sherlock interviewed her after the body was found, she was at the broodmare complex."

"Did she say how long she'd been there?"

Rose shook her head.

"So we don't know how much time elapsed between those two events," Peg mused. "Nor how easy it might be to travel between those two locations quickly and without being seen."

"I don't like the direction you're heading with these questions," Rose grumbled. "Now it sounds as though you're thinking of Lucia as a suspect."

"Nonsense. I'm merely keeping my options open." Peg's fingers continued to tap. "Next thought, the loose yearling. A farm like Six Oaks is exceedingly careful with its Thoroughbreds. They have to be, or they'd lose all their clients. I should think a loose horse is an unusual occurrence. So how was that related to what happened to Jim Grable?"

"It wasn't," Rose said. "I told you that earlier."

"No," Peg corrected. "You said Lucia told you that the yearling wasn't at fault. But that doesn't mean it wasn't involved. Maybe Grable was busy doing something with the horse, and that's why he didn't hear someone sneaking up behind him with a hammer."

"Or," Rose proposed, "maybe the killer opened the stall door and turned the yearling loose after Grable was already dead. Perhaps he thought the horse would serve as a distraction while he made his getaway."

"If so, it didn't work," Peg pointed out. "Since it was because of the horse that Grable's body was discovered."

"And yet the killer *did* manage to escape without being seen." Rose was pleased to be able to score a point of her own. "So I'd argue that the diversion he created was successful."

Peg frowned at her—she hated being out-argued—and changed the subject. "While we're talking about the hammer . . ."

Rose smirked. "Are we talking about the hammer? Because honestly, I don't have much to say on the topic of tools."

"I don't either," Peg admitted. "Except to wonder whether a hammer is the kind of thing that would normally be sitting out, in the aisle of a barn—"

"Pointing to a crime of convenience," Rose interjected.

"—or whether the killer would have had to bring it with him from somewhere else."

"Pointing to premeditation," Rose finished for her.

"Look at us." Peg sounded pleased. "It's almost as if we're on the same wavelength for once."

Rose smiled too. An event like that was worth noting.

"We should consider both possibilities," she said. "According to Lucia, there are plenty of potential suspects, since everyone at Six Oaks hated the man."

"Surely not everyone," Peg replied. "After all, Grable held a position of some responsibility. Somewhere, there must be a boss who thought he was doing a good job."

"Maybe Ben Burrell knows something about that." Rose got up from the bed. She'd been lounging long enough. Plus, having skipped lunch, her stomach was beginning to rumble.

"That's a thought—" Peg stopped and stared. "Is that your stomach growling?"

"Yes, sorry. I haven't eaten all day."

"No need to apologize. I was only worried it might be Hope." Peg stood up too. She was always happy to be on the move. "Why didn't you eat lunch?"

"I don't know." Rose shrugged. "I guess I forgot."

"You forgot." Peg didn't look convinced.

"Okay, maybe after all these years in the convent, when I was almost never by myself, and certainly not at mealtime, I guess I'm just not comfortable eating alone."

Yet another fascinating fact from the annals of Sister Anne Marie. Peg's brain boggled at the details about convent life that Rose occasionally revealed. She couldn't imagine living like that, always subject to someone else's rules and restrictions.

"In this case, you should stick with me," she said. "I heard about a good steakhouse that's not far from here."

Hope must have been listening, because she opened her eyes and lifted her head. "Yes, I said steak." Peg reached down to give the Poodle a pat. "We'll be sure to bring something back for you."

"I just need two minutes to change my clothes." Rose was already heading toward the closet. "And at the end of that time I'm going to ask for your decision."

"Filet mignon," Peg said promptly. "Medium rare."

"Not that decision." Rose glanced back over her shoulder. "Lucia. What are we going to do about her?"

"I don't need two minutes for that decision either. It's perfectly obvious that we have to do more than just talk to Officer Sherlock. We should start by going back to Six Oaks tomorrow morning and asking some questions. What do you say to that?"

"I couldn't agree more," Rose replied.

Chapter 10

Peg and Rose set out for Six Oaks again the following morning. Peg was driving the minivan. Rose was enjoying the scenery as it went flying past her window. Hope was stretched out on the back seat.

It was a beautiful early-September day. The sun was shining in a nearly cloudless sky. A light breeze cooled the air. In anticipation of doing plenty of walking, both women had dressed in casual clothes and comfortable shoes. They couldn't have asked for better weather for their visit to the farm.

"This really is horse country," Rose said. "Everywhere I look I see them. The land is beautiful too. But I don't understand why there are so many old black barns in the fields. Most are crumbling to pieces. They look like they're about to fall down."

"Those are tobacco barns," Peg said. "Remnants of an industry that's gone by the wayside. At one time Kentucky was one of the largest tobacco producing states in the country. The government buyout in 2005 changed that, however. Now most farmers here have turned to other crops, and the barns don't have a use anymore."

Rose turned in her seat. "How do you know so much about tobacco, of all things?"

"I read everything. And I ask questions. I'm always curious about why things are the way they are."

"I'm well aware of that." Rose laughed. "It's your curiosity that's gotten us embroiled in several investigations."

"And yours," Peg returned. "I'm not the one who interrogated Lucia yesterday. This one's all on you."

"Lucia needs help," Rose said simply. "And, luckily, we're in a position to be able to do that. Aside from a father in Mexico and a brother in Southern California, she's been on her own since the age of seventeen. It seems to me it would be nice for her to have someone to lean on for a change."

"You're a soft touch, Rose."

"You say that like it's an insult." Rose refused to be offended. "I happen to think that caring about other people's needs is a good thing."

Peg didn't have a comeback for that. So instead she concentrated on her driving. Minutes later, they arrived at Six Oaks' imposing front gate.

"I asked Ben if we could watch some of the final preparations before my colt ships to the sale tomorrow," Peg said. "I was hoping Lucia could take us around again, but Ben said she's unavailable. He'll be escorting us himself."

Peg pulled into the same shady spot where she'd parked the minivan on their previous visit. As she opened the vehicle's windows halfway, Hope sat up, looked around, and sighed. She knew what was coming.

"Just go back to sleep," Peg told her. "We won't be gone long."

When they entered the office building, Ben Burrell was in the paneled reception area waiting for them. He immediately smiled at Peg and came to greet them.

Ben was in his sixties and had a ruddy complexion that looked like a permanent sunburn. A Six Oaks ball cap covered his receding hairline, and a paunch was straining the efficacy of his belt. He was only an inch or so taller than Rose, which meant that his head was barely higher than Peg's shoulder.

"Nice to see you again, Peg," he said, before holding out his hand to Rose. His palm was callused but his grip was gentle. "You must be Mrs. Donovan. It's a pleasure to meet you. Peg tells me you don't have much interest in horses, but I always say, you never know until you try. Maybe you'll see something today that'll whet your appetite for the game."

"Spoken like a true salesman," Peg said. "If Ben had his way, I'd be increasing my investment in Thoroughbreds, rather than trying to reduce it."

"Hey, you can't blame a guy for trying." Ben grinned. "That's my job. As you know, we at Six Oaks are always available to help you out with whatever you need."

"I appreciate that." Peg hoped he'd still feel that way when she and Rose started asking questions about Jim Grable's death. "Let's get going, shall we?"

They exited the office together. Ben led the way to a truck that looked just like the one they'd ridden in with Lucia. Peg promptly climbed into the front seat. Rose had already resigned herself to sitting in the back.

Ben closed the door on their side, then walked around the truck, got in and slid behind the wheel. "There's one thing I want to mention before we get underway," he said. "With the Keeneland sale about to start, it's pretty hectic at the yearling division right now. Lots of things need to be taken care of in a short amount of time, and every single item is important. As you know yourself"—he nodded toward Peg—"this sale can be the one chance breeders have to maximize their profits for the entire year."

"Quite right," Peg agreed. She knew what her year's equine expenditures looked like down to the penny. She was counting on the proceeds from this sale to put her back in the black.

Ben put the truck in gear and pulled out of the parking lot. "While I'm happy to show you around, I hope you understand it would be best if we let people get on with doing their jobs. Observe but stay out of the way. The colts will be getting their first set of shoes this morning. That might be interesting for you to watch."

"We understand completely," Rose assured him. "We'll be delighted to see whatever you want to show us. Lucia did a wonderful job with us the other day. I was hoping we might be able to say hello to her?"

Ben glanced back at Rose over his shoulder. "I'm sorry you missed her. Lucia isn't on the farm today."

"Oh?" Peg asked. "Where is she?"

"She left for Keeneland early this morning. We're setting up our barn there so everything will be ready for our incoming horses. Book two, where your colt is being offered, is the largest group in our sales consignment. We'll have eight colts and nine fillies."

"Seventeen is a lot," Rose commented as Ben turned down the driveway that led to the yearling and training divisions. "What's involved in setting up a barn?"

"Basically, we ship in everything we're going to need for the care and management of those yearlings over the next four days. You name it, we're bringing it. For the barn itself: straw, buckets, hoses, pitchforks, rakes, brooms. Then we'll also need hay, feed, and supplements, as well as all our grooming supplies, the new sale's halters and shanks, and stall cards to hang outside each stall."

"Four days?" Peg asked. "I thought book two was two days long."

"The selling part is," Ben replied. "Keeneland will send four hundred yearlings through the ring on each of those days. But before the buyers bid, they first come back to the barns to inspect the horses and decide which ones they're interested in. After your colt ships in tomorrow, he'll spend the next two days being shown to prospective buyers."

"Four hundred a day?" Rose was shocked.

"It's the biggest Thoroughbred sale of the year," Ben told her. "Peg's nice colt is selling in book two, but there are six books total. The sale will run for nearly two weeks. More than four thousand yearlings will go through the auction ring during that time."

Ben parked the truck beside the nearer of the two yearling barns, and they all got out. The small paddocks beside the barn were empty, but Peg could see activity in a large pasture beyond them. A row of yearlings, each led by a handler, were walking around the perimeter of the field. One of the colts was tossing his head and playing around, but the rest were behaving beautifully.

Peg's gaze narrowed on a chestnut in the middle of the line. Even from afar, she recognized the way he carried himself.

"Is that my colt?" she asked.

Ben nodded, impressed. "You have a good eye to be able to pick him out from here."

"I should hope so. I've spent my whole life developing it."

"Peg also breeds and judges dogs," Rose explained.

"I remember hearing something about that. Poodles, right?" Ben grinned. "Although if you can find any similarities between those athletes out there and your lap dogs at home, I'd be pretty surprised."

"The notion that Poodles are nothing more than lap dogs is a misconception," Peg began.

Oh good Lord, thought Rose. *Here we go.*

She reached over and poked Peg. "We're here to look at horses. Maybe you could save your lecture for another time?"

"Maybe Ben is interested in what I have to say."

"Sure I am." Ben was always eager to humor a paying customer.

"Trust me," Rose told him. "You're not. If you let Peg get started talking about Poodles, she'll never stop. And I'm sure we have more interesting things to discuss. Don't we?"

"Yes," Peg agreed reluctantly. She and Rose followed Ben to stand beside the pasture fence, then gestured into the field. "Is that part of the yearlings' training?"

"Training and conditioning," Ben confirmed. He crossed his arms over the top of the fence. "The walking builds muscle. Up hill, down hill, it's all good for their development. The colts learn how to stride out and really use their bodies. At the same time, they're also learning how to pay attention to the guy at the end of the shank. That's useful when they get to the sales ground, where there'll be all kinds of distractions for them to contend with."

They quieted as the line passed in front of them. Manny, who'd shown Peg her colt on the previous visit, was once again handling him. He gave Peg a two-fingered wave of acknowledgment. She smiled in return.

"Some farms use electric walkers," Ben said when the colts had moved on. "But we like to do things the old-fashioned way. Walking the yearlings by hand is more labor-intensive, but it's also safer."

"Safer," Peg echoed. She'd been looking for an opening, and Ben had just handed her one. "Speaking of that, we heard that an accident took place here the other day. Can you tell us what happened?"

Ben stepped away from the fence. His lips flattened into a thin line. "Where'd you hear about that?"

"It was on the news," Rose said. "And people were talking about it back at our hotel."

"People?" Ben said carefully. "What people?"

"We don't know." Peg's shrug was deliberately casual. "We didn't ask their names. But they said Jim Grable's death wasn't an accident. Rose and I met Mr. Grable the last time we were here, so that came as quite a shock to us."

Ben sighed. He didn't look happy. "No, it wasn't an accident. Though I'd appreciate it if you didn't spread that around. Unfortunately, it seems that somebody knocked Jim on the head."

"Oh my." Rose widened her eyes. "Do the police know who did it?"

"Not exactly. Although I guess maybe they have a couple of ideas."

"What an awful thing to have happen at a beautiful place like this," Peg said. "Who do you think could have been responsible?"

Ben stared at her for a long moment before answering. "What I think is that it's none of my business."

He cast his gaze back to the yearlings in the field. The line had stopped walking and was heading back toward the barn. Ben took that as his cue. He turned away from them, strode twenty feet down the fence line, and opened the gate.

Peg and Rose shared a look.

"Is it my imagination, or was Ben your best friend until you brought up Grable's death?" Rose asked. "Then suddenly he couldn't get away from us fast enough."

Peg nodded as she turned to follow him. "Let's just say I don't think he's going to be spilling his guts anytime soon."

It was left to Rose to bring up the rear. "Spilling his guts? Who are you, Mickey Spillane?"

"You wish."

Ben trailed the yearling colts back to the barn. Peg and Rose followed. A medium-sized truck was parked outside the barn aisle. Beside it, a farrier was working on the feet of a big, burly brown colt.

The man was bent over and looking downward as he held one of the colt's legs braced between his thighs and applied a rasp to the bottom of the hoof. On the ground nearby, a wooden box was filled with other tools of his trade: hoof nippers, a farrier's knife and hammer, and a nail clincher.

"Fascinating." Peg sidled over for a closer look.

Ben slid his hand under her arm and gently drew her back. "Most yearlings I wouldn't mind, but Snow Cloud here can be a little unpredictable. I wouldn't want you standing too close if he got a notion to do something stupid. Your colt will be coming up next."

"Unpredictable." The farrier snorted under his breath. "That's one word for it." He carefully replaced the yearling's foot on the ground, then straightened to face them.

He was taller than Peg and as skinny as a rail. His hair was pulled back in a ponytail that was tied with a leather thong, and the bulge in his cheek was probably a wad of tobacco. Dressed in jeans and a faded denim shirt, he wore a leather apron that started at his waist, then split to cover his legs to below the knees.

He looked at Peg and Rose curiously. "Hi, I'm Abel."

"Peg," she introduced herself. The farrier seemed to be a first-name kind of guy. "And this is Rose."

"Lucky Luna is yours?"

"Yes."

"He's a nice colt."

"Thank you. I'm glad you think so." Peg had heard her colt praised so many times she'd begun to think that must be standard operating procedure when owners visited. Tell each one that theirs was the best, and everyone went home happy.

The brown colt was growing restless at the delay. When he stamped a front foot, the groom holding him looped the leather shank in his hand, then bopped the colt on the nose to tell him to pay attention. Watching the interplay between them, Peg recognized the handler as Sergio, another employee she'd met before.

Meanwhile, Ben had pulled Abel aside. "What are his chances?" he asked the farrier, nodding toward the brown colt.

"Slim and none." Abel shook his head. "There's no way that colt's going to be sound enough to ship to the sale tomorrow. That's a heck of a stone bruise he's got. It might turn into an abscess before it's done."

Ben stared at him. "The owners aren't going to be happy about that."

Abel shrugged. Not his problem. "We've been working on it for a week but there's only so much you can do."

"That's a shame," Ben muttered. "If we could have gotten him there, the colt probably would have topped the session. I'd hate to be the one to have to break that news."

Abel just shrugged again and got back to work. A few minutes later, the brown colt was led away, and then it was Peg's colt's turn.

"What's a stone bruise?" Peg asked Ben as Abel was resetting his equipment. She looked at her colt's hooves. They looked normal to her—which wasn't saying much. As far as she knew, the previous colt's feet had also looked fine.

"The bane of my existence at the moment," Ben groused. "That other colt's a pricey pinhook, owned by a partnership that does a lot of business with the farm. If he misses the sale, there's going to be hell to pay."

Peg nodded. She understood the theory of pinhooking: buying a horse early in its life in the hope of selling it for more money after it had a chance to mature—hopefully improving along the way. In this case, the colt would have been purchased the previous fall as a weanling with the intent to sell him now in his yearling year.

Of course pinhookers also assumed the risk that something might go wrong with the young horse in the meantime. Or that a weanling that looked promising might turn into a very average yearling. But when a pinhook was successful, it offered significant rewards for the gamblers who'd been willing to take the chance.

"I'm sorry," Ben said. "That's a terrible answer to your very reasonable question. Let me try again. Horses' hooves may look hard from where we're standing, but the sole on the bottom is much more sensitive. Just like the sole of your foot. If you step on something sharp, it's going to hurt. Right?"

"Right," Peg agreed.

"Same thing can happen to a horse, and when it does, it often causes a bruise. Most times, they're not too serious, but a bad bruise can take a while to heal. One small rock can put a horse out of commission for weeks."

Peg glanced back toward the field where they'd been watching the yearlings walk. From here, the surface looked like acres of lush green lawn. "It's surprising that a horse could get a stone bruise in pastures as pristine as these."

Ben just sighed. "That's Thoroughbreds for you. If there's one single rock in fifty acres of grass, they're going to find it and step on it. It's just too bad that in this case, the timing couldn't have been worse."

Chapter 11

As so often happened, Peg had gotten involved in a long boring conversation on a topic Rose had no interest in. Not only that, but Peg and Ben were now observing the farrier work on the chestnut colt's feet with the kind of rapt attention most people reserved for life-changing events. Which, as far as Rose could see, this most certainly was not.

While they were busy discussing pins and hooks, Rose strolled over to a paddock beside the barn that housed the yearling fillies. Earlier, the enclosure had been empty. Now it held a single occupant. A small gray filly was nibbling on the grass at her feet. She ignored Rose's approach.

"You must be hungry," Rose said. She leaned her arms on the top rail of the fence like she'd seen Ben do earlier. "Don't they feed you around here?"

"She gets plenty to eat," a voice said from behind her. "Unfortunately, it doesn't seem to help her grow none."

Rose turned around. Tammy Radnor was standing a few feet away. Her booted feet were planted on the ground and her arms were crossed over her chest.

"Something I can do for you?" Tammy asked.

Rose offered a friendly smile. The gesture did nothing to soften Tammy's stern demeanor. "Sure," she said. "You can tell me why this filly gets to come out here and all the others are stuck inside the barn."

Tammy walked over and joined Rose beside the fence. "All the sales yearlings stay up during the day. That keeps them looking sleek and shiny the way the buyers like to see 'em."

Rose nodded. She remembered Lucia mentioning something about that. "So this one isn't going to the sale?"

"Not anymore." Tammy frowned. "She was entered. Owners thought she might bring a good price. Filly's got the breeding to do it. Everybody kept hoping she'd grow, but here we are at sales week, and she's still a midget. Nothing you can do about that. Just Mother Nature having a laugh at our expense."

"So small is bad when it comes to Thoroughbreds?" Rose asked.

"It is if you want to sell for decent money," Tammy said. "The office broke the news to the owners yesterday, and they said go ahead and scratch her from the sale. Not much point in hauling her over there, only to buy her back and bring her home again."

"So you're saying no one would buy her because of her size?" Rose felt a sudden pang of sympathy for the unwanted filly.

"Nope."

"That doesn't seem fair."

Tammy flipped her long braid back over her shoulder. "Welcome to life. Lots of things aren't fair."

Just what Rose needed. A lesson in philosophy from a woman who appeared to think that Rose was slightly stupid, just because she was uneducated on the topic of horses.

Rose pressed on anyway. "Are small racehorses slower than big ones?"

"Nope."

"Do they win fewer races?"

Tammy gave her a withering look.

Rose figured that was another no. She was starting to feel like she was talking to herself. But now that she'd begun this line of questioning, she really wanted to make sense of it.

"Why are people prejudiced against the little ones?" Rose didn't bother to add that the gray filly looked like a big horse to her.

Tammy's lip curled. "Because small men like to buy big horses. Maybe they're compensating, you know?"

Rose smothered an unexpected laugh. "No. Really. That was a serious question."

"And I gave you a serious answer."

Oh. Rose had thought the woman was joking. "So what will happen to this filly if nobody wants her?"

"Geez." Tammy snorted. "There's no reason to make her sound like Little Orphan Annie. Just because she got scratched from the sale, things aren't anywhere near that dire. All it means is that her owners will hang on to her and race her themselves."

She looked over at Rose. "You must be new to the industry."

"Yes." *Obviously.*

"Then let me give you a piece of advice."

Rose was about to mention that Peg was the one who owned the Thoroughbreds, not her. But Tammy was already moving on.

"Hang on to your hat," she said.

Rose turned the expression over in her mind, trying to make it fit in this context. "Because I'm in for a wild ride?" she guessed.

"Because somebody will steal it from you if you don't."

Tammy cackled as if she'd said something witty. Once again, Rose didn't know if she was kidding or not. And considering the other answers she'd received thus far, she wasn't about to ask. Instead she changed the subject.

"Last time we saw you, you were with the broodmares and foals. Today, you're here working with yearlings. Which do you prefer?" That question seemed easy enough.

"Preference has nothing to do with it," Tammy said. "I just go where I'm told. Normally I work with the babies. I enjoy handling the foals and I'm good at it. But when sales time comes around, everything normal goes straight out the window. Right now, we're shorthanded all over the farm. It'll be that way until the sale ends."

"Why is that?" Rose asked.

Tammy stared, as though once again Rose's ignorance had managed to surprise her. "How much do you know about the Keeneland sale?"

"Nothing, other than that it's big." Ben had told them that, so Rose felt safe in repeating it.

"Right." Tammy chuckled, but she didn't sound amused. "It's big. And it has about a million moving parts. Not to mention hundreds of worker bees running around behind the scenes, trying to keep everything running smoothly while making it all look effortless."

"Worker bees," Rose echoed. Once again she was lost.

"Consignors, van drivers, card callers, grooms, showmen, vets, chiropractors, bloodstock agents . . ." Tammy paused for breath, then said, "Where do you think all those people are when they're not busy at a sale?"

"Home?" Rose ventured.

"Most of them are working at their real jobs. The ones that keep them fed and clothed for the rest of the year. Those showmen you'll see at the sale working at the Six Oaks consignment—you know, the guys who bring the yearlings out of the barns and present them to the buyers?"

Rose nodded. She didn't actually know, but it didn't seem prudent to bring that up.

"They're the grooms who are usually here at the farm. The people we rely on to get mostly everything done. Which works out fine when there's no sale going on. But then Keeneland comes around, and half the support staff here takes vacation days so they can go work over there."

"Why would they do that?" Rose asked.

"For the money, of course." Tammy spat out the answer as though it was obvious.

Maybe it should have been. Money seemed to be the answer to almost everything around here. Even so, Rose was still confused.

"But they're getting paid either way. Aren't they?"

"Sure, but it's not the same thing. Not even close. A lot of the guys here work for minimum wage. The money they get paid at the sale is a whole different ball game." Tammy lifted a hand and rubbed her thumb and fingers together to indicate a sizable sum.

"But," Rose sputtered, "isn't it basically the same work?"

"For the grooms, maybe. But not the show people. Nico, Sergio, Manny, they'll all be there. Because they're good at what they do. It takes talent to show off a yearling to its best advantage. That's a real skill. I might even go so far as to call it an art."

Art. Rose frowned. She doubted that.

"Imagine you're a busy buyer with lots of horses to see," Tammy said. "You're only going to devote a couple of minutes to looking at each one before deciding whether or not you're interested. That's a really short amount of time."

Rose nodded. Finally something she understood.

"Now imagine having a showman with the ability to make his horse stand out from all the others. The guy whose yearlings make shoppers' eyes light up as soon as they see it. Being able to grab a buyer's attention like that is special—and as far as consignors are concerned, it's just about priceless."

Rose started as a warm muzzle bumped her arm. She'd been so intent on listening to what Tammy was saying that she hadn't even noticed the gray filly approaching the fence. Now she felt foolish for jumping away. Up close, the yearling looked calm and friendly. Her dark eyes were framed by outrageously long lashes.

"Hello, pretty girl." Tammy extended an arm over the fence and scratched the filly's neck. "We were just talking about you."

Rose snuck a glance at Tammy. Speaking to the filly, the woman sounded just like Peg did when she was holding conversations with her Poodles.

"Do you think she was listening to us?" Rose asked.

"What? No." Tammy laughed at the thought. "She's been too busy eating all this nice grass out here."

"Of course," Rose mumbled. Once again she'd sounded like an idiot.

She glanced back toward the colt barn. Peg and Ben were nowhere to be seen. Maybe they'd gone inside. She wondered how long it would be before they reappeared and she could make her escape. In the meantime, she was wondering about something else.

"If there's so much money to be made at the Keeneland sale," she said, "why didn't you get a job there too?"

"Me?" Tammy scoffed. "You're kidding, right?"

"Umm . . . no."

"The women—girls—who get jobs as showmen at the sales don't look like me. For one thing, they're thirty years younger. For another, they're cute and perky, and they look good in short shorts." Tammy rolled her eyes. "Guys get hired for their skills, or sometimes because they're available when a warm body is needed. But the girls mostly get hired to look decorative."

"I assume you know how sexist that sounds."

"Hey—I'm not the one doing the hiring. Just someone who's observed the process from the sideline for years. Besides, I never said the girls aren't just as good as the guys at what they do. Only that it's not the first qualification they're judged on when a man is doing the hiring."

"That's terrible," Rose said.

Tammy shrugged. "And again, that's life. If you don't mind my saying so, you must come from some place pretty cushy if you don't already know that."

Rose had come from the convent, where there'd been plenty of women in charge. The Mother Superior of Divine Mercy could go toe to toe with any man and come out ahead. Although, since technically even she had to answer to the Big Man Upstairs, maybe she didn't possess the autonomy Rose was granting her.

As Rose took another look back at the other barn, Peg and Ben finally emerged from inside. Talking to Tammy had been a challenge, but Rose had enjoyed it. She was sorry her time was up.

"I'd better be going," she said. "It looks like my ride is ready to leave."

To her surprise, Tammy placed a hand on her arm to stop her. "Last time I saw you here, you were with Lucia."

"That's right."

"Was that because you're a client or because you and she are friends?"

Rose hesitated only briefly. "Friends."

"Good. Lucia's another gal around here who's had things tough. Usually when she gets beat down, she bounces right back up. This time it's going to be harder for her. Just so you know, she could use someone in her corner."

Rose paused. "You're referring to Jim Grable's death?"

Tammy nodded.

"How come nobody here is talking about that? It seems odd not to even mention it. People are acting like it never happened."

"That's exactly what the top brass would like you to think. As far as they're concerned, it didn't happen. And if it did, it had nothing to do with Six Oaks Farm. They put out a notice. Anyone who's heard talking about it will be fired on the spot."

"That didn't stop you," Rose pointed out.

"I don't know what you mean." Tammy held up her hands in a gesture of innocence. "All I said was if you happen to care about Lucia, now would be a good time to be there for her."

Peg and Ben were almost to the truck. Peg was staring over at Rose. She was probably wondering why she wasn't coming to join them. Another minute and the dratted woman would be waving her arms over her head to get Rose's attention.

"I have to go," Rose said quickly. "But Lucia and I have already had a conversation about what happened. Peg and I are going to try and help her."

Tammy's brow furrowed. "How are you going to do that?"

"Peg has some experience in these things."

"*Murders?*"

"Investigations," Rose corrected. "She's been involved in a few."

"Like she's a cop?"

"No, more like she's a talented amateur who's good at figuring things out."

Tammy smirked. "That's the dumbest thing I've ever heard. She actually thinks she can scoop the police?"

"Scooping the police isn't the point. Protecting Lucia is. I think we can both agree on that, can't we?"

"I suppose." Tammy still didn't look convinced.

"So if there's anything you'd like to tell me about Grable's death . . ."

Abruptly Tammy backed away. "Not me," she said firmly. "I'm not stupid enough to get involved. At my age I'm not putting my salary and benefits on the line. If anybody asks, I didn't say a thing."

Chapter 12

Peg and Ben were waiting for Rose beside the truck. "It took you long enough." Peg scowled to emphasize her impatience.

Rose brushed past them and climbed inside. Peg and Ben followed suit. "Tammy and I were having an interesting conversation."

"You were?" Ben cast a glance in Tammy's direction as if he wasn't even sure that was possible.

Rose bristled. "Tammy knows a lot about horses. As she should, since she's worked at Six Oaks just about longer than anyone else."

"Where'd you hear that?" Ben asked. He started up the truck and turned it around.

"Lucia mentioned it the other day," Peg said. "I wonder how many years Tammy's been here?"

"I wouldn't know," Ben replied. "It's not like I keep tabs on stuff like that."

"How long have you worked here?" Rose inquired.

He thought back. "Almost eight years. I can't believe it's been that long."

"You must have started around the same time Lucia did."

"Maybe." He was noncommittal. "She started out in the barns and my first job was in the office. Our paths rarely crossed until recently."

"That's interesting," Peg said. "What brought about the change?"

Ben kept his eyes trained on the road in front of him. He hesitated so long before answering, she wondered if he intended to ignore the question entirely.

"Lucia was promoted to the position of assistant yearling manager," Ben said finally. "The job should have been a good fit for her, but it turned out it wasn't. Unfortunately, she couldn't get along with the rest of the crew."

Rose leaned forward in her seat. Peg caught the movement out of the corner of her eye and raised a brow. They were both thinking the same thing. If Lucia was assistant yearling manager, that meant she'd reported directly to Jim Grable. Why hadn't she mentioned that earlier?

Ben was still talking. "Upper management gave it six months, hoping things would sort themselves out. When they didn't, the boss decided it was best to remove her from the post. Lucia's a good kid. She tries hard. So they kept her on, slotting her into different spots around the farm wherever someone needs a hand."

"It must keep things interesting for her," Rose said. "Never knowing where she'll be working next. You told us she's over at Keeneland today. Where will she be assigned tomorrow?"

Ben turned to look back at her. "Lucia will be at the sale all week, helping out around the consignment. Tomorrow, she'll probably be one of our showmen. Lucia has a wonderful touch with even the rowdiest yearlings. They really respond to her."

"In that case, it's a shame she couldn't manage to keep her job at the yearling barn," Peg mused, encouraging Ben to elaborate on his previous comment.

"Apples and oranges," he said. "Horse skills don't always translate to people skills, and vice versa. Actually, Lucia wasn't originally scheduled to be part of the sales team. But under the circumstances, it seemed like a good time for her to be away from the farm." Ben slowed the truck to pull into the small lot in front of the office. "I'm sure she'll do a great job with our yearlings over at Keeneland. And that's what matters, right?"

"Right," Peg and Rose both agreed, then shared a look. They were also in agreement about wanting to be alone so they could discuss what Ben had just told them.

Before the truck had even stopped moving, Hope was already standing on the rear seat of the minivan. Her tail swished from side to side as she woofed a delighted greeting. *You're back! You're back! It's about time!*

Peg was obviously torn between saying goodbye to Ben and going straight to Hope. Rose nudged her in Ben's direction. "Go," she said. "I've got this."

"Let me know if you need anything else," Ben told Peg. "As you know, your colt sells later in the week, but the sale starts tomorrow with the book one horses. For the next ten days, I'll be back and forth between there and the farm, but I'm available by phone if something comes up."

"I appreciate that," Peg replied. "And thank you for giving me so much of your time today. I've never been able to watch the sales process in person before and I'm finding it fascinating."

"It is that," Ben agreed. "But you should also keep in mind that horse sales can be the best thing that ever happened to you, or the worst. Thankfully, your colt vets a hundred percent clean, so we've passed that hurdle. He's big, he's correct, and he's got the right family. But even with all that in your favor, it still doesn't guarantee that someone's going to fall in love with him."

"Two people," Peg said with a twinkle in her eye. "After all, it's an auction. It'll take two bidders to drive the price up."

"Right. That's something else we'll need to discuss. But

we can cover it at the end of the week. Nice to meet you,
Rose." Ben waved to both women and went inside the office.

Rose already had the door to the minivan open, and a
leash fastened to Hope's collar. When Peg approached, the
Poodle leapt out of the vehicle and landed at Peg's feet
with an exuberant bounce. Peg took the end of the lead
from Rose.

"Just a little leg-stretcher," she told Hope, mindful of
the farm edict against visiting dogs. "We'll just circle those
two trees and be on our way."

Five minutes later, they were all back in the vehicle. By
mutual accord, neither Peg nor Rose brought up the topic
they were dying to talk about until they'd passed through
the Six Oaks gate and turned out onto the road. Then they
both spoke at once.

"Oh my God!" Peg said.

"Assistant yearling manager?" Rose squealed.

Hope sat up and looked back and forth between them.
It wasn't often she heard both women scream at the same
time. She hoped it meant something interesting was about
to happen.

"I can't believe Lucia neglected to mention that fact to
you," Peg said.

"Two facts, actually," Rose replied with a frown. She
wasn't happy about either omission. "One, that she worked
directly for Jim Grable. And two, not only didn't they get
along, their relationship was so acrimonious that it led to
her removal from his team."

Peg looked at Rose across the front of the van. "Then,
after Ben drops that bombshell, he goes on to say what a
hard worker Lucia is. I couldn't make sense of that at all.
So does the farm consider Lucia to be a good employee or
not? And if the answer is yes, why have they gotten rid of
her for the time being by banishing her to the sale?"

"I'm pretty sure you have that last part wrong," Rose

told her. "According to Tammy, being allowed to work at the sale is a perk, not a punishment. The grooms at the farm become showmen at the sale. They earn a whole lot more money there than they would at home."

"Good to know," Peg said. She hadn't realized that. Thank goodness there wasn't much traffic. Peg was paying more attention to the conversation than she was to the country lane she was driving on.

"Before we get sidetracked by the sale," she continued, "let's circle back to the assistant manager position that Lucia had—and then lost. It must have been a pretty important job, probably one she'd earned by working her way up. And now that it's been taken away, she's left doing what? Acting as Ben's go-fer?"

"For at least part of the time." Rose thought back to their conversation. "She told me that she also fills in at the barns and the training center. She goes wherever she's needed on any given day."

"That's even worse," Peg said. "Rather than just being Ben's lackey, it sounds as though she's become everyone's subordinate. This new job is clearly a demotion from her former position. What do you suppose Lucia did to deserve that?"

"I have no idea," Rose replied shortly. Why did Peg always come up with better questions than she did? "Nor do I think we should assume that what happened was Lucia's fault. However, rather than speculating aimlessly, I propose we table that query and ask her about it the next time we see her."

"I rather enjoy aimless speculation, myself," Peg said. "But in the interest of harmony, I will accede to your wishes and ask about something else. You spent a long time talking to Tammy. Considering the length of her tenure at the farm, she might be someone who knows where the bodies are buried—figuratively speaking, of course. Did she have any useful wisdom to impart?"

Rose's thoughts immediately went back to the pretty gray filly in the paddock. "Thoroughbred buyers don't like small horses."

"Noted," said Peg. "But not entirely useful. Anything else?"

"Only young, pretty girls can show yearlings at the sale. Old, crotchety women need not apply."

"I guess that lets us out." Peg looked disappointed. As if she'd been considering a change of profession and had just found out she didn't qualify.

"Tammy also offered me some advice," Rose added. "It's actually more applicable to you. She said if I wanted to be involved in the Thoroughbred industry, I should hold on to my hat so someone doesn't steal it."

"Interesting." Peg's tone implied that it was anything but. "But what I was really hoping was that you'd been able to steer the conversation around to the subject of Jim Grable's murder."

"I did."

"And?"

"Tammy shut me down immediately. She said the farm is behaving as if it never happened. None of the employees are allowed to talk about it under threat of being fired."

"Now we're getting somewhere," Peg said with relish.

"Where?"

"I don't know. But at least we're on the right topic. Or maybe heading in the right direction. Which is better than we were a minute ago."

That didn't sound like much progress to Rose.

"There was one other thing. Tammy's worried about Lucia. She said Lucia's had some tough breaks, and she needs someone on her side."

"Yes," Peg said brightly. "That's us."

"I told her that. I also told her you were going to solve Jim Grable's murder."

"That seems like a bold statement on your part." Peg

cast another glance in Rose's direction. "You may have more confidence in me than I have in myself."

"Don't be ridiculous. No one has more confidence in themselves than you do. It's one of the things that makes you so insufferable."

"One of them?" Peg said. "There are more?"

"A whole list," Rose confirmed. Let Peg ponder that in her spare time. "While I was busy with Tammy, what did you learn from Ben and Abel?"

Peg saw their turn approaching. She slowed the minivan and navigated the corner. "Ben is a born salesman. He likes to hear himself talk."

"To echo your earlier sentiment, that's not entirely useful. Especially since we were already well aware of it. What else did I miss? Did you and Abel get chatty about horse feet?"

"Hooves," Peg corrected.

"Whatever."

"Abel wasn't a particularly chatty guy. He's more the strong, silent type."

"Maybe that means he has hidden depths," Rose said hopefully.

"Or maybe he just has nothing to say."

"He may not be a talker, but I'll bet he sees a lot of things," Rose mused.

"How so?"

"If I'm understanding correctly, most of the farm workers have jobs that place them in a single location, like the broodmare barn or the training center. But Abel's different. All the horses have hooves. His job must take him all over the farm."

"I see what you're saying." Peg considered that. "Abel has a lot more access than the other employees."

"Which means I'll bet he knows plenty about what goes on around there."

"You're probably right."

"Try not to sound so surprised," Rose said. "I do come up with a decent idea every now and then."

"And sometimes even more often than that," Peg conceded. "You've brought up a good point. Maybe I should have tried harder to cozy up to Abel. He looked so busy that I didn't want to disturb him."

"The horses at the sale have hooves too." Rose was peering out her side window. "Maybe we'll get lucky and have another chance."

Peg had driven them to the tiny town of Midway, a picturesque hamlet named for its location halfway between Lexington and the state capital of Frankfort. The business district consisted mostly of one main street, bisected by a railroad track. Both sides of the road were lined with shops and restaurants. With its gabled roofs and colorful storefronts, the town looked as though it belonged in a fairy tale.

"Is there something you need here?" Rose asked.

"Yes. Food." Peg was heading for a parking spot. "I'm starving. Aren't you?"

"Now that you mention it, I suppose I am." Rose turned to the back seat where Hope was already on her feet. The big Poodle had no intention of being left behind again. "But what about Hope?"

"That's one of Midway's many charming attributes," Peg told her. "Hope can come and dine with us."

Rose stepped out of the vehicle onto the sidewalk. There was a lovely bistro with outside seating two doors down. Maybe after they ate, they could spend some time exploring the rest of the town.

"There's something else I forgot to tell you," Peg said, as she and Hope joined Rose on the sidewalk. "Tammy isn't the only one who's worried on Lucia's behalf. Inside the barn, while Ben and Abel were conferring about something, Manny came over and pulled me aside. Totally un-prompted, he also offered his support for her."

"Good for him," Rose said. "There's definitely something about Lucia that draws people in and makes them want to take care of her."

"I agree," Peg replied. "It makes me happy to know that young woman isn't as alone in the world as she thinks she is."

Chapter 13

After lunch, Rose spent nearly an hour window shopping in Midway. Hope enjoyed the excursion. Peg didn't. She was eager to be moving along.

"You're the one who brought us here," Rose pointed out.

"We came to eat. Which we've done. Now it's time to head over to Keeneland." In spite of her objections, Peg found herself leaning in for a closer look at a window display of quality leather goods. Trust people who knew how to make saddles to craft a fine purse.

"I thought your colt wasn't even getting there until late afternoon." Now Rose was eyeing an ice cream shop. She knew Hope would be on board with that stop too.

"You're right." Peg straightened away from the window and realized she was talking to herself. Rose had moved on down the sidewalk. Hope was tugging at her leash to go after her. Peg had no choice but to oblige.

"That's why this is the perfect time for us to go and scope things out," she said when the three of them were together again. "Tomorrow when the sale starts, things will get hectic and everybody will be stressed. It will feel like everything's happening all at once."

Rose turned to face her. "You make the experience sound so appealing. How can Hope and I possibly resist?"

"You're being sarcastic, aren't you?"

"I am."

"You never used to do that."

Rose was well aware that the more time she spent with Peg, the sharper the edges of her personality seemed to become. She hadn't yet decided if that was a good thing or a bad thing.

"You should be pleased I'm learning new skills," she said.

"When you start learning new skills that benefit me, then I'll be pleased," Peg retorted. "In the meantime, acquiescence would be better."

She turned around and headed back to where she'd left the minivan. Hope had no choice but to go with her. Peg could only hope that Rose was following too.

"Uh-oh," Rose said on the way to Keeneland. "I just realized there's something we neglected to do."

"What's that?" Peg hoped Rose wasn't angling for another detour.

"The whole reason Lucia came to see me yesterday was because she wanted us to speak to the police on her behalf. We were supposed to corroborate her version of the conversation she had with Jim Grable."

"I didn't forget," Peg told her. "I declined."

Rose swiveled in her seat. "What do you mean?"

"I can't see how doing so would be a useful move on our part."

"But . . ." Rose sputtered. "Lucia thinks it will help to prove her innocence."

"I disagree. For starters, we don't know anyone in the local police force."

Rose frowned. It wasn't like Peg to make silly excuses. "There's an easy solution to that. Officer Sherlock is the person who interviewed Lucia. We can ask to speak with him."

"And say what?" Peg asked. "That we're a couple of busybodies visiting from the East Coast and we'd like to poke our noses into your investigation?"

"That sounds rather harsh."

"Not really. You know as well as I do that even on our home turf, Detective Sturgill doesn't take kindly to our interference."

"He should," Rose muttered. She and the detective were not the best of friends. "After all, we've solved two cases for him."

"I very much doubt that he sees it that way."

"Nevertheless, Detective Sturgill likes you. Maybe he could put in a good word for us."

Peg cocked a brow in Rose's direction. "He'd be more like to warn the local constabulary to steer well clear of us."

Peg was probably right, Rose realized unhappily. "So where does that leave us?"

"Right where we started. Doing all we can to aid Lucia's cause in our own way. We'll ask some questions and see what kinds of answers turn up."

Rose nodded. At least they were good at that.

"As for local law enforcement, I recommend that we stay out of their way. I learned on my previous visit that Southern sheriffs don't like outsiders telling them what to do."

"It's not just Southern sheriffs," Rose told her. "Nobody likes it when you tell them what to do."

"That's not true." Peg sounded offended. "Many people enjoy my guidance."

"That's what they want you to think. Most people are too intimidated by you to tell you the truth."

"Oh well then, that's all right." Peg enjoyed a good intimidation every now and again. She wasn't about to give up that source of satisfaction. Then a thought struck her, and she looked over at Rose. "I hope that group doesn't include you."

"Not anymore."

"But once?"

"Of course," Rose replied. "You know that's so, or you wouldn't have asked. You used to scare the heck out of me. You did it on purpose."

Perhaps she had, Peg reflected. She just hadn't expected to be called to account for doing so. At least not now, so many years later.

"It was a long time ago. Am I too late to apologize?"

"No." Rose said firmly. "You're not."

"Then I'm sorry."

"Apology accepted. Better late than never."

"You could have handled that more graciously," Peg told her.

"Yes," Rose agreed, and left it at that.

The Keeneland Race Course was a national historic landmark located in the heart of the Bluegrass. Its vast acreage housed two racetracks, a sales pavilion, more than fifty barns, and a library containing almost everything there was to know about breeding and racing Thorough-breds.

Two race meets were held each year, one in April, and one in October. Between those times, Keeneland hosted weddings, corporate events, musical entertainment, and four Thoroughbred auctions. The September Yearling Sale was Keeneland's premier event, attracting buyers from all over the world.

"This place is huge," Rose said as Peg drove through Keeneland's main gate. The stone clubhouse with its wide portico was straight ahead of them. The grandstand rose majestically behind it, the boxes and tiered seating all painted Keeneland's signature shade of green. The race-track itself was to their left. In the other direction, Rose could see numerous rows of low white barns. "How are we ever going to figure out where everything is?"

"I've come prepared," Peg said practically. "And if we still get lost, we'll ask for directions."

She drove around the side of the clubhouse and found a tree-lined parking lot near the sales pavilion. Much of it was already full. With the sale not yet in progress, most of today's activity would be taking place in the barn area. Judging by the look of things, there was quite a crowd on hand.

Peg drove down a small slope and parked in a spot adjacent to several rows of barns. When she hopped Hope out of the minivan, the Poodle immediately dropped her nose to the ground and began to sniff around. Peg didn't blame her. Everything felt new and strange to her too.

"Are you coming?" she asked Rose, who was still in the front seat, staring at her phone.

"In a minute. I'm checking to see if there have been any updates about Jim Grable's murder."

"You mean his 'accident.' "

"I'd settle for that, but I still can't find anything."

"Of course not," Peg said. "Who's going to update a story about a presumed accident? What will they say? 'Jim Grable is still dead'?"

"You're terrible," Rose grumbled. She climbed out of the minivan and shut her door.

"No, I'm pragmatic," Peg returned. "If Six Oaks was able to muzzle the press when the story was fresh, it's unlikely the media will print something about it two days later."

"I don't care. I intend to keep checking anyway. You never know when I might find out something interesting."

Peg stood beside her and waved a hand to display the vista before them. "What's interesting isn't on your phone, it's right here in front of you. Look around. This place is amazing."

More horses, Rose thought. *Yippee.*

Each of the Keeneland barns was numbered. Barn 1 was nearby, and the consignors stabled there were doing a brisk business. The walking rings beside the barn were full. Handsome yearlings were being posed, or paraded back and forth, by their handlers. Agents and buyers stood off to the side, taking notes and discussing each horse's merits and flaws among themselves.

The people managing the consignments directed traffic with a sure touch. A steady stream of yearlings entered and exited the shedrow barns. Occasionally buyers lingered over a particular horse, and a log jam formed behind it. When that happened, the other handlers pulled their charges out of line, moving them away to await their turn. Peg felt like she was observing the performance of an intricate and carefully choreographed dance.

"That looks like chaos," Rose said.

"Not chaos." Peg continued to watch with admiration. "Clockwork. Look at the guy in charge. He knows exactly where each one of his yearlings is now, and where it needs to go next. He's an orchestra conductor, only with horses."

"If you say so." Rose sounded dubious.

"You would too, if you were paying more attention."

Rose had no idea why Peg was so fascinated by animals. If she were forced to pay more attention to this scene, her eyes would probably glaze over. Judging by the stubborn expression on Peg's face, however, there was no point in arguing.

"Where to next?" she said.

"Up the hill, then we take a right down the driveway

and go through another set of barns," Peg told her. "The Six Oaks consignment is in barn 14. This way."

Peg had already taken off, with Hope trotting happily beside her. Rose had to trot a few steps herself to catch up.

"Are you sure you know where you're going?" she asked. It would be just like Peg to strike out in a random direction, assuming that everything would fall into place.

Peg held out her sales catalog. "I got this from Ben. It lists the pedigrees of all the yearlings that are selling in the first book, and there's a site map in the back. If you like, we can stop in the sales pavilion, and you can pick one up for yourself."

"No, thanks." Seeing the sale in person was more than enough. Rose didn't need to read about it too.

Each barn they passed looked similar to the one they'd paused to observe. Traffic was brisk everywhere. Yearlings came outside, were presented to potential buyers, then went back in the barn at a rapid pace. Showmen jumped from one horse to the next seamlessly.

Every barn sported colorful signs and banners announcing the names of the consignors stabled there. Handlers and grooms were dressed in the farm colors. Everyone had a job to do, and all of them were busy.

"And I thought dog shows looked frenzied," Rose said. "I wonder if anyone here ever gets to pause and take a deep breath."

"These people have a great deal of work to accomplish in a relatively short period of time," Peg replied. "Considering the tight schedule and the amount of money that's on the line, right now, breathing probably seems like a luxury to most of them."

They reached the top of the hill and started down the driveway. Their next turn would take them through the middle of two barns where yearlings were currently being shown. Peg tightened her hand on Hope's lead, pulling the Poodle in close to her side for safety.

"I have a question," Rose said.

"Good." Peg thought it was about time Rose showed an interest in all the activity going on around them. "Shoot."

"Since all these horses are here already, how come your colt isn't coming until later?"

"My colt is in book two."

"You say that as if it should mean something to me."

Peg had thought perhaps it might. She tried again. "These are book one horses."

"Again . . . not entirely clear," Rose said. "Aside from understanding that one comes before two, I'm still baffled. Explain it to me like I'm in kindergarten."

"This could take a minute."

"I'm not going anywhere." *More's the pity,* Rose thought. "How about the Cliff Notes version?"

"The twelve days of the sale are divided into six books. Each book covers two days."

Rose sighed. *Seriously?* Well, maybe it was her own fault. After all, she had mentioned kindergarten.

"That much math I can do," she said.

"Four thousand yearlings are entered in the sale. And they can't all fit on the Keeneland grounds at the same time."

"No?" Rose looked around. She saw lots of barns.

"No," Peg replied firmly. "Do the math."

Throwing Rose's own words back at her? That was just mean. As if she was supposed to know how many horses could fit inside a barn. This was beginning to feel like one of those riddles people told when they were drunk. Rose had never understood the hilarity of that either.

"Enough math." Rose flapped a hand, causing Hope to look at her with interest in case she was waving a dog treat. "Move along."

"Before each group of yearlings is offered for sale, they're on the grounds to be shown to buyers for two days. The book one horses started showing yesterday. They'll begin selling tomorrow. While the book one horses sell, the book two horses will be showing. When it's their turn to sell, the book three horses will be in the barns. And so on."

"Sheesh," said Rose. "You made it sound like it was going to be complicated. That makes perfect sense. Anything else?"

"Yes," Peg replied. "Two things."

Rose should have known she wasn't going to escape that easily.

"It takes time to get the yearlings moved into and out of the barns. So only half the available stalls are used for each book. Book one horses are in the lower barns. Book two are in the upper barns, and they switch off again with each change of book. Which means that most consignors are usually running two barns at once."

"Luckily, that's not my problem," Rose said. She sounded so cheerful that Hope wagged her tail. The Poodle was still hoping for a biscuit.

Peg wasn't finished. "Last thing—and perhaps the most important."

"Maybe you should have started with that."

"Maybe I was building up to a big finish."

"One can only hope," Rose said.

"Not surprisingly, quality matters. Keeneland inspects the yearlings that are entered in the sale and ranks them according to their potential value. The best ones—those expected to bring the highest prices—are cataloged in book one. The second best group—"

"Is in book two," Rose finished for her.

"And so on down the line."

"So the yearlings in the last book are the ones who will never win a horse race?" That seemed like a shame to Rose.

"Not necessarily. If there's one thing I've learned about horses, it's that every day is a new surprise."

"Somehow I don't find that the least bit reassuring," Rose said.

Chapter 14

Like the others they'd walked past, barn 14 was a low, white, shedrow barn that was bustling with activity. A white sign with bright blue letters, saying SIX OAKS FARM, hung above the entrance. Below it was a table covered in a matching blue cloth. One end of the table was stocked with information about the Six Oaks yearlings. The other held an array of snacks for buyers to munch on while they shopped.

When Peg and Rose approached the barn, Lucia was standing beside the consignment table. Once again, she was dressed in the farm uniform. Her long hair was loose and a pair of sunglasses on top of her head acted as a hairband. She was holding a bunch of long, narrow cards—fanned for visibility—in one of her hands. In the other was a pen that she was using as a pointer. Lucia was concentrating as she surveyed the busy courtyard in front of the barn.

"Jenny, you're first in line for Mr. Beckett," she said, as a handler exited the barn with a rangy gray colt. The pen moved to indicate an empty show ring where two men were waiting. "Nico, did the Maybees see your filly? Yes? Then you're done for now. Go back inside."

Lucia's gaze skimmed around the area again to make

sure she wasn't missing anything. The available walking rings were all full, and three additional yearlings were lined up, ready to show. No one else was waiting to ask for her attention. When she saw Peg and Rose standing nearby with Hope, she smiled and sketched a small wave.

There was an empty bench on a strip of grass beside the Six Oaks' table. Peg and Rose made their way over to it, being careful not to walk across a show ring or impede anyone's view of the yearlings. Hope's head swung from side to side as they crossed the courtyard. She was eager to see everything at once.

Lucia came over as soon as they sat down. "Do you need me to pull something for you?" When Peg looked at her blankly, she tried again. "Would you like to see a horse?"

"Oh!" Peg laughed as comprehension dawned. "No, thank you. Rose and I are just spectating, while I try to figure out how everything works. Is it all right if we just sit here and watch for a bit?"

"Of course. Stay as long as you like. In a few minutes, maybe I'll be able to come over and chat. These crowds always seem to come in waves. For half an hour we'll be totally inundated by lookers, then suddenly they all seem to disappear at once. Manny, wait!"

Lucia had been keeping one eye on the action while she talked to them. Now she signaled in the direction of a yearling who was about to enter the barn. "Cecil's waiting to see that colt. Far ring on the left."

As Manny spun the colt around, she turned back to them. "Sorry."

"No problem," Rose said. Like Hope, she was fascinated by the commotion going on around them.

"Just one quick question," Peg said before Lucia could turn back to her job. She nodded toward a pair of men standing a few feet away, their heads bent over a looseleaf notebook that one of them held in his hands. "Who's the man on the left? He looks familiar. I feel like I should know him, but I can't quite place him."

"That's Walter Tausky. He's the sales manager at Six Oaks. You've probably seen him back at the farm. He works in the office, and manages all our sales consignments. In fact, if you have any questions about your colt after he arrives, Walter would be the person to talk to."

"Of course," Peg replied. "I met him on my last trip here."

She remembered Walter as a heavyset man with dark bushy eyebrows and a direct gaze. In the time since she'd last seen him, Walter had lost quite a bit of weight. He also looked considerably older. His brows were now more gray than brown, and his once fleshy cheeks were sunken and sagging. No wonder Peg hadn't recognized him.

"Is that someone important?" Rose asked after Lucia left.

"For Six Oaks, yes." Peg got Hope settled in the grass at her feet. "Walter is Ben Burrell's boss. He's here managing the sales consignment."

"Probably a good person to know, then." Rose sat back in her seat. The bench's slats had been heated by the sun, and their warmth felt good through the thin cotton of her blouse. "What do you suppose he and that other man are looking at? How odd to be reading a book in the midst of all this. The horses are supposed to be the important thing, aren't they?"

"As far as I know." Peg watched as Lucia greeted an incoming group of shoppers. She pulled a card out of a box on the table and handed it to one of the men. Using a pen that hung from a string around his neck, he made several check marks on the card, then gave it back to her. "Although the more I see, the more questions I have about what's going on."

Now Lucia was sending the group to an empty walking ring. Then she turned to the barn and called out a series of numbers. Two grooms were standing in the aisle. Their heads were tipped back to watch a horse race showing on a TV screen up beside the hayloft. Hearing Lucia's voice behind them, both men leapt to comply.

Peg turned to Rose. "I just figured something out."

"You've figured out many things in your life. Is this one cause for particular celebration?"

"Yes, actually. Because I'm usually the person who knows what's what."

Rose snorted inelegantly.

"Scoff if you like, but you can't deny it."

Sadly, Peg was right about that.

"But here, when I'm surrounded by horse people who've worked with Thoroughbreds their whole lives, I feel like such a greenhorn. You have no idea how annoying it is, having to ask for explanations about everything."

"Of course I do." Upon leaving the convent, Rose had quickly discovered that the cloistered decades had left huge gaps in her adult education. Knowledge and experiences that most women her age took for granted were often mystifying to her.

Peg turned and stared. Then abruptly she realized what Rose meant. "I never considered that before."

"And there's no need for you to do so now," Rose replied tartly. It was never a good thing to admit a weakness to Peg. "Instead, tell me what you learned."

"Those cards Lucia is holding? I think they're a list of the yearlings in the consignment. People use them to mark down which ones they want to see."

"If you say so," Rose replied.

She hadn't been paying attention to that detail. Why? Because she didn't care. Plopped down in the midst of this microcosm of weird human behavior, Rose was much more interested in people-watching. It was too bad Peter wasn't here to experience it with her. He'd be having a field day.

Now Walter and his fellow reader had moved on. Their place at the end of the show ring had been taken by a trio of shoppers: two men and a woman who looked as though they were waiting for a horse to be brought out for their inspection.

All three were in their forties, or maybe a bit older. Two were holding catalogs in their hands. The third had an iPad. One man wore slacks, loafers, and a button-down shirt. The other was in jeans and sneakers. Both had on ball caps, one red, one blue.

In Rose's opinion, the woman was the most interesting person of the three. Her blond hair had been professionally styled; her dress appeared to be silk. Numerous items of gold jewelry—on her earlobes, at her throat, around her wrists—glittered in the sunlight. She looked as though she'd dressed for a fancy occasion, rather than to visit a barn.

Perhaps the woman felt the tug of Rose's gaze. She looked up and their eyes met briefly. Clearly she was unimpressed by what she saw, because her focus slid away as a yearling emerged from the barn.

This one was a bay filly. Nico was leading her. Rose watched as the filly tossed her head and danced at the end of the shank. The three people quickly straightened up and began to pay attention.

First they watched Nico move the filly down and back on the peastone walkway. Then the trio strolled around to the side of the path. Nico stopped the yearling in front of them, posing her in an even stance, with all four of her legs visible and her head facing forward.

Now that they'd changed their position, the three shoppers were standing almost on top of the bench where Rose and Peg were sitting. Eyes trained on the filly in front of them, the trio appeared to be oblivious to their presence, even when Peg was forced to move Hope between her legs to accommodate them.

Their dismissive attitude spoke volumes: Two old ladies sitting on a bench weren't worthy of notice. Rose and Peg obviously couldn't be anyone important because all the important people at the sale were busy doing *something.*

When the three began to critique the filly, it was easy for Rose and Peg to hear what they were saying.

"She looks fine," the woman said, sounding bored. "As she should, considering what we paid for her."

"Now, Zara," the man with the red ball cap said in a placating tone. "Let's give credit where credit is due. She looks a good deal better than *fine.* Midnight Magic is a beautiful filly. The buyers are going to love her conformation."

Blue Ball Cap cleared his throat. "Yes, but—"

Both gazes swung his way. Rose was sure she saw a quelling look pass between the two men. Abruptly, Blue Cap shut his mouth.

"But what?" Zara asked. She dipped her head in the first man's direction. Her smile didn't quite reach her eyes. "Was there something you wanted to say, Leo?"

"I was just going to remind you of something I know you're already aware of." Leo pressed on, ignoring the other man's glare. "A small issue came up on this filly's X-rays—"

"A tiny issue," Red Cap broke in. "Minuscule."

"Sesamoiditis," Zara said, turning to face him. "That's a big word for something you're calling a tiny issue, Martin."

Peg and Rose shared a smile. Having spent plenty of time bickering with each other, they didn't mind listening to someone else argue for a change.

"It's not a deal breaker," Leo said quickly. "She'll still

scll well. Perhaps very well. We'll all make a little money on her. But she just won't be the slam dunk we were envisioning."

"That's the second time I've had to hear bad news about a presumed 'slam dunk' this week." Zara was still staring at Martin.

"Now, Zara," he said again. "It's not like you walked into this blind. You knew there were risks with getting involved in the horse business."

"High risk, high reward," she recited as if repeating something she'd heard numerous times before. "I get it. But you also assured me that your years of experience as a bloodstock agent put you in a position to be able to mitigate those risks."

Peg glanced at Rose as if she wanted to say something. Which, no doubt, she did. Peg had opinions on everything. But interrupting this conversation—which they weren't even supposed to be listening to—was a little much, even for her.

Rose grimaced. Not only that, but the hard bench was feeling more uncomfortable the longer she sat on it. So she really wasn't in the mood for any of Peg's crap. She shook her head firmly and hoped Peg would listen.

"It's true, my experience does count for a lot," Martin said with confidence. "And let's not forget how well this partnership started. You made money last year, didn't you?"

"You're right." Zara drew in a deep breath, then slowly exhaled. "I did. Now I'm hoping that wasn't just beginner's luck. Anyway, my annoyance really has nothing to do with this filly. I'm sure she'll do fine in the sales ring."

"She will." Martin nodded encouragingly.

"It's the Snow Cloud colt that I'm depressed about. We all had such high hopes for him. He was supposed to be our star. And he was doing so well, right up until the very last moment. I can't believe he isn't going to make it to the sale because of a stupid accident."

Peg had been reaching down to give Hope a pat. But now her ears perked up. She recognized that name. Snow Cloud was the big, muscular colt she'd seen Abel attending to the day before. The one who had a stone bruise.

Leo reached over and laid a hand on Zara's arm. "That's horses for you. When you're dealing with yearlings, some things just can't be helped. They need to run around and exercise in order to grow, develop, and stay sane. You can't wrap them up in bubble wrap just because they're going to a sale."

"I know," Zara replied with a frown. "But it still hurts to think about how much money that colt would have brought. Let me remind you that we have him insured for a million dollars."

"Since I handle the policy, I'm well aware of that," Leo told her. "But let's also not forget—that million is only real money if you can sell the horse for it."

"Which we would have done," Martin said. "Easily."

"Easily," Zara grumbled. "As if anything about this feels easy. The next time I see Jim Grable, I'm going to give him a piece of my mind. He's the guy in charge of that yearling barn. He's the one who assured us that with the colt in his care, nothing could go wrong."

Leo and Martin shared a look. For a moment, neither one of them spoke.

"When did you get into town, Zara?" Martin asked finally.

"Last night, why?"

"I guess maybe you haven't heard then."

"Heard what?" she asked.

"Jim Grable's dead. He died a couple of days ago in an accident on the farm."

Zara rounded on him in shock. "That bastard is dead?"

"Yup," Leo confirmed the news.

"Good riddance," she said.

Chapter 15

Nico and the filly were still waiting patiently on the walkway for someone to give them further instructions. Apparently Peg and Rose weren't the only ones listening to the trio's conversation. When Zara snapped out her comment about Jim, the showman's head lifted. He quickly smothered a laugh.

Martin glanced over, frowning. He waved his fingers in the air, dismissing the horse and handler. Nico turned the filly around and walked her back into the barn.

In the time that they'd been sitting on the bench, the courtyard between the Six Oaks consignment and the one beside it had gradually emptied. The shoppers had moved on to the next set of barns. Peg stood up to stretch her legs. Hope did the same.

"See what I mean?" Lucia said, coming over. "It's always like this. Everybody shows up at once, then they all leave the same way. Peg, let me take you over and reintroduce you to Walter. Don't be offended if he doesn't remember you. Walter's a busy guy, he's always got a lot on his mind. But he's the person to talk to if you need anything."

"Thank you," Peg said, handing Hope's leash to Rose. "I'd appreciate that."

Rose supposed that meant she and Hope were remaining behind. That was fine with her. On this trip, she'd already met plenty of horse people, more than she'd ever expected to know in her entire life. Rose could find common ground with just about anyone. But she was quickly discovering that horse people were like dog people. They only seemed to be able to talk about one thing.

Peg followed Lucia inside the barn. Now that there was a lull in the activity, a cluster of grooms and showmen were standing in the aisle watching the TV, where another horse race was in progress. Walter was among them. Eyes still on the screen, he noticed their approach and held up a finger, asking them to wait.

"Keeneland broadcasts the live feeds from racetracks all around the country," Lucia said to Peg in a low voice. "There's always racing happening somewhere. As you might imagine, it's a popular pastime around here."

Peg looked up at the screen. On a turf course, a closely bunched group of horses was racing down the homestretch. People around her were gesturing at the TV and calling encouragement to their favorites. When the horses crossed the finish line, she heard several people groan and one or two cheer.

"Sorry about that," Walter said, turning to Peg and Lucia. "There was a Six Oaks filly in the race. One we sold here two years ago."

"Did she win?" Peg asked.

"Second," he replied, scrubbing a hand across his cheek. "But it was a good effort. She'll get 'em next time. Is there something I can do for you?"

"Walter, I just wanted to introduce you to Peg Turnbull," Lucia said. "She's Lucky Luna's owner and she's here from Connecticut for the sale."

"Yes, Ben told me you were in town." Walter reached out and shook Peg's hand. "It's a pleasure to see you again. Your colt's done everything right so far. We're hoping for a good result when he goes through the ring."

"As am I," Peg agreed.

"If there's anything you need, please feel free to let either me or Ben know. We're always here to help."

"Thank you. I'll remember that."

Walter turned to Lucia. "If you want to take a short break, now's your chance. The guys and I can hold down the fort for twenty minutes or so while you give your feet a rest."

"Great idea," Peg said. "Lucia, why don't you join Rose and me in the pavilion for a cold drink?"

Lucia smiled. "That sounds perfect."

Rose and Hope were standing next to the bench, waiting for them. "Where are we going now?" she asked.

"The sales pavilion." Peg pointed across the way. "Lucia's going to join us for a drink or something to eat."

It seemed to Rose that she and Peg had eaten rather recently. But since Peg seemed to have come up with a way for them to speak with Lucia privately, Rose wasn't about to argue.

"There were three people looking at a filly Nico was holding, near where Peg and I were sitting," Rose said once they were underway. "Who were they?"

"Do you mean Midnight Magic?" Lucia asked.

"Yes," Peg said. "That's the one."

"They're a pinhooking partnership. Leo Grainger, Martin Shrady, and Zara King. The three of them pooled their money and bought several weanlings last fall. The idea is to hold them until this year, and then sell them for a profit as yearlings."

"Does that work?" Rose asked curiously.

"Sometimes," Lucia said. "If the pinhookers chose the right horses to buy, it can turn out spectacularly well. Like maybe they get a price break initially because the weanling looks small and weedy, or has an X-ray issue. But then by the time the September sale rolls around, the baby has blossomed, or outgrown its vetting problem. Then the sellers make a killing."

"And what happens if they chose the wrong horse?" Rose asked.

Lucia shrugged. "Then they lose money instead. Usually what these partnerships do is purchase enough weanlings so they can spread the financial risk across all of them. That way, the ones that do well end up covering the losses on those that tank."

"They own the filly they were looking at," Peg said. "And also a nice colt I saw back at the farm. Ben called him Snow Cloud."

"That's right," Lucia agreed. "Unfortunately, it looks as though the colt won't make it to the sale. But Leo, Martin, and Zara have two additional yearlings that are entered in book two. Their colts will ship in this afternoon when yours does. All three of them will start showing tomorrow morning at barn 31. I'd be happy to introduce you to the partners the next time we run into them. Then, if you have any more questions, you can ask them directly."

They strolled past the sales pavilion's back walking ring, then entered the building through an open door. Since Lucia knew where she was going, she led the way. A long hallway circled the auction ring and tiered seating in the gallery. After that, they came to the Limestone Café, a round room that was brightly lit by a row of large windows. High on the curved walls, a dozen television sets ringed the room—all tuned to horseracing at various venues around the world.

Peg kept Hope close to her side as they headed toward an empty table, but it didn't seem to matter. The people in the room were intent on their own business. No one paid any attention to the Poodle. Rose went to the Coffee Bar and came back with tea for Peg, coffee for herself, and a selection of scones, including a plain one for Hope. Lucia went into the Grill and returned with a hamburger and a soda.

Peg was keeping an eye on her watch. By the time they were all settled around the table, they'd already used up eight minutes of Lucia's break.

"I got the impression you wanted to talk to me," Lucia said as she took a bite of her hamburger. "Does that mean you had a chance to talk to Officer Sherlock?"

"I'm afraid not," Rose replied. "But I told Peg everything you and I discussed yesterday, and we both agreed that we want to help you."

"That's good. I guess." Lucia paused uncertainly. "But if you're not going to tell the police I'm innocent, how are you going to help?"

"By figuring out what happened to Jim Grable," Peg said.

"We know what happened," Lucia replied. "Someone killed him."

"Precisely. And we intend to find the person who did it."

Slowly Lucia laid down her burger. "How will you do that?"

"By asking lots of questions," Rose told her. "And then putting the answers together until a pattern emerges that points us in the right direction. We've done it before."

"You have?"

"Twice." Rose held up two fingers. Peg had even more expertise than that, but Rose didn't want to sound like she was bragging.

"That's not a lot of experience." Lucia returned to eating her hamburger.

"It's enough," Peg said firmly. "But if we're going to help you, you need to help us too."

"I don't understand." Lucia didn't sound convinced by any of this.

"Whether you understand or not, the main thing is that

you have to trust us," Peg told her. "Then you can help by telling us everything we need to know. And by answering our questions completely and honestly."

"I can do that." Lucia hesitated briefly, then said, "Of course I can."

"Good." Rose had yet to touch her coffee. But she'd crumbled up a scone and slipped it to Hope under the table. "Because it turns out there were a few things you neglected to mention yesterday."

"Like what?" Lucia asked warily.

"Like the fact that you used to be assistant yearling manager at the farm," Peg said. "I assume that means you reported to Jim Grable."

"I did."

"But you no longer have that job."

"No." The reply was whispered so softly that Rose barely heard it.

"Ben Burrell told us you were removed from the job because you had a hard time getting along with the team."

Lucia's head snapped up. Her eyes blazed. "That's not true!"

"So you didn't have trouble fitting in?" Rose asked.

"No, of course not. Why would I? I'm a hard worker and I'm good at what I do. The other guys at the yearling barn appreciated that."

"But Jim Grable didn't?" Peg said around a sip of tea.

"No, he thought I was great at my job too." Lucia huffed out a sad little laugh. "He said I was the best assistant he'd ever had."

Peg and Rose looked at each other across the table. Clearly they were missing something.

"And yet you were demoted from that job," Peg said. "So something must have gone wrong. What was it?"

"Jim Grable," Lucia snapped. "He's what went wrong. I tried telling him no. I pushed him away. I warned him not to touch me again. But Jim thought the fact that he was my boss meant that he could do whatever he wanted. He was sure there was nothing I could do to stop him."

Rose's heart dropped. Maybe she should have suspected something like that. But she hadn't. Not even close. She reached around the table to lay her hand gently on Lucia's shoulder.

The girl ignored the gesture of support. She wouldn't look at Peg either. Instead, Lucia lowered her gaze and stared hard at the table.

Rose suspected she knew what that meant. Lucia was used to fighting her own battles. Maybe she'd had to be because so many people had let her down. Now she looked as though she was afraid that Peg and Rose might be the next ones to walk out on her.

When Lucia spoke again, her words were defiant and her tone was filled with venom. "Jim thought he could break me, but I wasn't about to let that happen. I stuck it out as long as I could, and then I filed a complaint against him for sexual harassment."

"Good for you," Peg said stoutly.

Rose nodded in agreement.

Finally Lucia lifted her head. "And then he fired me."

Chapter 16

"Fired you?" Peg said, outraged. "He's the one who should have been fired."

"I thought so," Lucia replied softly, as if all the fight had suddenly gone out of her. "But apparently that's not how things work."

"The hell it isn't!" Rose swore. Coming from her, those were blasphemous words.

"If that man wasn't already dead, I'd like the chance to make him wish he was," Peg growled.

"And I'd hold him down for you," Rose added.

The mutual offer brought a small smile to Lucia's face. "Thank you."

"There's no need to thank us." Peg was still angry. "We haven't done anything yet."

"Just . . . thank you for taking my side. Most people didn't."

"How is that possible?" Rose asked.

Lucia shrugged. "Jim was in a position of power, and I wasn't. People were afraid to stand up to him—and with good reason. Look at the outcome. Jim kept his job. I didn't."

"Okay, Grable fired you," Peg said. "But the farm must have overruled his decision, because you still have a job there. I suppose that's better than nothing."

"Don't credit them with too much goodwill," Lucia replied. "I didn't give them a choice. If Six Oaks had let me go, I was going to hire a lawyer. And I made sure they knew it."

"They didn't want the bad publicity," Rose realized.

"Of course not. Image is everything around here." Lucia sounded bitter. "It was more palatable for them to find ways to keep Jim and me apart on a thousand acre farm than it was for them to deal with the fallout from a lawsuit."

"Just like Grable's murder," Peg said. "They hushed it up."

Lucia nodded. She picked up her hamburger and took another bite.

Peg wasn't the only one who was aware that time was passing. Rose also didn't want to get Lucia in trouble by keeping her away from her duties for too long. But it felt as though they weren't even close to being finished with this conversation.

"Why didn't you tell me about this yesterday?" she asked.

"I assumed you knew," Lucia said.

Peg and Rose had had people lie to them before. Lucia wasn't even particularly good at it.

"No, you didn't," Rose said.

"Okay." She sighed heavily. "Here's the rest of it. Jim told everyone that I came on to him. That I'd made it clear I was eager to get ahead in my job by any means possible. He said I'd promised him a very good time."

"Yuck." Peg shuddered.

"I figured if I told you about what Jim said, maybe you'd continue to believe me, or maybe you'd switch sides and believe him. And if that happened, I knew you wouldn't be willing to talk to Officer Sherlock. Which is what I really needed you to do."

"Young lady, you didn't give us enough credit," Peg said sharply.

Lucia didn't wilt beneath Peg's harsh tone. "Maybe not, but I had to assume the worst. After all, we'd just met. There are people on the farm that I've known for years, who believed Jim's version of the 'truth' over mine. Trusting people to do the right thing hasn't served me particularly well lately."

Rose picked up her coffee. When she'd first brought it to the table, it was too hot to drink. Now it was cool to the touch.

"You know this gives you an excellent motive for murder," she said.

Lucia scowled. "Everybody realizes that."

"Except for Rose and me," Peg said drily. "Because we just got clued in two minutes ago. I don't suppose there's anything else you like to confess?"

"No."

"How about why Ben told us this morning that you'd be showing yearlings at the sale, and instead we arrive to find that you're"—Peg had no idea what the name of that position might be—"doing something else entirely."

"Calling cards," Lucia supplied.

"I hope *this* demotion doesn't mean you've managed to get yourself on someone else's wrong side."

Rose gasped. "Peg, that was a low blow."

"No, it wasn't." Peg was unperturbed. "Lucia has promised us the truth and that's what I intend to hear. I'd hate to discover at a later date that there's been another omission in her story."

"My story?" Lucia looked surprised. "It's not a story, it's my life. And anyway, I wasn't demoted. All I did was fill in for someone who went to oversee the setup of our next barn. Dealing with people—even entitled horse shoppers—is way easier than dealing with fractious yearlings.

There's less chance of getting hurt too. And I make good money either way. If that's a demotion, I'll take it."

Rose cocked a brow in Peg's direction. "I think you owe Lucia an apology."

"No, she doesn't," Lucia said before Peg had a chance to reply. It was just as well. Rose was sure Peg would have refused anyway. "I like people who speak their minds. It's a pleasant change from dealing with the ones who sneak around and do stuff behind your back."

"Are you talking about anyone in particular?" Peg asked.

Lucia pushed back her chair and stood up. She'd finished her soda, but her burger was only half-eaten. "I have to get back. Walter will be calling cards while I'm gone, and that's bound to make him grumpy. Maybe Hope would like the rest of this?"

"Thank you. She would." Peg accepted the leftover sandwich.

"What you told us about Jim Grable's behavior changes things," Rose said quickly before Lucia could step away. "It gives you a motive—but I'm guessing you're not the only one."

"I'm not." Lucia grimaced. "You can ask just about any woman who's ever had to work with him. Talk to Jenny. She'll tell you. None of us were upset when we heard what happened to him."

"Did those other women speak up for you when you filed your complaint?" Peg asked.

The thunderous expression that briefly crossed Lucia's face was more than answer enough.

"That explains why she came to us," Peg said when Lucia had left the café. Hope was under the table, polishing off Lucia's hamburger. "When she needed support before, it sounds as though everyone turned their backs on her."

"Why do you suppose that is?" Rose asked.

"The most likely reason is that they thought speaking up in Lucia's defense might jeopardize their own jobs."

"That's one possibility."

Peg peeked beneath the table to check on Hope. "Are there others?"

"Maybe they hadn't witnessed Grable's bad behavior for themselves, and they didn't believe her."

Peg's head popped back up. "Except that Lucia implied they didn't have to witness his interactions with her, they'd experienced the same thing."

"The women, anyway," Rose pointed out. "It does makes me wonder, though . . ."

"About what?"

"If, despite your efforts to pin Lucia down, there isn't more to the story than she told us."

"Of course there's more." Peg stood up. She was ready to move on. "There's always more. Haven't you learned that by now?"

Peg, Rose, and Hope left the sales pavilion. Offered a choice of either returning to the busy sales barn, or taking a stroll to familiarize themselves with Keeneland's expansive grounds, they opted for the latter. Peg led the way up the hill toward the facility's historic racetrack.

"It would be ridiculous to be here and not even see it," she said.

They walked through the stone entrance, then up a stairway. That brought them to a wide path that cut between the paddock—where racehorses were saddled—and the neighboring walking ring that led to the track. Ahead of them was the back of the grandstand, with the racetrack itself just beyond it.

"This is lovely." Rose stopped to admire the mature trees and perfectly trimmed hedges. "If I were a horse, this is where I'd want to live."

Aside from the three of them, the place was deserted.

Peg reached down and unsnapped Hope's leash. The Poodle shook her head, realized she was free, and trotted over to investigate a stone wall with a row of custom painted lawn jockeys on top of it.

"The racetrack is this way," Peg said.

Once again, she was in front as they crossed the grandstand's ground floor and emerged on the other side, at the top of the track apron. The vista that spread out before them was breathtaking. The racetrack—with an outer dirt oval, inner turf course, and manicured infield—occupied center stage. Behind it, the hill on which it was built sloped away, leaving a boundless expanse of bright blue sky as its backdrop.

Rose stopped walking. She peered first in one direction, then the other. Then she looked perplexed.

"But . . . where are the racehorses?" she asked. "Isn't this where they're supposed to be?"

"Not at the moment." Though Hope knew better than to stray too far, Peg was keeping a close eye on her. She snapped her fingers and the big Poodle came trotting back to her side.

"Why not?"

"Because there's no race meet going on now. The barns on the backside are filled with sales horses. The racehorses will be back at the end of the month for Keeneland's October meet."

"Well, that's disappointing."

Peg reattached Hope's leash. "If you want to see live racing, we'll have to return another time. Now let's head back to the Six Oaks barn. I want to have a word with Manny, if I can. It would be interesting to see how his version of events compares to Lucia's."

"Don't forget about Jenny," Rose said as they skirted about the end of the grandstand and found themselves almost immediately returned to the backstretch barns. "We should talk to her too."

"I agree," Peg replied. "Lucia mentioned her, but I didn't know who she was. I meant to ask if you knew."

"You should be paying more attention." Rose smirked, pleased to be the one with information for once. "Jenny is one of the Six Oaks showmen. Young? Blond? Cute?"

Peg shook her head. Her memory was still blank. For the most part, she'd been looking at the horses, not their handlers.

"She had a yearling out when we were there earlier," Rose said. "Lucia gave her an instruction about something and said her name."

"Good. Then you'll be able to pick her out for us."

But when they arrived back at barn 14, neither Manny nor Jenny was anywhere to be seen. It was after four o'clock. They'd started showing yearlings before eight that morning. Now everyone, including the horses, was tired. The barn was closing for the day.

Lucia was standing next to the consignment table, packing up the box of cards, the farm brochures, and the notebooks. Most of the food had already been eaten. She pulled off the blue tablecloth and folded it into a neat square.

"Back so soon?" She smiled as they approached.

"We were hoping to catch Manny," Rose said. "Has he already left?"

"No. We've stopped showing here, but we're still setting things up at barn 31. We have to finish tonight because we'll start showing the book two yearlings bright and early tomorrow morning. I just got word that those horses have arrived at the loading dock. Manny and a couple of other guys went to pick them up and bring them to the barn. The first group includes your colt, Peg."

"My colt is on the grounds?" Peg's eye lit up. "Until now, the sale has felt like a mirage, shimmering somewhere off in the future. But now it's finally happening. Is it okay if I go over and take a look?"

"Sure," Lucia told her. "But there's a lot that needs to be done up there, and everyone's pretty busy. So maybe try to stay out of the way?"

"Don't worry about us," Rose said. "I'll make sure Peg doesn't go poking around anywhere she's not supposed to be."

"Really?" Peg slanted a scornful look at Rose once they were on their way. Even Hope appeared to be amused. "You're a pipsqueak compared to me. How do you intend to enforce that promise?"

"I haven't the slightest idea." Rose laughed. "But it sounded good. At least to someone who doesn't know how forceful you can be."

Lucia had stated there was still much work to be done, but to Rose, the next barn appeared to be in good shape when they arrived. Not that she actually knew what a well-stocked barn should look like, but she'd imagined some level of barnyard disarray: maybe farm equipment lying on the ground or piles of hay bales blocking their way. Nothing like that could be seen here.

"Look out." Peg grabbed Rose's arm and pulled her to one side.

It was then that Rose heard the sound of hoofbeats on the macadam road behind her. She turned and saw a line of four yearlings approaching. The first colt was dark, almost black. The second in the line was Peg's chestnut. Two bays followed behind him.

The colts' ears were pricked, and their nostrils flared as they high-stepped down the road. For most yearlings, this sale would be the first time they'd left the farm where they were born. Everything looked, smelled, and sounded different. None of them were sure they liked that. All four handlers had their hands full as the colts checked out their new surroundings.

"There's Manny," Rose said. The young Hispanic man

was leading the colt in the rear. Though the horse pranced and played, issuing a small squeal as he bounced in the air and kicked out a hind leg, Manny didn't appear to be bothered by the ruckus.

"Better him than me," Peg murmured.

"Me, too," Rose agreed.

The men walked past them, then entered the barn and delivered the colts to their stalls. Each stall had a sign on its open door, announcing the yearling's hip number and breeding. Peg's colt was on the end. She handed Hope's lead to Rose, then walked over to the low concrete wall that bordered the shed row and peered inside.

The doorway to her colt's stall was secured by a metal gate that enabled her to see within. The enclosure was heavily bedded with straw. A full water bucket hung from one wall, and there were several flakes of bright green hay on the floor. Her colt was busy examining everything about his temporary home.

"Three more to pick up," one of the men said, heading back toward the drop-off point. Manny waved the trio on their way and went to join Peg.

"Don't worry about your colt," he said. "He's smart, and he'll settle down soon enough. By tomorrow he'll be showing like a champ."

Manny was shorter than Peg but not by much. He had dark eyes and a great smile. One of his earlobes held a small gold earring.

"I hope so," she replied. "There's a lot riding on this."

Manny nodded. She was sure he'd heard that before.

"Do you have a minute to talk?" Peg beckoned Rose over.

"I can probably spare five," Manny told her, taking a quick look around.

Two grooms were bedding stalls at the other end of the barn. Another was unloading bags of feed from the back of a truck. A man was up in the hayloft, stacking bales of straw. But where they were standing, things were relatively quiet.

"You said earlier that you'd be willing to help Lucia," Peg said.

"I am," he confirmed. "She and I are friends. I don't want to see her get into trouble for something that wasn't her fault."

"So you don't think she's responsible for what happened to Jim Grable either?" Rose asked.

"No way. Lucia told me about the policeman questioning her. That was Ricky's fault. He's a groom at the farm. He threw Lucia under the bus because he has his own problems. Ricky didn't want the authorities looking too closely at him, so he told them they needed to talk to her."

"Problems," Peg said. "You mean with Grable?"

"Nah." Manny shook his head. "No more than the usual crap we all went through with Jim. Ricky's visa's expired. Last thing he wants is INS hearing his name. Lucia was just an easy out for him. Everyone knew she and Jim hated each other."

"Because she filed a complaint about him?" Rose asked.

"Yeah." Manny looked uncomfortable. "That and maybe some other stuff."

"What other stuff?"

Manny turned his head away and listened. A moment later, Peg and Rose could hear the sound of hoofbeats too. The next group of yearlings was about to arrive.

"Look," he said, "I'm not the right person to ask about this. Maybe there was a little side hustle happening back at the farm. You know, things ending up places other than where they were supposed to be. But I didn't know what was going on, and I didn't want to know. Safer for me to mind my own business."

"If you're not the right person," Peg said doggedly, "who is?"

Three fillies and their handlers came walking around the corner of the barn. The fillies were better behaved than the colts, but not by much. There was still plenty of snorting and head tossing going on. The guy in the middle looked at Manny and grinned.

Manny waited until they'd passed, then jutted his chin in that man's direction. "Nico," he said. "Guy's had a crush on Lucia for years. It's never come to anything but he's still hopeful. Talk to him."

Chapter 17

"That was interesting," Peg said, after Manny had left to help with getting the fillies settled.

Rose handed her Hope's leash. The Poodle was asleep on the grass beside them. "It would have been more interesting if you'd asked him about what Lucia told us earlier."

Peg got Hope up and the three of them began the long walk back to the parking lot. "I meant to. But then I got sidetracked."

"You always get sidetracked. You start out intending to do one thing and then you do something else entirely."

"Which often leads us in new and unexpected directions." Peg defended herself. "As it did today. What do you suppose Manny meant by a side hustle?"

"As if I would know. You know perfectly well I was in the convent during the Studio 54 days."

"Not that kind of hustle." Peg laughed.

"Are you sure?" Rose glanced over at her. "That's the only kind I know. Didn't John Travolta have something to do with it?"

Peg was still chuckling. "Has anyone ever told you that your grasp of pop culture leaves a great deal to be desired?"

Rose stopped walking. She disliked it when Peg made fun of her. It reminded her of their interactions decades earlier, when Peg was married to Max and Rose was still in the convent. At the time, Peg had seemed so worldly and sophisticated, while Rose always felt awkward and immature in comparison.

"If you'd rather discuss politics, I'm quite well versed in that area," she said.

"Politics?" Peg hooted. "No, thank you!"

Then abruptly she stopped too. Taken by surprise, Hope had to quickly double back. Now they were all discombobulated.

"You're angry," Peg said. It had her taken a moment to get it. And she still didn't entirely understand. "Now what's the matter?"

"Sometimes you treat me like I'm a child."

"Don't be ridiculous."

Peg started walking again. Rose didn't. Hope paused between them, undecided. Normally, she'd have followed Peg. But this time she suspected Peg was in the wrong. The Poodle decided to wait and see what was going to happen next.

"You're doing it again." Rose still hadn't moved. "You're dismissing something I said because you'd rather not deal with it."

Peg reached the end of Hope's leash. That made her halt. She turned back to see Rose and *her* Poodle standing together, as if the two of them were aligned against her. Rose's fit of pique was one thing. Their relationship had always had its ups and downs.

But Hope taking Rose's side? There was no way she could allow that to stand.

Rose looked down at the Poodle and smiled. "Good girl."

Peg came stalking back. "Don't talk to my dog."

"Why not?" Rose asked reasonably.

"Because you're always complaining that you don't understand her. So I know you're just doing it to annoy me."

"I didn't used to understand her. Now I do." Hope looked up at Rose and wagged her tail.

"Stop that," Peg said rudely. "Both of you."

Rose laughed. "Now who's acting like a child? Surely you can't be jealous over a dog."

Of course Peg could. Especially when the dog in question was Hope.

The bond she and the Poodle shared was more than a decade in the making. She and Max had bred Hope's parents and grandparents, nurturing the family of Poodles through meticulously curated generations. The moment Hope was born, Peg had been emotionally involved. Coming from Peg's first litter after Max's death, Hope was special to Peg and always would be.

Hope looked up at Peg and whined softly. She took two steps then pressed herself against Peg's leg. Peg got down on her knees. She used both hands to cup Hope's head and ruffle her fingers through the Poodle's ears.

"I know," she said softly. *I'm your favorite.* The words didn't need to be spoken aloud to be true.

"You know what?" Rose asked. She couldn't read Peg's mind the way Hope could.

Peg levered herself up. "That Hope thinks we're both acting like a pair of ninnies."

"Ninnies? Really? That's the word she used?"

"It's a perfectly fine word," Peg said. "Besides, I'm paraphrasing."

"I see."

"What she actually said was that we both need to grow up and figure out how to get along. All this bickering is upsetting her."

They still had quite a hike to get to the parking lot where they'd left the minivan. Peg started to walk again.

Rose fell in beside her. Hope nudged them apart with her nose, then wedged herself in between the two of them.

"It's upsetting me too," Rose said.

"Not me," Peg replied stoutly. "I enjoy a good dustup. I can't help it if you're too soft."

"And I can't help it if you're disrespectful."

This time, Hope was the one who halted. Both women took several steps before realizing the Poodle was no longer with them. Together, they turned and looked back.

"I'm sorry," Peg said.

"Me too," Rose added.

Hope let them think about that for several seconds before she decided they were forgiven, and they could all start moving again.

"Do you suppose Hope might be the smartest one of the three of us?" Rose mused.

Peg barked out a laugh. "I never doubted that for a minute."

Later that evening, Rose spent almost ten minutes on the phone with Peter. It was longer than the combined total of their two previous conversations, yet she still managed to learn almost nothing about what was happening at home. Instead, Peter spent most of the call reminding her to relax and have fun. As if she hadn't heard that before.

Peg, who was sitting in her hotel room with a book in her lap, glanced up once or twice during the course of the call. Since the door was open between their two rooms, and Rose hadn't seen Peg turn a single page since she sat down, she wasn't fooled by that ploy. Her suspicion was confirmed when Peg spoke up as soon as Rose disconnected the call.

"You don't need to look so disgruntled," she said. "Peter only wants what's best for you."

"I know that. But I feel fine. I wish he'd believe me."

Rose stood up and walked over to the doorway. "And by the way, you shouldn't be eavesdropping on other people's private conversations."

"Pish," said Peg. "That's how I find out all the best things. If you don't want me to listen in, you should close the door."

Rose laughed. They both knew that wasn't going to happen.

"Tomorrow's going to be another long day," Peg reminded her. "Between the start of the sale, and my colt showing to buyers back at the barn, we're going to have lots of things to see and do. I'm ready to make it an early night if you are."

"Fine by me," Rose agreed.

Peg and Rose were both awake shortly after sunrise the next morning. After Hope had eaten her breakfast and had a long walk, the two women went to the hotel coffee shop to feed themselves.

Peg ordered a pot of Earl Grey tea and an extra large, frosted cinnamon bun. Rose asked for scrambled eggs, toast and jam, and a very large cup of coffee. She knew she'd need the extra caffeine to keep up with Peg today.

"Have you noticed how often people we've met in Kentucky talk about money?" Rose asked after their meals had been set in front of them. She slid a small mound of scrambled egg onto her fork. "I suppose there's nothing wrong with that, but it does seem unusual."

"There's a lot of wealth in the horse industry," Peg said. "Purses are increasing, multimillion dollar stallion syndications aren't unusual, and massive amounts of money are bet on horseracing, because people love to gamble. All those facts and figures are reported daily by the Thoroughbred press. Since everyone already knows everybody else's business, why not talk about it?"

Rose nodded. She hadn't realized that.

"Also, there's the bragging aspect to consider. Men who are able to spend large sums of money on their hobbies often enjoy flaunting their wealth. It's no different than wanting to own the largest yacht in the marina."

"Surely you're not involved on that level?"

"Heavens, no." Peg had been using a knife and fork to eat her breakfast, but it was beginning to seem like eating the big bun with her fingers might be a more economical use of her time and effort. She tore off a piece and popped it into her mouth. "Did I ever tell you how I came to own a Thoroughbred broodmare?"

"I believe you alluded to a bequest at one point." Rose paused to put jam on her toast. "But you never elaborated beyond that, so I was forced to invent my own backstory for Lucky Luna's presence."

"Really?" Peg looked up with interest. "Where did your version say she came from?"

"I was thinking elves. Or maybe something to do with a lottery ticket."

"Unfortunately, the truth is more prosaic than that. Years ago, Max and I had a friend named Anthony Stone. Tony was a bit of a Renaissance man. Everything interested him. We never knew what he might decide to dabble in next."

"Dabbling?" Rose said. "In racehorses? That seems like a risky venture."

"I agree. But Tony loved it. When he passed away three years ago, it came as quite a shock when I found out that he'd left Lucky Luna to me in his will."

"Did he say why?"

"Apparently he thought my background in dog breeding made me the right person to oversee Luna's broodmare career."

"I suppose that makes sense," Rose considered. "If you don't mind my asking, how have you done so far?"

Peg's fingers were delightfully sticky with frosting. Now

that she'd finished her cinnamon bun, she was thinking about licking them clean. Rose probably wouldn't approve. Peg couldn't decide whether that made the prospect appear more, or less, appealing.

"Probably due more to beginner's luck than skill, I've just about managed to break even. The sales of Luna's previous foals have covered both her expenses and the stud fees I paid to produce them."

"Good for you." To Rose, that sounded like a win. Actually, not owning a horse at all sounded like even more of a win. But there was probably no point in bringing that up.

"That's why this week's sales result makes all the difference," Peg continued. "The hope is that the money this colt brings will pay all of Luna's bills for the upcoming year. But as you mentioned earlier, there's always a risk. Racehorse ownership is all fun and games when it's going well . . ."

"And when it's not?"

Peg winced slightly as she signaled for the check. "Then it's more like a bottomless money pit. Do you remember the big colt we saw yesterday at Six Oaks—the one the farrier was working on beside the barn?"

"Only vaguely," Rose admitted. "There was something wrong with one of his feet, wasn't there?"

"Yes. That was Snow Cloud. He belongs to the three partners we overheard yesterday."

"He's the expensive colt that won't make it to the sale?"

Peg nodded.

Rose thought back. "The woman partner was very upset about that."

"She should be. It sounded as though they expected to get a lot of money for him. But this sale was their opportunity to cash in, and now he's going to miss it. The partners took a chance and it didn't work out for them."

"No wonder she was unhappy," Rose mused.

"Depending on how the sale goes, she won't be the only one," Peg said. "I suspect these next few days are going to feel like we're sitting on top of a pressure cooker in more ways than one."

This time when they drove onto the Keeneland grounds, the lot where they'd parked the previous day was already full. As was the one next to it. And the one after that.

"Where did all these people come from?" Rose asked when Peg finally found an empty spot behind the track kitchen.

"Everywhere." Peg hooked the leash to Hope's collar and hopped her out of the minivan. "Don't forget, yesterday the sale hadn't started yet. The people on the grounds then were those looking at book one horses. Now, both book one and book two yearlings are available to be seen. So the pool of shoppers has grown."

Rose and Peg started down the long driveway that led to barn 31. Hope cavorted happily at Peg's side. Both women had dressed that morning with practicality in mind. Rose was wearing slacks and a long-sleeved tunic in a flattering shade of pink. Peg had on a lightweight denim dress that was belted at the waist. They were both wearing sturdy shoes.

As they walked, Peg was still speaking. Long-winded explanations were her specialty. In another life, she might have enjoyed being a college lecturer. The notion of people paying to listen to her words of wisdom seemed eminently appealing.

"Inside the sales pavilion, the auction is about to begin. The bidding wars that take place during these first few sessions are exciting to watch. I think I mentioned that all the best yearlings are offered first?"

"You did."

"So aside from the buyers and sellers, spectators show up too. Everyone enjoys watching the top horses go through the ring and bring six- and seven-figure prices."

When Peg said things like that, Rose couldn't help but think back to the time she'd spent in Honduras. Where she and Peter had worked, a man was considered rich if he had a roof over his head and enough money to feed his family. The price of just one of these "top horses" would have been enough to support several villages for an entire year.

"You're looking very pensive," Peg commented. "I hope you're not thinking about bidding on a horse."

The ridiculous idea banished Rose's dreary thoughts. She looked at Peg and laughed. "Certainly not. If we venture near the sales ring, I'll be sure to sit on my hands."

"You don't need to go that far," Peg said. "As long as you're careful not to catch the eye of a bid spotter, you'll probably be safe."

"Safe." Rose smirked. "Around here, that seems to be a relative term."

Chapter 18

"The first thing we should do is see if we can find Nico and ask him about what Manny told us yesterday," Rose said as they approached barn 31.

"Nico, right." Peg nodded in agreement, but she sounded as though she was only half listening.

"Do you have a better idea?"

"No, that's fine. But I also want to check in with Lucia, or whoever's calling cards at this barn, and find out if anyone has come to look at my colt yet."

"He just got here," Rose pointed out. She didn't want Peg to get her hopes up too high. "And he doesn't sell until Thursday. That's still two days away. There will be plenty of time for buyers to see him."

Peg glanced at her watch. "The barn's been open for more than an hour. I might as well ask."

Barn 31 was the last in the long row, and the Six Oaks stalls were on the far side. With no barn opposite them, the consignment had a large courtyard all to itself. Fortuitously, that gave the crew private access to four show rings.

All the rings were in use when Peg, Rose, and Hope walked around the barn, then through a gate, to enter the courtyard. Nico was showing a yearling in one of them. A young man Peg didn't recognize was standing beside the consignor table. Since he was holding a handful of cards, Peg assumed he was the person in charge.

Naturally he was dressed in the farm attire: khaki pants and a royal blue polo shirt with the Six Oaks logo. His body was tall and lanky. To Peg's eye, he barely looked old enough to shave. She handed Hope's lead to Rose, pointed them toward a nearby bench, then marched over to say hello.

"Good morning." The man greeted her with a friendly smile as he offered her a card. "Can I help you?"

Peg accepted it and saw that she'd been right. The card listed all the Six Oaks yearlings that were in book two. There was a space beside each yearling's hip number for buyers to check off the ones they wanted to see. A signature was requested at the bottom.

"You may," Peg said. "My name is Peg Turnbull. I own the colt out of Lucky Luna. I came by to see how he's doing."

"Nice to meet you. I'm Bryce Hardin." The man's smile widened. "Your colt's doing great. We've already had a dozen all-shows so far this morning." He took a quick glance at the walking rings. "He isn't out right now, but I can get him for you if you'd like to see him."

"Thank you, but there's no need. I saw him just the other day at the farm. What do you mean by an 'all-show'?"

"When buyers initially come to see what we have, they usually look at everything in the consignment. That's called an all-show. Then having seen all the horses, they narrow down their lists to the ones they're interested in. Those yearlings will merit a second, and perhaps a third, look over the next couple of days before they sell."

"So what you're saying is the fact that a dozen people

have asked to see him doesn't really mean much. Correct?" Peg was disappointed to hear that.

"Yes and no," Bryce told her. "It's true that nobody pulled him out specifically—although it would be early for that to happen. But when I watch the shoppers, I can usually tell which yearlings have caught their eye. Maybe they'll ask for another walk, or touch their throats, or step in close to measure how tall they are. If I had to speculate, I'd say that Lucky Luna has already drawn some interest from the right people."

"Thank you for the explanation." Peg hoped he wasn't just telling her what he thought she wanted to hear. She tucked the card in her purse to examine more closely later, then gestured toward the bench. "Will Rose and I be out of your way if we sit and watch for while?"

"Sure, that's fine," Bryce was already looking past her to a new group of arriving shoppers. "Let me know if you need anything. And if you have more questions, Walter is your man—you've met Walter Tausky?"

"Yes, I have."

"He's busy at barn 14 at the moment, but he'll be by to check on us later."

"Perfect," Peg said. "Thank you."

She went over and joined Rose on the green-slatted bench. Peg reached down to give Hope's head a pat, then wiggled back and forth, trying to get comfortable. "Why don't these things have cushions on them?"

"Probably because they don't expect anyone to use them," Rose said. "Between yesterday and today, you and I are the one people I've seen sitting down. Everyone else is running around this place like Alice's White Rabbit—as if they're all late for a very important date."

"More likely, they all just want to look as though they are." Peg was more of a cynic than Rose.

"By the way, we're not the only ones who've dropped by to observe the activity." Rose nodded toward Martin Shrady, one of the three pinhooking partners they'd seen the day before. He was leaning casually against the white board fence that bordered the courtyard, eyeing a chestnut colt who'd been out for several minutes. "Didn't Lucia tell us that he and his partners have two yearlings in this consignment?"

"Yes, she did," Peg agreed. "I think I'll go over and introduce myself."

"Why am I getting the impression that you're going to do all the interesting things today, while I just sit here on this bench?" Rose grumbled.

"Well, we can't both go talk to him because it's better for Hope to be over here out of the way, so she doesn't accidentally spook a horse or distract the buyers. But if you'd prefer to meet Mr. Shrady yourself, I'll be happy to stay here and keep Hope company while you do so."

Rose frowned as she immediately saw the problem with that idea. "You know perfectly well I haven't got a single intelligent thing to say on the subject of Thoroughbreds. What would I talk to him about?"

"Good question." Peg stood up and smoothed her skirt. "My plan is to let Mr. Shrady do most of the talking."

When Martin Shrady saw Peg heading his way, he immediately pushed himself off the fence and stood up straight. He was a handsome man, with a full head of dark, curly hair, even features, and a disarming smile that he directed at Peg as she drew near.

"Martin Shrady," he said, extending a hand. "I saw you yesterday at the other barn. I apologize for not stopping to introduce myself then."

"Peg Turnbull," she replied as they shook hands. "There's no need to apologize. You and your friends were quite busy at the time. I understand that several of these handsome horses are yours."

"That's correct." Martin turned around to have a look. "The bay colt at the far end is one of them. He's by Curlin. The other is by Bolt d'Oro. He's not out right now, but he should be along in a minute. How about you? I assume from your level of interest that you also have a yearling here?"

"Yes. Mine's a colt too. He's out of a mare named Lucky Luna."

Peg's colt had just exited the barn. Bryce directed his handler to an empty ring near the hedge. A man with an iPad and an impatient look on his face was waiting there for him.

"There." Peg pointed. "The chestnut."

Martin didn't reply right away. Instead he took his time, observing the colt both standing and walking before offering an opinion. "He's very nice. I'm sure you'll do well with him."

"I hope so," Peg said, then laughed. "Just like everyone else here.'

Martin nodded, acknowledging the truth in that.

"I'd say something nice about your colt except I'm very much a newcomer to Thoroughbred sales," Peg told him. "As a dog breeder and dog show judge, I know better than to voice an opinion on an animal when I don't have a solid base of knowledge with which to back it up."

"A newcomer?" Martin sounded pleased. "Good for you. This industry could use some fresh blood. Especially people who don't already think they know everything. If you have any questions, feel free to ask."

Peg moved over to stand beside the fence. That way, they could both watch the yearlings show as they talked. "Actually, there is something I'd like to know."

"What's that?"

"Someone mentioned yesterday that you, and the people you were with, are a pinhooking partnership. How does something like that come together?"

"Good question," Martin said. "It starts with a group of individuals who have common interests and some spare cash that they'd like to invest. In my day job, I'm a bloodstock agent. Basically, that means I use my expertise to help my clients buy and sell horses. I also do appraisals and sell stallions seasons. Glengellen Associates, maybe you've heard it?"

"I'm sorry, no," Peg sounded properly regretful. "I'm afraid I don't have a chance to spend much time in Kentucky."

"Well I'm glad you're here now," Martin told her. "To continue with what I was saying, the woman I was with yesterday is Zara King. Like you, she's new to the industry. She loves horses and is happy to have the opportunity to be involved with them. Our third partner is Leo Grainger. He has a small breeding operation in Versailles. He sells most of his stock as weanlings, though occasionally he'll stay in for a piece on a horse he particularly likes. Leo also sells equine insurance on the side."

Peg glanced over at Rose and hoped she was listening. Later, they were going to have to compare notes about all this.

"So between the three of us, we pretty much have all the bases covered." Martin preened, while trying to appear modest about their accomplishments. "That's why I put the group together. We each brought something useful to the table—and that's a good foundation on which to build a successful partnership."

Peg's ears perked up. She loved useful people. It was easy for her to understand about the broad-based expertise and hands-on experience that Leo and Martin brought to the equine partnership. However, Zara King's sole contribution appeared to be financial. Perhaps in Martin's view, that was an equally valuable addition to the proceedings.

"So the partnership was your idea?" she said brightly.

Like all salesmen, Martin was eager to air his accomplishments. "Indeed it was. In fact, it's been so successful that I'm thinking about putting a second group together. Is that something you might be interested in hearing more about?"

"Possibly." Peg played coy. She didn't dare look at Rose again in case the woman was laughing. "Let me give it some thought. At my age, I obviously need to be concerned about unnecessary risk. I believe something was mentioned yesterday about a colt that won't be making it to the sale?"

Martin frowned. "You heard about that?"

"I'm afraid so."

"That particular situation is a huge shame. We expected great things from the Snow Cloud colt—"

"Snow Cloud?" a voice said behind them. "Has something happened? Martin, if there's been an update you should have called me."

Peg and Martin turned as one. On the other side of the fence, Leo Grainger was coming toward them. There was a hopeful expression on his florid face. He was a chunky man, dressed in faded jeans that rode low on his waist and pooled around his ankles. His gaze slid over Peg briefly before snapping back to Martin.

"Leo, I'd like you to meet Peg Turnbull," Martin said. "She has a colt in the consignment too."

"Nice to meet you." Leo was still staring at Martin. "Has there been news?"

"Leo, maybe take it down a notch." Martin sounded annoyed. "What news could there possibly be? If Snow Cloud isn't on the grounds by now—which he isn't—it's too late to salvage the situation."

"Bruises heal," Leo said stubbornly. "Maybe he recovered overnight. Did anyone check to see if he was sound this morning? He could still ship in for the second show day. We could put an ad in the *Thoroughbred Daily News* to let everyone know that he's here."

"I'm sure someone examined him this morning," Martin said.

"Who?" Leo demanded. "Not that guy Abel. I don't want him touching the colt again. Or any of our yearlings, for that matter."

"Why not?" Peg asked, surprised. Abel had struck her as a perfectly pleasant, if somewhat taciturn, man.

Leo's gaze slid her way. For the first time, he seemed to fully register Peg's presence. She provided a fresh audience for his complaint.

"Because I suspect this whole disaster is his fault. I don't think the colt ever had a stone bruise. I think Abel accidentally quicked him with a nail and that's why he's lame. The farm doesn't want to deal with the fallout so they're covering up for him."

"Leo, be quiet," Martin said sternly. "Stop talking right now. I know you're upset that the colt isn't here. We're all unhappy about it. But you can't go around spewing unfounded accusations."

"Who says they're unfounded?" Leo demanded. "Have you seen the colt for yourself? I haven't. Nobody's seen him. We're just taking Walter's word about the information that came from Grable. Maybe that's a mistake."

"Please let me apologize for Leo." Martin turned his back on his partner, facing Peg instead. "If you haven't already discovered, emotions tend to run high at horse sales. People get carried away. They say things they don't really mean. Then later they wish they'd never opened their mouths."

Leo grunted something rude under his breath. Peg and Martin both pretended they didn't hear a thing.

"I understand completely," she replied. "The same thing has been known to happen at dog shows. I think it's time for me to go rejoin my friend."

"It was a pleasure meeting you," Martin said. "I hope we run into each other again. Perhaps under more favorable circumstances."

Peg smiled. "Don't worry, Martin. I'll make sure of it."

Chapter 19

"That turned out to be more excitement than I expected to see," Rose commented when Peg returned to the bench. "Maybe I should have gone over there myself."

"It was more than I expected too." Hope was napping beneath the bench. Peg leaned down to give her a proper greeting. "It's a shame you had to miss it."

Rose stood up and moved over. There was plenty of room on the seat, but Peg seemed to be indicating that the only spot she'd accept was the one beside her Poodle. It figured.

"Hopefully your aged memory took it all in, because I could hardly hear a thing until Leo showed up. Then I'd imagine everyone heard them. But let's start at the beginning with a recounting of your conversation with Martin. Perhaps with some color commentary on the side."

"You were supposed to be taking it all in while it was happening live," Peg complained as she sat down. "I probably don't remember everything Martin said, but I'd imagine I can give you the gist."

"The gist it is," Rose agreed, then laughed unexpectedly. "Oh my. Try saying that three times fast."

"I'd rather not, thank you very much. What I'll say instead is that having now met both Martin Shrady and Leo

Grainger, I wasn't terribly impressed with either one of them."

Rose nodded. Peg's assessment wasn't unexpected. "It looked from here as though things were going fine until Leo arrived."

"They were. And do you want to know why?"

"Yes, please."

"Because it turns out that Martin Shrady is a blood-stock agent. And, as I'm sure you're aware, people who want to sell you something are the friendliest people in the world."

"What did he want to sell you?" Rose asked curiously.

"There was mention of another, upcoming, partnership to be formed. He asked if I might be interested."

"I see." Rose bit back a laugh. "How could you possibly resist when his current partnership is proceeding so smoothly?"

"I know." Peg smirked. "He was not at all pleased when Leo showed up and tossed a spanner into the works, by claiming that their supposed big-money colt—who didn't make it to the sale due to being lame—doesn't have a stone bruise as the people at Six Oaks contend, but rather was quicked with a nail by Abel the farrier."

"Stop right there." Rose held up a hand. "There are so many things in that sentence I don't understand that I hardly even know where to begin asking questions."

"Fire away," Peg said. "I'm on top of at least part of it."

"Start with a definition of a stone bruise and work your way over to the quick nail. Then explain to me why the farm people say one thing about it and one of the horse's owners says another."

"A stone bruise is pretty much self-explanatory. It's when a horse steps on a rock and bruises the underside of his hoof. As for the next part, I believe the word Leo used was *quicked* and it seemed to describe the colt, not the nail." She paused to pull out her phone. "I'm afraid I don't know what that is, but I intend to learn all about it shortly."

Rose waited while Peg spent what seemed like an inordinate amount of time scrolling through items on her phone. If there was one thing she'd learned in her life, it was patience. Now Rose sat in the shade and watched a stream of pretty horses pass by. There were worse ways to spend a sunny September day.

"I think I've got it," Peg said finally. "Being 'quicked' is something that happens to a horse's hoof. It means that a farrier hammered a nail in too deeply, and it went through the hoof wall into the sensitive laminae."

"Ouch." Rose shuddered. "That sounds painful."

"Hence the resulting lameness." Peg put her phone away. "Either way, it sounds as though what happened to Snow Cloud was an accident. Surely no reputable farrier would quick a horse on purpose."

"Maybe not, but there *is* a difference between the two scenarios," Rose pointed out. "A stone bruise is an injury the colt would have done to himself. While a quicked hoof would be an injury inflicted by a person, in this case Abel the farrier. Maybe it's a matter of negligence. Then the question would become: Was Six Oaks Farm responsible for the colt missing the sale, or were they not? And don't forget, if there was negligence, then you might also have liability."

"It's interesting you should mention that," Peg mused. "Leo said something yesterday about having written the insurance policy on the colt."

"He did." Rose remembered too. Then her voice dropped to a hushed tone. "And it was for a million dollars."

"Too rich for my blood," Peg muttered. She glanced up to see her own colt standing virtually right in front of her, as he was being shown on the walking path near their bench. "Oh look, there's my handsome boy now."

The shopper who was inspecting the colt, looked over

at her and smiled companionably. Then he marked something in his catalog and gestured for the colt to take another walk.

Rose waited until the man had finished his examination and moved on, then said, "What do you have your colt insured for?"

"Not a million dollars!" Peg hissed under her breath.

"No, of course not. And anyway, I'm not asking about his valuation. What I want to know is what kind of policy you have on him. Is it life insurance? Health insurance? Maybe loss of use? And would your policy cover a problem like the one the partners are experiencing with their yearling?"

Peg thought for a moment, then shook her head. "I can't imagine that missing a sale is the kind of thing that would be covered under any normal policy. And it seems unlikely in Snow Cloud's case. Why would the partners be so upset, if they could simply put in a claim and collect their money?"

"I suppose you're right," Rose said. "I hadn't thought about that."

Hope moved out from beneath the bench. She stood up, then rocked back onto her hind legs for a long, luxurious stretch. Her pomponned tail was high in the air as she finished the movement with a big shake, then turned her head to look up at Peg.

"I think that's Hope's way of telling us we've been sitting still for too long," Rose said.

"She's probably right." When Peg looked around the courtyard beside the barn, she was surprised to see that all but one of the show rings was empty. "It's nearly lunchtime. That seems to have caused a lull in the activity."

"Surely you don't want more food," Rose protested. "I feel like we just ate breakfast."

"No, I'm not hungry either. But I wouldn't mind taking a look around the barn for Nico," Peg said, standing up.

"Every time I've caught a glimpse of him this morning, he was busy with a horse. Now, when things have slowed down, he seems to have disappeared."

"Maybe he's gone to lunch," Rose said, getting up too. "Let's go find out."

A small crowd had gathered in the pass-through in the middle of the barn. Heads tipped upward, everyone was watching a race on the TV screen above the aisle. Rose let her gaze skim over the assembled group. She didn't see Nico there, but a blond-haired girl caught her eye.

"Who are you staring at?" Peg asked.

"That's Jenny, the woman Lucia mentioned yesterday. The one who's supposed to back up her story about Jim Grable's bad behavior."

"Well done, you." Peg sounded pleased, which in turn made Rose feel the same. Peg didn't often offer praise for something Rose had done right. There was no time to enjoy the moment, however, because Peg was already hurrying on. "What are we waiting for? Surely watching television isn't all that interesting. Perhaps Jenny would like to join us for a stroll. We could buy her lunch from one of the food trucks."

A race was ending as they approached. Its conclusion was accompanied by the usual chorus of groans and cheers. Peg remained outside the barn, keeping Hope well away from the milling crowd.

Rose went in and skirted around the edges of the rowdy group. She was forced to pause when a man dressed in the Six Oaks colors poked the person standing beside him. When he extended his open hand and wiggled his fingers, she realized it was Manny. "Pay up," he said to the other man.

The second man, Sergio, just laughed. "No way, not yet. That was just the first race. I still have plenty of time to get even."

Rose dodged around the pair and kept moving. They weren't the only ones who were settling bets on the race.

By the time Rose got to Jenny, the young woman was on the fringes of the group. She looked surprised when Rose suddenly stopped in front of her.

Jenny's wheat-hued hair was contained in a neat French braid. Her eyes were cornflower blue. The farm polo shirt and khaki shorts looked as though they'd been tailored to her lithe body. Rose recalled Tammy's description of the women who were hired to act as showmen for Six Oaks. Jenny fit the bill perfectly.

"Hello," Rose said. "I'm Rose Donovan. Lucia Alvarez told me you might be able to help me with something."

"She did?" Jenny looked confused, but not unwilling. "Umm, sure, I guess. What do you need?"

"Just a few minutes of your time." Mentioning their connection to the Six Oaks consignment might lend her request some legitimacy. Rose nodded toward Peg who was waiting outside the barn. "That's Peg Turnbull. She owns one of the colts in your consignment. We'd just like to ask you a couple of questions."

"About the colt? Then I should probably have Bryce call Walter for you. I wouldn't want to give you the wrong information." Jenny started to turn away.

"Not about the colt." Rose lowered her voice. "About Jim Grable."

Jenny paused and bit her lip. "Lucia sent you?"

"That's right. We promise to be quick. Peg and I would be happy to buy you lunch."

"Umm . . . let me check."

Jenny walked over to Bryce, who was leaning against the waist-high outer wall of the barn, frowning over an iPad. He barely looked up when she spoke. Seconds later, she was back.

"I've got ten minutes," Jenny said. "And you don't have to worry about lunch. We always order in for the whole crew. Today there's pizza and barbecue in the tack room. I'll grab something to eat when I get back."

Rose introduced Jenny to Peg when they exited the barn. Jenny smiled politely at Peg, but when she saw Hope her face lit up. She immediately knelt down in front of the big Poodle.

"Hello, gorgeous girl," she said. "What's your name?"

"Hope," Peg supplied. She liked this young woman already. "And she's happy to meet you too."

"Of course she is." Jenny grinned. "Look at her tail. It's wagging so hard her whole body's shimmying. Hope, you poor thing. Are you bored at the sale? Is no one paying enough attention to you? Let's go take a walk and see if we can find some excitement for you."

Rose glanced at Peg and pointed to her watch. They needed to be moving along.

"I thought we might head over toward the grandstand," Peg said. Since barn 31 was at the end of the row, it was the one closest to the racetrack. "You can hold Hope's leash if you like."

"Absolutely." Jenny stood up and took the leather strip from Peg. Then she looked at Hope and patted her leg. "Come with me, Hope."

The three of them left the courtyard and headed toward the entrance to the track area.

"I hope Rose didn't take you away from something fun," Peg said, watching with approval when Jenny's free hand rested on Hope's withers as they walked along.

"No way," Jenny replied. "I was just hanging out with the guys. We're making good money here at the sale, so of course they're all placing bets on the races. Things can get pretty wild when there's a big pot at stake. I was just as happy to get out of there when I did."

Rose waited until they'd gone far enough to be well out of earshot, then asked Jenny, "Are you and Lucia friends?"

"Yeah, sure." She shrugged. "I mean, we don't hang out after work or anything. But we see each other around the farm, and we get along fine."

"You're aware that the police questioned Lucia in connection with Jim Grable's death?" Peg said.

"Yes. They talked to lots of people."

"Did they question you?"

"No. I wasn't at the yearling division that day. I didn't even know about what happened to Jim until later."

"What was your reaction when you heard the news?" Peg asked.

Jenny didn't reply right away. They walked past the ticket booths that marked the entrance to the track area, then went up the steps to the terrace behind the grandstand. Several white, wrought-iron chairs were scattered around, but none of the three women sat down. They wouldn't be there that long.

"Of course I was shocked," Jenny said finally. "I mean, who wouldn't be?"

"Lucia suggested that you might also have been relieved," Rose said.

"She did?" Jenny attempted to look surprised. She didn't quite manage to pull it off.

"Yes, she did," Peg replied firmly. "I assume you know about the sexual harassment complaint that Lucia made against Grable."

Jenny sucked in a deep breath. "We all knew about that."

"By 'all' you mean all the employees at the farm?"

Jenny glanced over. "Actually, I meant all the women employees. But that was only at first. Because everyone else heard soon enough."

"Why did the women know before anyone else?" Rose asked.

"Why do you think?" Jenny handed Hope's leash back to Peg, then strode to the end of the terrace to stare back at the Six Oaks barn. It was still quiet there. "Because Lucia talked to us about it beforehand. You know, in case we wanted to add our names to hers."

"But no one did, did they?"

"No." Jenny heaved a sigh. "It was just Lucia. She did it all on her own."

"Men like Jim Grable look for opportunity," Rose said. "In his position at the farm, he must have found plenty. Surely Lucia wasn't the only woman he was harassing."

Rose and Peg walked over and joined Jenny at the edge of the terrace. She was still gazing at the barn. Peg was on one side of her. Rose was on the other. Jenny didn't look at either of them.

"No," she said after a minute. "Of course she wasn't."

Rose knew that Jenny had to be around the same age as Lucia—in her mid-twenties—but suddenly she seemed much younger. No doubt Lucia had a great deal more real-world knowledge than Jenny did. It was probably the reason Lucia had learned how to fight back.

"I take it you're speaking from experience," Peg said gently.

Jenny just shrugged.

"I don't understand." Rose also moderated her tone. "What Lucia did could have helped all of you. Why didn't anyone support her?"

Jenny took a step back. That way, she could see both of them. "Because Tammy Radnor told us not to."

Chapter 20

"Tammy Radnor." Peg and Rose shared a look.

"She's an old lady who's worked at Six Oaks for years," Jenny said. "Mostly she just handles the foals now."

"Yes, we've met Tammy," Rose said. "Aside from her yearling, Peg also has a mare and foal on the farm."

Jenny perked up. "What's her name? I wonder if I know her."

"Lucky Luna," Peg told her.

"Really? I love her. Lucky Luna is a real doll."

"Yes, she is." Peg smiled. She loved hearing her animals praised. But Jenny was attempting to change the subject, and Peg wasn't about to allow that to happen. "Let's get back to Tammy, though. She had to have understood what Lucia hoped to accomplish. Why would she tell you not to support her?"

"Tammy's not only been at Six Oaks forever, she knows everything about the place. Probably a whole lot more than most of the men who've gone on to be promoted above her." Jenny paused to split a look between Peg and Rose. "I'm saying that to make it clear that when Tammy gives me advice, I know I should take it."

"Of course," Rose agreed.

"Tammy admired what Lucia was trying to do. Honestly, we all did. But Tammy told us—all of us, including

Lucia—that if we went ahead with the complaint, there would be repercussions."

"Are you saying you'd have lost your jobs?" Peg asked.

"No, nothing that blatant." Jenny frowned. "Although Lucia did end up getting reassigned. But trust me, there are worse things that can happen to a person on a horse farm than being demoted."

"Like what?" Rose prompted when Jenny turned away from the terrace wall. She looked like she was ready to head back to the barn. Rose was determined to hear more before they lost their chance.

"Maybe we'd start being assigned the worst shifts. Instead of working days, we'd be put on night watch. Or we'd be given all the tough horses to handle. The mares that bite or kick, or the yearling colts that think they're already stallions. Those guys can be nasty." Jenny grimaced at the thought.

"Jim Grable might have been the worst offender," she continued, "but he certainly wasn't the only guy who took advantage. Or who thought women didn't belong in jobs that could have gone to men instead."

"That kind of thinking is archaic," Peg said.

"And destructive," Rose added.

"Tell me about it," Jenny grumbled. "Also, a critical report on one man would have been seen as criticism of all of them. Tammy made that abundantly clear. 'Don't rock the boat,' she told us. 'It's better to stay safe.' "

"I don't suppose there's any possibility Tammy was exaggerating?" Peg asked.

"None," Jenny said firmly. "We all knew what she was referring to. Last year, a girl named Iris came to work at Six Oaks. She'd grown up riding horses, jumping, eventing, the whole deal. Nothing fazed her. Iris was a natural for the yearling division because even the rowdiest colts just made her roll her eyes. But then she got herself on

Jim's bad side. After that happened, nothing she did was ever good enough for him.".

Peg's eyes narrowed. She swore under her breath.

Jenny started walking back toward the terrace steps, but at least she was still talking. Rose fell in beside her. Peg and Hope brought up the rear.

"Jim assigned Iris to care for a colt who was really rank. I mean, this guy was a nutcase. Previously, when the men had to handle him, they'd always done it two at a time, with one of either side of him. But Jim just told Iris to stop complaining and deal with him. So she did. One day when she went to turn him out, the colt reared up and struck out at her. He came down on her leg and broke her femur."

Rose winced. "That's a bad bone to break."

"Yup. And it took her forever to heal. In the end, she never did come back to the farm."

"Please tell me there were repercussions for Jim when that happened," Peg said.

Jenny glanced back at her. "You're kidding, right? As far as the farm was concerned, Iris was the one who'd screwed up. If she didn't think she was competent to handle the colt, she should have asked for help."

"But—" Rose began, then stopped when Jenny glared at her.

"Who do you think reported the incident?" she asked. "And described how it happened?"

The answer was self-evident. Neither Peg nor Rose bothered to reply.

They went back through the ticket booths, and out to the driveway. Barn 31 wasn't far away. Just two yearlings were being shown. Bryce appeared to have everything under control. Jenny quickened her pace anyway. It was as if, having recounted what happened to Iris, she wanted to be certain not to make any mistakes herself.

"Wait," Peg said suddenly. Everyone stopped walking.

"You never said what Iris did that got her on Jim's bad side."

"It was something stupid," Jenny muttered.

"Go on," Peg prodded.

"She'd noticed that things were going missing around the barn. New halters, tubs of expensive supplements, stuff like that. Iris didn't want to say anything about it to Jim, because she was afraid he'd find a way to blame her. Instead, she went over his head and told Walter."

"Walter?" Peg was surprised. "I thought he was the farm's sales manager."

"He is. But lots of people at Six Oaks have more than one title because the management at the top is only like three people. Walter is also the farm COO. Iris thought the situation was something he should know about."

"Why do you think she was stupid to tell him?" Rose asked.

"Because it's a barn," Jenny said practically. "There's always stuff getting misplaced, or tossed in the back of a truck and ending up somewhere else. And sure, maybe sometimes things walk out on their own. But Iris should have just let it go. And when she didn't, it ended up causing a huge flap. Of course Jim found out she'd talked to Walter. Iris should have known that was inevitable. After that, it was only a matter of time before she was gone."

They'd reached the white board fence that bordered the barn's courtyard. Jenny headed for the gate, then paused. She glanced at the barn. No one was paying any attention to them.

"I'll tell you something else," she confided. "That all happened a year ago and things are still going missing. I pretend I don't notice and so does everyone else. Nobody ever says a word."

"I have something to say," Peg announced after Jenny had disappeared back into the barn. She and Rose had decided to walk over to the sales pavilion and watch the sale in progress. As always, Hope was happy to be on the move.

"Go ahead," Rose said. "You already have my undivided attention. What are you waiting for, a drumroll?"

"That would be grand." Peg peered down at her. "Do you think you can come up with one?"

"I doubt it. So just move along."

"I found our conversation with Jenny discouraging. Even at her young age, she's already resigned to the inequality in opportunities offered to men and women. She didn't stand up for Lucia—or for herself, either. I got the impression she also had a history with Grable. And yet she just accepted the status quo."

Rose nodded in agreement.

"Women's liberation probably seems like an anachronism to young people now. But I remember those days vividly. The protests, the bra burnings . . . we fought hard for the advances we gained. It seems a shame for this generation to allow things to backslide without a fight."

Rose was sorry she'd missed out on all that. "Did you really burn your bra?" she asked curiously.

"I would have. Except the only time I was in a situation where such things were happening, I wasn't wearing one."

Rose burst out laughing. After a minute, Peg joined in. Then she glanced down at her chest. Gravity had definitely had its way with her body since then.

"Those were the days!" she cried, which only made them giggle all the more. Hope bounced up and down at her side. The Poodle didn't know why everyone was so excited, but she was pleased to be part of it.

"But seriously," Peg added, as they approached the sales pavilion, "what I really wanted to say is this. The things Jenny told us have made me even more determined to stand up for Lucia. Because someone should have stood up for Iris, and apparently no one did."

"I fully agree," Rose replied.

They entered the pavilion through the front door and stepped into a lobby that was crowded with people, both coming and going. Though they couldn't see the sales ring from there, the sound of the auctioneer's steady patter was already audible. "Who'll give me six, who'll give me six hundred, six hundred thousand . . ."

Rose looked over at Peg, her eyes wide. *"Dollars?"* she whispered.

"I told you so," Peg said.

She and Hope crossed the lobby and went through another set of doors into the hallway that circled the auction ring and the tiered seating around it. When Rose followed, she saw that in contrast to the quiet of the day before, now the whole area was brightly lit and buzzing with activity. From where they were standing, they had a perfect view of the sale happening live in front of them.

The auction ring itself was a semi-circular, raised platform. Green horsehead hitching posts, strung with thick ropes between them, marked its boundary. The floor was laid with rubber bricks. A tall, wooden podium where the auctioneer was seated was at the back of the ring. Large monitors, hung high on the walls, flashed the rising bids in quick succession.

Now the number was at seven hundred thousand. Rose looked at it and thought she might faint.

A gray colt was standing in the ring, his shank held by a Black man wearing dark slacks and a green Keeneland jacket. The colt's head was high in the air. To Rose, he appeared to be watching the proceedings too. Every so often, the handler turned the yearling in another direction so everyone in the seats around the ring would have a good view.

"Seven hundred," the auctioneer intoned. "Going once, going twice. Sold for seven hundred thousand."

A door slid open in the back wall of the ring. A man dressed in the colors of the yearling's consignor took the shank from the Keeneland handler and led the colt out. Another door opened, and a new yearling was led in. An announcer began to read a description of the horse's pedigree.

"We can't stay here," Peg said, as traffic in the busy hallway was forced to eddy around them. "Let's sit down and get out of the way."

"In there?" Rose could hardly fathom it. Now that she'd seen the sale in action, the process seemed both faster, and scarier, than she'd imagined when she joked about sitting on her hands. What if she accidentally placed a bid by blinking or scratching her nose?

"No, not while we have Hope with us. Over here."

A row of cushioned benches, just outside the sales arena, offered the perfect spot for spectating. Large windows gave a clear view of the activity, but since bids couldn't be placed from out there, the area was excluded from the sales process. The seats inside the arena were nearly full, but the benches were mostly empty. There was plenty of room for Hope too.

As they settled into their seats, yet another yearling was led into the ring. Rose was amazed by how quickly the sale was proceeding, and said so.

"They average forty horses an hour." Peg turned her catalog to a new page. "That's just ninety seconds per horse. It may seem fast, but Keeneland has everything down to a science. As you can see, it all flows like clockwork."

Rose glanced at Peg's catalog. Each page appeared to be little more than a list of horses' names. "And you actually understand all this?"

"Not *all* of it," Peg replied carefully. "But enough not to feel like a total novice. I've owned Lucky Luna for three years, and I've sold her two previous yearlings through this sale. Those times, I watched the proceedings online. This is the first opportunity I've had to be here in person."

By the time Rose looked up again, another yearling had been sold. The number on the monitors was $250,000. She wondered if she'd eventually become inured to the sight of these huge numbers. If so, it hadn't happened yet.

"Are there any horses that don't sell for a fortune?" Rose couldn't believe that the people in the arena looked so blasé about the prices. Many were texting, or talking, or not even paying attention at all.

"This is book one," Peg reminded her. "These yearlings are the best of the best. Competition to buy them is fierce."

They sat in place for several hours, watching a steady parade of yearlings come and go. Peg paid avid attention to the sale. Rose amused herself by gazing around the inside gallery and trying to pick out which people were the ones doing the bidding. She was terrible at it. It turned out she was wrong in almost every instance.

After a while, the auctioneer's spiel became just background noise, a stream of syncopated babble that echoed inside Rose's head. Hope appeared to have tuned out too. She was fast asleep on the floor. Rose began to wish she could do the same.

Once again, a yearling exited the ring. Almost immediately, another was led in. Rose wasn't paying attention. Instead, she was checking out the bid spotters. She wondered how hard it would be to do a job like that. They must have to be constantly on their toes. And what would happen if they missed a bid?

Beside her, Peg suddenly sat up straight.

"What?" Rose glanced over.

Peg gestured toward the ring. To Rose's eye, the bay filly there looked much the same as those who'd proceeded her.

But the handler who'd brought her inside was wearing the Six Oaks uniform.

"Is that one we know?" Rose was whispering. She wasn't quite sure why.

"Yes, don't you remember? We saw her at barn 14 yesterday. She's the filly the partners were looking at right in front of us."

"Midnight Magic," Rose said. "I remember that because I thought it was such a pretty name."

"It will be interesting to see what price she brings." Peg had lowered her voice too. "Zara King, the partner we haven't met yet, was complaining about an issue that turned up in the filly's sales X-rays. Martin and Leo were assuring her that she would sell well anyway."

Peg and Rose leaned both closer to the window as the auction began. The opening bid on the filly was twenty thousand. After that, the number progressed by tens. It didn't take long for the bidding to end at one hundred and forty thousand. The auctioneer pronounced the filly sold, and she was led from the ring.

"It's lower than most of the others we've seen," Rose commented as she and Peg both sat back on the cushioned bench. "But it's still a good price. One hundred and forty thousand dollars is a lot of money."

"I'm not sure the partners would agree with you," Peg said. "I wonder if she sold."

"Of course she sold. We just watched it happen."

"No. We watched the filly go through the ring. But that doesn't necessarily mean that she sold."

Rose was perplexed. "The auctioneer said she did. I heard him."

"They always say that. It doesn't always mean it's true." Peg held up a hand to shush Rose before she could object again. "Before each yearling goes through the ring, their owners decide what's the lowest price they're willing to accept. That amount is called the reserve. The auctioneer will carry the bid to that number, regardless of whether there are live bidders or not. His job is to encourage the bidding to go past that point, but he isn't always successful."

"So what happens if he isn't?" Rose was interested in spite of herself.

"Then the yearling has been bought back by its owners. It's listed in the sales results as an RNA, which stands for 'reserve not attained.' "

"But the owners wanted to sell the horse."

"Yes, but only above a certain price," Peg said. "So now they have to explore other options. Maybe they'll sell her privately. Or they'll point her toward a two-year-old sale next year. But based on the conversation we heard yesterday, I can tell you one thing I'm sure of. Those three partners are not happy about this outcome."

Chapter 21

They left the sales pavilion shortly after that.

Peg went reluctantly. She could have watched the proceedings for several more hours. Rose and Hope all but danced out of the building. They both felt as though they'd been set free.

"Now where are we going?" Rose asked. She was holding Hope's leash. The Poodle paused to watch a squirrel scamper down a tree, then think better of that decision and run back up.

"Barn 31," Peg told her. "The consignment should be getting ready to close for the day and I want to get an update from Bryce about how my colt has done. Plus, we still haven't had a chance to talk to Nico."

When they reached the barn, all its walking rings were empty. Several grooms were setting feed; another was up in the hayloft tossing down bales of hay. Bryce was packing up the table. Nico was nowhere to be seen.

Peg strode across the courtyard. Bryce turned around when he heard someone coming, then smiled when he saw it was Peg. "Hello, Mrs. Turnbull. Have you had a good day?"

"It's Peg, please. And my day has been fascinating on several fronts. But I want to hear how things progressed here. How's my colt doing?"

'Very well. I don't have the exact numbers at my fingertips." He gestured toward a thick stack of cards. "But I'd say he's in our top five as far as interest goes."

"When we spoke this morning, you said there'd been a dozen all-shows." Peg was pleased to be able to use the new terminology she'd learned. "I hope there were more after that?"

"Yes, absolutely. At least another dozen during the day." A lock of dark hair had fallen forward over Bryce's brow. He raked it back with his hand. "More importantly, your colt had four second looks from buyers. I believe there might have even been a third look from one agent."

"That sounds promising," Peg said. "I assume that indicates a higher level of interest on their part?"

"It does indeed. Especially this early. Of course, we'll have to wait and see what his vetting looks like, but right now I'd say you have every reason to be hopeful that he'll do well."

"Thank you. That's delightful to hear. If you wouldn't mind, could you explain your statement about the vetting?"

"Sure." Bryce leaned against the table as if he had all the time in the world to chat. "You're aware that before he shipped to the sale, your colt's joints were X-rayed, and his throat was scoped for possible abnormalities, right?"

"Yes, Ben told me about that. As I understand it, the X-rays are in a repository that's here on the grounds?"

"That's correct." Bryce nodded. "We also have a vet sheet here at the consignment that summarizes the findings, but most buyers like to have their own vet examine the actual films. And of course, the buyers are charged for that. So when someone who's looked at your colt is willing to spend money performing additional due diligence, we know he's serious."

"I see," Peg said happily. She was learning all sorts of new things.

"Assuming the X-rays are acceptable," Bryce continued, "the buyer's vet will come to the barn to do his own scope. When that happens, we're pretty sure we've got a live bidder who wants to buy the horse."

"Thank you for the explanation," Peg said. "I'll let you get back to work. I was hoping to have a word with Nico, but I don't see him around."

"No, he's already left for the day. He'll be back tomorrow morning. Is there something I can help you with in the meantime?"

"No, that's all right. I'll just check in again tomorrow."

Rose and Hope were waiting for her beside the fence at the edge of the courtyard. Somewhere Rose had found a rubber ball. She and Hope were playing catch. At least Rose was. Hope was making it clear that she would rather chew on the toy.

"All done," Peg said. "I'm ready to leave when you are."

"Not yet." Rose pointed toward the other end of the barn. "Look."

Abel's truck was parked on the far side of the last walking ring. The farrier was beside it, working on a yearling. Bent over at the waist with the horse's leg tucked securely between his own, Abel was tapping the horse's hoof with a horseshoe hammer. When he finished the job, he lowered the foot gently to the ground, then straightened and stretched out his back.

Rose thrust Hope's leash into Peg's hand and started walking. She'd missed out on meeting Abel at the farm—okay, maybe that was her own fault, but still. Then she'd managed to hear just bits and pieces of Leo's rant about the farrier from the other side of the courtyard. Rose was tired of getting her information secondhand.

By the time Peg caught up to her, Rose had already reached the back of Abel's truck. A groom was leading away the yearling the farrier had been working on. Abel was packing up his tools and preparing to leave.

"Hello," she said. "I'm Rose Donovan."

Abel glanced up. "Saw you the other day," he said. "I'm Abel."

"Yes, I know. You're the farrier."

Abel didn't reply. Of course he didn't. He already knew he was a farrier. Rose felt like an idiot.

"Hello, Abel," Peg said cheerfully, stepping up beside her. "It's nice to see you again."

"Ma'am." He dipped his head, then lifted his wooden toolbox and carried it around to the back of the truck. When he realized both women were watching him, he stowed his gear, then said, "Something I can do for you?"

"Yes." Peg decided to take the lead. "We'd like to ask you a few questions. That is, if you have time."

"Got nothing but time." The wad of tobacco in Abel's mouth shifted from one side to the other. "Now that I got that shoe tacked back on, I'm done for the day."

"Good," Peg said. "Since we last saw you, Rose and I have met the partners who own the Snow Cloud colt you were working on at Six Oaks the other day."

Abel stood and waited impassively for her to come to the point.

At this rate, they'd be here through dinner, Rose thought.

"One of them, Zara King, was very upset that the colt was going to be missing this sale."

"Makes sense," Abel allowed. "If I owned that colt, I'd be upset too."

"Another partner, Leo Grainger, doesn't think the colt has a stone bruise," Rose chimed in.

She expected Abel to be disturbed by the news. Or maybe to become defensive. Instead, he just shrugged.

"Leo's no dummy. He bred that colt, he's known him since he was a bitty foal. To tell you the truth, I'm not sure he has a stone bruise either. The contusion seems awfully deep for something like that."

"The thing is," Peg prodded, "Leo's telling people that you quicked the colt with a nail."

"Is he now?" The farrier pondered that.

Peg and Rose both nodded. And waited. Then waited some more. There didn't seem to be much else to do.

"Here's the thing about partnerships," Abel said eventually. "Pooling your money to make a profit sounds like a great idea, right up until something goes wrong. And with horses, more often than not, something goes wrong."

That seemed to be a common refrain. A fact which made Rose wonder why anyone ever got started doing this.

"As soon as there's a problem, each partner begins to look around for somebody to blame," Abel continued, in his slow, measured voice. "If I had to guess, I'd say Leo thinks putting me in the crosshairs shifts some of the criticism away from him. But that doesn't make what he said true."

"Leo said they have an insurance policy on the colt. Is that the kind of thing they could make a claim foi?" Rose asked.

"I don't see how. Mostly what that hoof needs to heal is time."

"Yes, but that time is causing the colt to miss this sale," Rose pressed. "And that's going to cost them money."

"There'll be another sale coming along soon enough," Abel said. "It seems like there always is. I'd imagine they'll put Snow Cloud into training at Six Oaks and aim him toward a two-year-old sale next spring."

"That's what Ben Burrell wants me to do with my colt," Peg mentioned.

Abel looked surprised. "You'd be crazy to do that. Especially when your colt's going to sell well here. Get your money out of him while you can, and let someone else take the risk."

"Those are my thoughts exactly," Peg said. "But Ben's been pushing pretty hard."

Abel frowned. "Never forget that Ben works for Six Oaks, and that's where his allegiance lies. Sure, he's probably given you some good advice. But you need to bear in mind that he isn't always looking after your best interests. In this case, it sounds like he's trying to drum up some extra business for the farm."

"I don't understand." Rose looked at Peg. "I assume you pay the farm a commission when the colt sells?"

"That's correct."

"So what's the difference if you pay it now or on a sale next year?"

"Big difference." Abel stepped in before Peg could answer. "Aside from the extra liability with holding on to the colt for another for six to eight months, the costs go up too. Basic board is one thing. Training fees are double that, or even more."

"Ben never mentioned it was that costly to put a horse in training," Peg said. "Now I'm even happier that I made the decision I did."

"That's another reason why those partners are trying to shift the blame onto someone else," Abel muttered. "You ask me, those guys are in way over their heads. First Snow Cloud got pulled from the sale. Then earlier today, their filly didn't sell either."

"Midnight Magic," Peg said. "Rose and I saw her go through the ring. Rose thought she sold, but I wasn't so sure."

"A hundred and forty thousand dollars. That's a lot of money!" Rose wondered how many times she would have to repeat that before she found someone who would agree with her.

"In the real world, I'd say you're right," Abel told her. "But not here. And not today. Today that figure sounds like chump change. The partners bought that filly for two hundred last year. Based on the lack of interest buyers were showing in her, Leo and Martin decided to cut their losses and let her go for one-fifty. Their reserve was one forty-five, and the live money ran out a lot lower than that. So far at this sale, they're oh for two."

Abel looked at Rose. "If you thought Zara King was upset yesterday, you probably don't even want to see her today."

Then he turned his gaze to Peg. For the first time since she'd met him, Abel managed a small smile. "Martin's desperate to get that filly sold privately, so they don't have to hold on to her until next year too. You didn't ask for my advice, but I'll give it to you anyway. You see Martin coming, you better hide until he goes by. Otherwise you might just find yourself owning a filly that nobody else seems to want."

"I like Abel," Rose said as they headed back to the lot where they'd left the minivan that morning. "It took a while to get him started talking, but once he got warmed up, he had plenty to say."

There were few people around, so Peg let Hope off her leash. Nose to the ground, tail in the air, the Poodle was bounding from one side of the long driveway to the other. Her joy in simply being able to choose her own path was a pleasure to watch.

"Abel's an interesting person," Peg mused. "He seems to know a lot about what goes on behind the scenes at Six Oaks. Which make sense, I suppose. His job doesn't just take him all over the farm, it also puts him in a position to be working in the background, unnoticed, while events unfold around him."

"Maybe we should have asked him about Jim Grable's death," Rose said. "I bet he overhears plenty of things that people don't want someone else to know."

"Good thought," Peg agreed. "Although Abel chooses

his words pretty carefully. I suspect he wouldn't have given us an answer. He doesn't seem to think much of the Leo, Martin, Zara partnership, does he?"

"You can hardly blame him for that. Especially since Leo tried to throw him under the bus. What interested me was the way he spoke about them. Abel seemed to think of Leo and Martin as a unit, with Zara being someone apart."

"That's an astute observation," Peg said as Hope came galloping back to them with a rubber bell boot in her mouth.

When the Poodle shook her head fiercely, the circlet flipped from side to side, smacking her in the face. For some reason, she seemed to enjoy that. Peg clipped the leash back onto her collar, and Hope fell in beside them.

"You needn't sound so surprised," Rose remarked. "I'm an astute person."

Peg grinned. "Quite true. I especially enjoyed watching you tell Abel that he's a farrier."

"Okay, so I got a little flustered. We don't all have your sangfroid when dealing with potential suspects."

"Is that what you think Abel is? A suspect?"

Rose thought for a bit before replying. "I did before. But now, not really. If he has a motive, I have no idea what it might be. Also, he didn't seem at all upset by Leo's accusation. I expected him to defend himself. Instead, he just dismissed it out of hand."

"Which means one of two things. Either Abel is innocent, or he's smarter than we are."

Rose laughed. "I wouldn't discount either of those options."

"Back to your astute observation for a moment," Peg said. "When I was talking to Martin earlier—before Leo arrived and blew everything up—he was explaining what each of them contributes to the partnership. Martin brings the equine and sales expertise. Leo does the insurance and—as Abel just told us—he's also Snow Cloud's breeder."

"And Zara?"

"She's the money."

Rose smirked. "How lucky for her. No wonder she's not thrilled by the way things are going."

"She's also the newbie," Peg added. "Martin and Leo both make a living in this industry while Zara only recently decided to become involved."

"Why do I feel like there's a conclusion you'd like me to draw from that?"

"Perhaps because there is. Keep thinking. I'm sure it will come to you."

"Leo and Martin know what they're doing. Zara doesn't," Rose mused aloud. "The men's contribution to the partnership is more skill-based, which means they're probably making most of the important decisions. That leaves Zara spending money to finance an operation she doesn't entirely understand and has almost no control over."

Rose turned and looked at Peg. "You suspect they're taking advantage of her."

"Of course I do," Peg replied. "I don't doubt it for a minute."

"Okay, smarty-pants, but what does that have to do with Snow Cloud's injury and Jim Grable's murder?"

"That's the part I don't know. Considering everything else I have going on here at the sale, I thought you should be the one to figure that part out."

"Of course." Rose sighed. "I'll get right on it."

Chapter 22

Peg fell into bed that night feeling as though her thoughts were careening in a dozen different directions. Though she was exhausted from the long days she and Rose had spent at the sale, sleep eluded her. The more she learned about the people who inhabited Jim Grable's world, the more questions seemed to arise.

Hope's warm presence on the bed beside her brought comfort, but even that wasn't enough to quiet Peg's niggling suspicion that there was something right in front of her which she was overlooking. The problem was, she had no idea what it might be. The only solution Peg could come up with was to dig in and try harder. She woke up and jumped out of bed the next morning like a woman on a mission.

"I have an idea." Peg opened the door between her room and Rose's without knocking.

"Now?" Rose was still tucked under her covers. In fact, until several seconds earlier, she'd still been asleep. She opened one eye. Opening both eyes seemed like something Peg might take as an invitation to come in. "What time is it?"

"Time to get up!" Peg entered the room anyway.

Hope did too. She scampered across the room and jumped up onto Rose's bed. Rose dodged to one side just in time. The flying Poodle missed her by inches. That was yet another reason why Rose herself had a cat.

"Aren't you going to ask?" Peg demanded. She was throwing open Rose's curtains.

Morning light came streaming into the room. Rose groaned and rolled over. "Ask what?"

"About my idea."

"I've never needed to ask before. Usually you just tell me what's on your mind." *Whether I want to hear it or not,* Rose added silently.

"I can do that." Peg sat down at the foot of the bed.

Hope hopped over Rose's body to join her. The two of them looked very pleased with themselves. Probably because they had no idea that Rose felt like murdering both of them.

"We're going to go talk to Officer Sherlock," Peg announced.

That got Rose's attention in a hurry. "We are?"

"We are," Peg confirmed. As though she had a real plan that made sense. Which Rose was seriously beginning to doubt she did.

"I thought you didn't want to do that. I recall a conversation about Southern sheriffs and their resistance to outside interference."

"I've changed my mind."

Rose wanted to ask why. She suspected that wouldn't get her a straight answer, however. After a minute, she came up with one on her own.

"You're stumped, aren't you?"

"No," Peg said quickly. "Well, maybe a little."

Welcome to my world, Rose thought.

"Usually when we ask questions, we get answers that make sense. We come up with clues that we can look at with fresh eyes, or maybe combine in different ways. And those things lead us to a solution."

Rose gave up on going back to sleep. She braced her pillow against the headboard and sat up. The bedcovers pooled around her waist.

"As always, you're being too impatient. Maybe we haven't asked enough questions yet. Maybe we haven't asked the *right* questions. Maybe we haven't talked to the right people."

"That's a lot of maybes," Peg grumbled. "And not a single answer among them. Maybe Officer Sherlock has answers."

"If he does, he'd hardly be likely to tell us."

"Fair point." Peg frowned. "Maybe we can convince him to pool our resources."

"I can see how Sherlock would be delighted by that idea," Rose scoffed. "Especially considering that we don't really have any resources."

"He doesn't know that."

"Not yet, anyway. It probably wouldn't take him long to figure it out."

Peg stood up. "You're a real spoilsport first thing in the morning. Lord knows how Peter puts up with you." She snapped her fingers and Hope jumped off the bed and went to her side. "Okay, then how about this? We'll simply pay the man a visit. We'll tell him we've come because Lucia asked us to, and we'll back up her story that she and Jim weren't arguing before he died. After that, if Sherlock wants to share any information about how his investigation is proceeding, so much the better."

Rose pushed back the covers and climbed out of bed reluctantly. "Good luck with that."

Woodford County was serviced by the Versailles Police Department, which was located in a brick-and-glass building on a downtown corner beside the railroad tracks. Peg, ever organized, had called ahead and made an appointment with Officer Sherlock. Upon entering the building,

Rose and Peg were shown to a small meeting room. Officer Sherlock joined them there several minutes later.

He was a heavyset man with direct, gray eyes, and a commanding presence. One look at him, and Rose realized how intimidated Lucia must have felt when she'd been called upon to answer his questions. Sherlock hadn't yet said a word and Rose already felt the same way.

She and Peg were seated at a table in the middle of the room. They both started to rise, but he waved them back to their seats. The officer pulled out a chair and sat down opposite them.

"I understand you have information about Jim Grable's death?" he said without preamble.

"Yes, we do." Just because Sherlock had forgotten his manners didn't mean that Peg was going to do the same. "I'm Peg Turnbull, and this is Rose Donovan. We're here visiting from Connecticut."

"And you have a connection to Mr. Grable?"

"No, not to him, exactly. But I board several horses at Six Oaks Farm. Rose and I met Mr. Grable earlier on the day that he was killed."

Officer Sherlock didn't look impressed by any of that information. He waved a hand, motioning for Peg to continue.

"We were wondering about the progress of your investigation into his death. Is your department close to naming a suspect?"

He folded his fingers together on the table in front of him. "I'm afraid I can't comment on that at this time."

"As you can probably imagine," Peg said, "with so many people gathered at Keeneland for the sale, there's been a lot of talk about Mr. Grable's death." She and Rose had prompted most of it. Peg didn't think it was necessary to mention that.

"Oh?" Sherlock's interest level rose fractionally. "What have you heard?"

"A valuable colt that was intended to go to the sale was injured in Mr. Grable's care. The group that owns the colt is quite angry about that."

"Horses get hurt all the time, Ms. Turnbull. They're like accidents looking for a place to happen. If you lived in central Kentucky, you would already be aware of that."

Peg and Rose shared a look. This wasn't getting them anywhere.

Peg decided to change tactics. "Are you aware there've been a number of thefts from the barns at Mr. Grable's yearling division over the past year?"

That got the officer's attention. "Thefts like horses going missing?"

"No," Peg admitted. "More like tack. And feed."

"Small stuff, then. Pilfering." He frowned. "Six Oaks is a big operation. I'd imagine petty theft like that doesn't put much of a strain on their budget. Nobody said anything about it to me when I was there, so they must not be worried about it. Is there anything else you'd like to tell me?"

Sherlock braced his palms on the table. He looked as though he was ready to rise. Peg didn't seem to be accomplishing anything, and Rose was tired of waiting for her to get to the point.

"Lucia Alvarez," she said.

He settled back down. "What about her?"

"She was assigned to show us around Six Oaks last Friday morning. Peg and I witnessed the supposed argument that took place between Lucia and Jim Grable. I believe one of the grooms reported it to you as a possible motive for murder?"

"Whether or not it constituted a motive isn't something for a groom to decide," Sherlock said firmly. "Nevertheless, I was made aware of the altercation and I intend to look into it further."

"But that's the thing," Rose said. "It wasn't an altercation. There were no harsh words spoken. Indeed, hardly any words were said at all."

"Before you go any further," he interrupted, "you should know that this isn't the first time Ms. Alvarez and Mr. Grable have come to blows. I have witnesses who are willing to attest to that. The two of them share an acrimonious history, one that is apparently well known among the people who work at the farm."

"That's not Lucia's fault—"

"In fact," he said as if she hadn't spoken, "their continuing dissension led to Ms. Alvarez being transferred to another, lesser, position at Six Oaks. She'd also been warned that if she caused any additional trouble, she would be let go from the farm entirely."

This time Officer Sherlock did rise to his feet. "So you see, the question of whether or not Lucia Alvarez had a motive for wanting Jim Grable dead isn't dependent upon the testimony of the groom. It's Ms. Alvarez's own actions that have caused her to become a suspect in the investigation."

"That didn't turn out the way I thought it would," Peg said, after they'd exited the police station.

Hope was waiting for them in the minivan. She jumped to her feet on the back seat and danced in place impatiently, waiting for Peg to open the door.

"It was my fault," Rose said glumly. "Things were going fine until I started talking."

"Nonsense." Peg reached the door and opened it, then let Hope leap out into her arms so they could reconnect with each other properly. "What happened in there wasn't anyone's fault. Officer Sherlock already had his mind made up before we even arrived. He had no interest in anything we had to say."

Rose walked around the other side of the minivan and got in. "Do you think Lucia and Grable actually had some kind of physical altercation? He was big man and she's barely my size. I can't imagine that would have ended well for her."

"It didn't," Peg pointed out. "We already know that. But rather than speculating, I propose we ask her about it the next time we have a chance."

Peg dropped Hope back down on the seat, gave her one last pat, then joined Rose in the front of the minivan. "Before we do that, however, I have another idea."

"Wonderful," Rose muttered.

Peg's first idea of the day had yanked her out of bed. There was no telling where this one might take her. Not only that, but it still rankled that she'd performed so poorly with Officer Sherlock. Every time she thought she was getting the hang of this detecting business, it was made clear just how much she still had to learn.

Then came an even worse thought. What if the real problem was that she was wrong about Lucia? Officer Sherlock was so firmly convinced that his suspicions had merit. What if Rose's propensity to root for the underdog had blinded her to the truth? Was it possible that she might be trying to protect a murderer?

"You're stewing about something," Peg said. "What is it?"

"What if I'm mistaken about Lucia's innocence?" Rose asked.

"You're not."

Rose turned in her seat to face the driver's seat. How like Peg to be so very sure of herself. Belatedly it occurred to Rose that it had been her turn to drive. Except that Peg had commandeered the steering wheel before Rose even had a chance to think about it. *Darn it.*

"How do you know?" she asked.

"Because I agree with you. And I'm a wonderful judge of character."

"Besides that."

"There's is no 'besides that.' The girl is innocent. So either she was in the wrong place at the wrong time, or someone is trying to make her look bad so they can escape scot-free. Which brings me back to my brilliant idea. Remember that?"

Peg cocked a brow in Rose's direction. Like maybe it was Rose's fault they'd gotten off track. Which it probably was.

"I remember there was an idea. I don't believe you mentioned brilliance."

"It was assumed," Peg said blithely. "This morning while you were taking your time in the shower, I got in touch with Ben Burrell. I told him I had my camera with me and that I'd love the chance to take some pictures of my foal frolicking in the pasture."

"Frolicking? Really?" Rose said. That didn't sound like Peg at all.

"Really." Peg smirked. "I asked if I could stop by the farm this morning and snap a few photographs. Ben said it was fine, except that he's at the sale so he can't escort me around the farm."

Rose suspected she knew what was coming next. "Did you ask for Lucia to take us instead?"

"No, she's at the sale too. I told Ben it wasn't a problem. I know my way around perfectly well. I said I'd be in and out in a matter of minutes and didn't need to bother anyone at all."

"So now we're going to Six Oaks so you can take pictures," Rose summed up. She still didn't understand what was brilliant about that, but at least it was a lovely day for a detour into the countryside.

"No, we're going to Six Oaks so we can have a chat with Tammy Radnor who works with the foals. Maybe there's more to her objection about the women employees supporting Lucia than Jenny told us. I think we should hear Tammy's story for ourselves."

"The last time I spoke with her, Tammy said she didn't want to be involved," Rose pointed out.

"Pish." Peg snorted. "She's already involved. Now we just have to figure out how to make her talk."

Rose wished she possessed even a fraction of Peg's boundless confidence. "I'll leave that part up to you."

"Of course you will," Peg said.

Chapter 23

The first time they'd pulled up in front of the tall stone gateposts that marked the entrance to Six Oaks Farm, Rose had felt apprehensive. Everything about the upcoming experience felt foreign to her. Plus, the thought of being surrounded by so many horses seemed scary. All that was behind her now. This time she was tingling with anticipation.

"I hope Tammy's here," Peg said, as the gates swung open to admit them.

"Where else would she be?"

"Maybe at Keeneland? It seems as though many of the farm employees have been going back and forth since the sale started."

"Not Tammy," Rose said. "She's too old."

Peg's head whipped around. "What does *that* mean?"

"I mentioned this the other day. Don't you remember?"

Peg thought back, then frowned. "No, although considering the topic, maybe I blocked it out. Refresh my memory."

"It was something Tammy told me when she and I were talking on Monday. When men get hired as showmen for the sales, it's their skill at handling yearlings that counts. When women get hired for the same job, what matters is what they look like in short shorts."

"That's ridiculous."

"I agree. But don't try arguing the point with Tammy. Because I did and she talked circles around me."

Peg had come to a fork in the long driveway that bisected the farm. She turned in the direction of the broodmare barns. "Not to denigrate your debating skills, but as I recall, Officer Sherlock just did the same thing."

"Sure," Rose said. "Kick me when I'm down. That's another reason why I'm letting you take the lead with Tammy. You can start with all the easy questions."

"Are there easy questions?" Peg asked. She didn't sound convinced. "There certainly haven't been any easy answers."

Peg parked the minivan beside the low, U-shaped, barn and they both got out. Hope began whining under her breath as soon as Peg and Rose opened their doors. She'd been left behind earlier. She didn't intend for it to happen again. Peg didn't disappoint her. She quickly hopped the Poodle out of the van and attached her lead.

On their previous visit, the barn had been humming with activity. Now, with the sale in progress, it looked almost deserted. All the stalls that ringed the center courtyard were empty. Their doors stood open; straw from their bedding spilled out into the aisleway. A cat was lying in the shade, one hind leg extended up in the air as it turned to lick its stomach.

As one, Peg and Rose turned toward the pasture where Lucky Luna and her colt had been turned out before. There, mares were grazing contentedly in the sun. Their heads were lowered, and their tails swished at the occasional fly. Several foals were asleep in the grass around them. Others were playing, yanking on halters and challenging each other to race.

"That's Lucky Luna," Peg said, pointing.

Rose had no clue how Peg was able to find her mare in a sea of horses who all looked mostly alike. Still, she was happy to play along. "Where's your camera? You should snap a few pictures to make this look good."

"It's right here." Peg was already striding toward the fence with Hope trotting along in her wake. "And look, Luna's colt is one of the babies that's running around. It's amazing how fast they are, even at this young age."

"Young or old doesn't matter," Tammy said, coming out of the barn to join them. "They're all Thoroughbreds, which means they love to run."

She walked over to stand next to the fence, watching as Peg focused her camera and took a picture. Tammy had on blue jeans and a denim shirt with the sleeves rolled back. There was a smudge of dirt on her cheek and her eyes looked tired.

"I didn't expect to see you here today," she said.

Peg tore her gaze away from the activity in the field. "Why not?"

"Because all the important people are over at the sale." Tammy looked as though she was waiting to see if Peg would register the subtle dig.

Peg did, and nearly smiled. Tammy was a tough old bird. Peg liked that.

"I guess I don't rate then," she said easily. "On a beautiful day, I'd much rather be here than there."

"Nice dog." Tammy looked at Hope. "That's gotta be about the biggest Poodle I've ever seen."

"Hope's a Standard Poodle," Rose told her. Hope wagged her tail obligingly when she heard her name.

"Standard or irregular doesn't make a difference to me," Tammy said. "Just don't let her get away from you. Around here, we shoot dogs that chase horses."

Insult number two, Peg thought. She liked that one less.

"This one told me you're some kind of investigator." Tammy addressed Peg, but she nodded toward Rose.

This one indeed.

"Rose," she supplied. "My name is Rose. And that's Peg."

Tammy blinked at her and pointed downward. "And that's Hope. It's not like my memory's impaired."

"No," Peg muttered, "just your manners."

"Very funny." Tammy cackled. "Rose here said the two of you meant to do something to help Lucia. How's that working out?"

"So far, not great," Peg admitted. "The police still think she's their best suspect."

"Last time we spoke, I got the impression you wanted to help Lucia too," Rose said. "Have you reconsidered your decision to talk to us?"

"About what?" Tammy suddenly looked wary.

"About who you think might have had a reason to want Jim Grable dead," Peg said. "You've been at Six Oaks a long time. You probably know everything that happens around here."

"You're right about that."

"So how about sharing some of that information with us?" Rose said. "For Lucia's sake."

Tammy thought for a minute. Then she shrugged. "There's probably no harm in telling you that it wasn't Lucia's fault that she and Jim didn't get along. In case you haven't figured it out, he wasn't the most popular guy on the farm."

"Because he liked putting his hands on women?"

Tammy leaned her arms on the top rail of the fence and stared out over the field. She felt more comfortable talking when she wasn't looking at them. "The thing about Jim was, he felt entitled. And there weren't many people around here who were willing to stand up to him."

"He sounds like a big bully," Rose growled. "Surely Lucia wasn't the first person to call him on his obnoxious behavior."

"No, she wasn't," Tammy allowed. "But people who went against Jim had a habit of disappearing."

"Disappearing?" Rose gulped. "Like dead?"

"Good Lord, woman! My, you have an active imagination." Tammy's shoulders shook with mirth. "No, not dead. Mostly they were just gone from the farm. Fired for some trumped-up reason. Injured somehow. Quit because they'd had enough."

Abruptly Tammy's laughter died. As if she'd realized there was nothing funny about what she'd revealed.

"Go on," Peg said. "We're listening."

"What was different about Lucia, is that she was the first person to actually file a proper complaint about Jim. One that worked its way up the ladder and got read by someone who mattered."

"Apparently that didn't help," Peg pointed out. "Because she still lost her job."

"Not exactly," Tammy corrected her. "Lucia lost *a* job. After that, she wasn't Jim's assistant anymore, but she was still on the farm."

"Only because she threatened to sue them if they let her go," Rose said.

Tammy looked surprised. "Did she really? I had no idea. Good for her, holding their feet to the fire. They deserved it."

"If Jim was such a problem, why did management keep him on?" Peg asked. Beside her, Hope got tired of waiting for them to do something interesting, and lay down on Peg's foot.

"Why do you think? Because he was white, and a man. And because, more's the pity, he had a good hand with the horses."

Tammy sounded bitter. It wasn't hard to understand why.

"Also, because he was buddies with the guys at the top. They'd hang out together, go drinking or to the races. They ran betting pools on Kentucky basketball games. There's a whole social component to the horse business that women like Lucia and me will never have an opportunity to be part of."

Rose hated hearing that. If Tammy had been a less prickly person, she'd have been tempted to give her a hug. As it was, Rose kept her hands to herself.

"Do you think Lucia really would have sued if the farm had fired her?" she asked instead.

"To tell the truth, I'm not sure about that," Tammy considered. "She's a bright girl and a hard worker. But mostly she got along the same way the rest of us do—by keeping her head down and minding her own business. I doubt she'd have even known where to look for a lawyer. And it seems unlikely she'd have the money to hire one. It was lucky for her that making the threat worked well enough."

"There's something else we were wondering if Jim was involved in," Peg said. Her colt went zooming past the fence and she turned and snapped a quick picture.

Tammy glanced at Peg. "You know if you wait to take the shot until after your colt's already gone by, the only thing you're going to get is a close-up of his butt."

"Point taken." Peg lowered her camera. "Rose and I heard that things are being stolen from the barns at the yearling division. Equipment, supplements, stuff like that. Do you think that was Jim's doing?"

Tammy took her time before replying. "Here's what I know. If that's been happening—and I assume it has, since you're asking about it—it would have been Jim's job to shut it down. He was in charge of everything that goes on over there."

It wasn't exactly an answer. Tammy was being evasive again. Peg put that line of inquiry aside and moved on.

"Tell us about the Snow Cloud colt."

Was it Peg's imagination or did Tammy relax when Peg changed the subject? She glanced at Rose, wondering if she'd noticed the same thing.

"What about him?" Tammy asked.

"He was supposed to go to the sale, but he didn't. The

partnership that owns him isn't happy about that. Leo Grainger thinks it was Jim's fault."

"Leo," Tammy said with a smirk. "I've known that guy since he was in short pants. And in all these years, he's never changed. Whenever he does something stupid, his next move is to look for someone else to pin it on."

"What was stupid about what happened to the colt?" Rose asked.

"Not that," Tammy said. "Before. Leo never should have allowed himself to get sucked into that deal in the first place. Leo thinks he's a smart guy. That's another mistake. Even on a bad day, Martin Shrady can outthink him by a mile. And he usually does. Leo bred that colt. You aware of that?"

Rose and Peg both nodded.

"So he takes him to the sale last November to sell as a weanling. He's expecting good money, and he gets it. So far, so good. But Leo doesn't just take his money and go home happy. Instead, he lets Martin buy him a drink in the Keeneland bar. He listens to Martin talk about how well he expects the colt to mature and how much his value is going to increase by September. Pretty soon, wouldn't you know it, Leo has a bad case of seller's remorse."

"I take it that was Martin's intention," Peg said.

"Hell, yeah." Tammy snorted. "By the end of the day, Leo is practically begging Martin to let him stay in for a piece. Eventually, Martin says he might let Leo come back in for a third. But there's a condition."

"Did Martin need Zara's approval?" Rose guessed.

Tammy just laughed. "You might think so, but no. She might not realize it yet, but Zara's just along for the ride. Martin's the one driving that train, and if she's really lucky she won't fall off and land in the dirt."

Rose would have asked for clarification, but she didn't want to interrupt. Not when Tammy was on a roll.

"No, the condition had to do with the three other weanlings Martin had already purchased to pinhook with Zara. If Leo wanted back in on Snow Cloud, he had to buy in on the others too. Let's stop and think about that for a moment. Of course Leo knew everything there was to know about his own colt. But the other three? At that point they were just pages in a catalog to him. He'd never even seen them."

"Or had them vetted," Peg mentioned.

Tammy pointed a finger her way. "That too. By now Leo's probably had a couple of bourbons and he's feeling great about himself. So he shakes on the deal. Leo—who'd gone to the sale that morning thinking he's going to end the day with a nice pile of change in his pocket—instead finds himself owning not one whole weanling, but separate pieces of four."

Rose snickered. When Tammy put it that way, the situation sounded pretty amusing. At least to her. Possibly not to Leo.

"But," Peg interjected, "that's not necessarily a bad thing, is it? I mean, that's what pinhookers do. They buy young horses and gamble that they're going to improve so they can sell them for more money later on."

"*Gamble* being the operative word." Tammy chuckled. "Would you trust Martin Shrady to buy a horse for you?"

Peg shrugged. "I'm not sure. I barely even know the man."

"Then let me answer for you. What you should have said is 'no'. And you should have answered a whole lot faster than you did."

Peg just stared at her.

Tammy stared back. "I'll spell it out for you. That partnership group had two of their yearlings in book one. The remaining two are in the next book. Let's look how their first two horses did. Snow Cloud missed the sale altogether."

"And the Midnight Magic filly went through the ring

and was bought back." Rose was happy to finally be able to contribute something.

"That's right," Tammy said. "Even if their next two yearlings both sell well, the chance that Martin, Leo, and Zara will be able to recoup all the money they've put into the partnership is practically zero."

Rose sighed. Once again, she was lost. "But if they all lose money on the deal, isn't that just as big a problem for Martin as it is for Zara and Leo?"

Tammy gave Rose a pitying look. She reached over and patted her shoulder. "Do you own any horses, honey?"

"No. Of course not."

"Good," Tammy said. "Keep it that way."

Rose laughed. How could she help it? "Believe me, I intend to."

Peg, meanwhile, looked annoyed. "I do own horses. And I don't understand either. Why don't you explain to us what's going on?"

Four foals went flying past. Hope lifted her head, pricked her ears, and watched them go by. She wished she could race with them, but there was no chance of that. Peg was oblivious to everything but her conversation.

"First of all," Tammy began, "Martin isn't spending his own money, he's spending Zara's—and to a lesser extent, Leo's. Second, he's the managing partner of the group, which means he's not only raking in management fees, he's also the one making the decisions."

Peg started to interrupt. Tammy held up a hand to stop her. "Think about it. Even if they decided to take a vote on something, of course Zara is going to side with Martin. He's the person she knows and presumably trusts, whereas Leo's just a guy who got added in later."

Peg nodded. She supposed that made sense.

"Three of their current yearlings were bought before Leo signed on, which means that Martin was solely responsible for choosing them. I'm sure he took a commission on those purchases—after all, that *expertise* doesn't come cheap."

Tammy rolled her eyes, in case Peg and Rose hadn't picked up on the fact that she was being sarcastic. "I wouldn't be surprised if he also took a kickback from the weanlings' sellers last fall. If that's the case, he'd have been more inclined to buy from consignors who were willing to do a deal, rather than those who were selling the best stock. Because who's going to stop him? It's not as if our newbie, Zara, would be able to tell the difference."

"No," Rose agreed. Even if Zara knew a lot more than she did, the woman still probably couldn't pick out a great weanling from among a multitude of good ones.

"So now we have three different ways that Martin is making money on the partnership and we haven't even sold a single yearling yet," Tammy pointed out.

"This is illuminating," Peg said. "But also depressing. What happens next?"

"Maybe the partnership manages to sell both of their book two yearlings," Tammy said. "If so, yippee. Now there's finally some money coming in. If not, the horses that haven't sold will be rolled over into next year's two-year-old sales."

"And between now and then, the owners will have to pay training fees," Peg said. She'd just learned that part.

"And what do you know, Martin is once again the man in the middle. No doubt he negotiates lower fees with the training center, while billing Zara and Leo for full freight. So failure at the yearling sale becomes yet another money-making opportunity for our enterprising managing partner."

"That's crazy," Peg sputtered. "How does he get away with that?"

"Mostly by doing business with people who are either dumber than he is, or who don't understand how the horse industry operates. Even when guys like Martin get caught, there's almost never any consequences because the people they've duped are too proud to admit that they got taken for a ride."

Tammy stepped away from the fence. It looked as though she'd given them all the time they were going to get. When Hope peered up at her, Tammy paused to reach down and scratch beneath the Poodle's chin. "Pretty girl," she said. "Just don't go chasing any horses."

"She won't," Peg replied firmly.

"Before you go . . ." Rose said. "Zara King mentioned that the Snow Cloud colt is insured for a million dollars. I figured she had to be exaggerating. Is that even possible?"

Tammy chuckled. "It's possible, all right. It's not even that unusual. But that colt? A million dollars is a pie-in-the-sky number for him. On a good day, he's maybe worth half that. I'd imagine Leo wrote that policy, and he knows better. Could be he's pulling a scam of his own. Despite what Zara King thinks she knows, there's no way they have Snow Cloud insured for that amount."

Chapter 24

"The people around here aren't very nice," Rose said when they were back in the minivan and on their way out of the farm.

"We already knew that, didn't we?" Peg asked. "Considering that one of them is dead, and it's likely that another one is responsible."

"Yes, well, at the risk of pointing out the obvious . . ." Rose shuddered. "Eww."

"You need to toughen up." Peg was unimpressed by her theatrics. "As you may recall, our bridge club also included a murderer, as did the ladies' support group we attended last month."

"Based on that recap, I think we need to cultivate a better circle of friends," Rose said with a frown.

"That can be a goal for when we get home. But in the meantime, you and I still have work to do. I'd like to head over to Keeneland now. We'll check and see how my colt is doing, then maybe have a quick word with Lucia. After that, we should take another shot at trying to track down Nico."

"Don't forget about lunch," Rose said. "Considering that you made me skip breakfast, I'm starving. How about if we try out the track kitchen?"

"Hope and I had a lovely breakfast." Peg drove out

through the Six Oaks gates. She turned onto the road that led to Midway, and beyond that, Lexington. "It's not my fault you slept until nearly noon."

"Seven-thirty," Rose corrected. She looked back over her shoulder. "Right, Hope?"

The Poodle was always pleased to be consulted. She lifted her head and woofed in agreement.

"Traitor," Peg grumbled. "You're supposed to take my side."

Hope woofed an affirmative reply to that too. As far as she was concerned, she was everyone's best friend.

Because Rose refused to budge otherwise, Peg parked the minivan near the track kitchen again. The two of them got out and went inside. Food was served cafeteria-style in the main section of the low building. The room's walls were covered with photographs of famous horses who'd raced at Keeneland, and famous trainers who'd trained there. A television in the corner was broadcasting the sale in progress.

Rose nabbed a Cobb salad. Peg, who'd already eaten earlier, ordered a double cheeseburger. They had their food wrapped to go. After paying, they carried it outside to eat on a nearby grass-covered hill where Hope could join them.

"Here's the plan," Peg said as she handed a chunk of her burger to Hope.

"I thought you already told me the plan." Rose plucked a piece of chicken out of her salad.

"I did, but now that I've had time to consider, I'm revising it. Did you notice how uncomfortable Tammy became when I mentioned the items that were disappearing from the yearling barns?"

Rose thought back. "No, not really."

"Well, you should have. Tammy was happy enough to talk to us about other things, but as soon as that topic arose, she shut it down. I'd like to know why. Manny was the person who first mentioned it to us. He called it a side hustle."

"Oh yes. The hustle." Rose remembered that.

"Manny's also the person who told us to talk to Nico, which makes me wonder whether those two things are connected. So I'm proposing that we do that first."

"Fine by me." Rose was poking around in her lettuce looking for more chicken. She seemed to have eaten all of it. She handed Hope a tomato instead. To her surprise, the Poodle ate it. "In the past couple of days, we've seen Nico at both Six Oaks barns. Where do you suppose we might find him now?"

"Either of those places or maybe somewhere else entirely." Peg stood up and dusted off the back of her cotton skirt.

It wasn't a particularly useful answer. Rose thought about pointing that out, but knowing Peg, it would probably start a whole thing. It seemed easier to refrain. They threw away their garbage, then headed down the driveway toward the sales pavilion with Hope bouncing at the end of Peg's leash.

Having finished with their book one yearlings the previous day, the Six Oaks crew was clearing out their equipment from barn 14. Peg and Rose stopped there first and got lucky. Nico was one of three men loading supplies into the bed of a blue pickup truck.

He was a good-looking man in his twenties, with heavily lashed eyes, full lips, and black hair that was long enough to curl down over his ears. Medium height, he was strong for his size. Muscles shifted beneath the shoulders of his blue polo shirt as he easily hefted a fifty pound bale of hay onto the truck.

"Nico," Peg called, pausing at the end of a walking ring. "Can we have a word with you?"

He turned to look in their direction. "Sure. I'll be right there."

Nico said something to the other men, then strode toward them. He moved with the easy confidence of a man who knew he was attractive to women. Even women Peg's and Rose's age.

"Something I can do for you?" he asked with a friendly smile. He leaned down and said hello to Hope, who showed her appreciation by giving him a doggy grin.

"I'm Peg Turnbull and this is Rose Donovan," Peg reminded him. Though she and Nico had occasionally spoken at the farm, they'd never been formally introduced. "I own the colt out of Lucky Luna."

"Sure, I know that. That's a nice colt, lots of people asking to see him. He's going to do well for you when he goes through the ring."

"I hope so." No matter how many times someone from Six Oaks repeated that assurance, Peg wasn't about to count her chickens just yet. "Rose and I were talking with Manny the other day. He told us you and Lucia Alvarez and friends."

"Sure." Nico's cheek dimpled when his smile widened. "Everybody likes Lucia. She's a great girl."

"Are you aware that the police consider her a suspect in Jim Grable's death?" Rose said.

Abruptly Nico's smile died. "Yeah. Everybody knows about that. It's crazy, what's going on. Lucia would never have done something like that. No matter how badly Jim deserved it."

"So you think what happened to Jim was his own fault?"

Nico hesitated. "He wasn't a good man. He made life hard for a lot of people who worked for him. Lucia wasn't the only one who hated having to put up with him."

"She was the one who held him to account, however," Rose said.

"Right," Nico growled. "And look where it got her. Lucia tried to do the right thing, and in the end, she was the one who had to pay."

"Rose and I are trying to help her," Peg said. "Like you, we'd hate to see her blamed for something she didn't do. We've had some success solving crimes before."

"For real?" Nico didn't look convinced.

"For real," Rose assured him. "So if there's anything you know that might help us exonerate her, we'd appreciate your cooperation."

"You're talking to the wrong guy," he said quickly. "I don't know a thing."

"That's not what we heard."

"From who?"

"We're not at liberty to say." Peg's voice was firm. "Just as any information you're willing to share with us would also remain confidential."

"Meaning you won't say where it came from?"

"Precisely." Rose reached over and placed a hand on his shoulder. Connection built trust. She'd learned that from Peter. "Please. We really need your help. And so does Lucia."

Nico's gaze skittered away. For a moment, Peg thought they'd lost him. Then he straightened his spine and lifted his eyes. "Give me your word that you won't use my name. After that, you can ask me what you need to know."

"I promise," Peg said solemnly.

"I do, too," Rose echoed.

"Jim wasn't a good person," Nico said.

"You already told us that."

"Anything that wasn't right around the farm, Jim probably had a hand in it."

"Give us an example," Peg said.

"You already know what happened with Lucia. And she wasn't the only one."

"We know about that too," Rose told him.

Nico glanced back over his shoulder, checking to see

where the other guys were and what they were doing. Peg wondered whether he didn't want to be overheard—or if he was looking for an excuse to leave the conversation and go back to work.

She wasn't about to let that happen. "We also know there was a problem with things going missing at the yearling barns."

"Yeah." He didn't meet her gaze.

"Maybe you were involved in that?"

"Maybe I didn't have a choice," Nico grunted.

"What do you mean?" Rose asked. "How could you not have a choice?"

"Those barns, they're filled to the brim with stuff. More tools, more tack, more equipment, than we could use in a year. Jim was in charge of requisitioning the supplies we needed. He'd put in a request and all kinds of things would just show up. Like nobody at the top was keeping track, or even cared how much he asked for."

Nico looked back and forth between Rose and Peg as if he wanted to make sure they understood what he was saying. "The guys that run that place have tons of money. I guess that's why they don't bother to pay attention to what's going on in the barns. It's like they think it's beneath them. So if some of that stuff left the farm and got resold elsewhere, maybe they deserved it."

"And you're saying you were involved in that?" Peg asked.

"Yeah, I guess." Nico didn't look happy. "In the beginning, it was an accident. Jim would point me toward a truck with a tarp over some equipment in the back, and tell me to drive it Midway and make a delivery. So I did. It's not my job to ask questions."

"Of course not," Rose agreed. Nico needed to know that they were on his side. "So that happened more than once?"

"Yeah," he admitted. "It did."

"Eventually you must have begun to wonder what was going on," Peg prompted.

"Sure. Because it didn't make sense, you know? Maybe once a month Jim would send me on a run. Why would I be taking supplies *off* the farm?"

"What did Jim tell you?" Rose asked.

"At first he just said I should mind my own business. So I did, for a while. Next time I asked, Jim told me that now I was just as guilty as he was. He said if I told anyone what was going on, he'd turn it around and blame everything on me." Nico scowled. "And if he did that, who do you think would have been believed?"

"Probably not you." Rose remembered how things had turned out for Lucia.

"Jim told me there was some money he needed to repay. He said when that was done, we'd be able to stop."

"And did you?" Peg asked.

"Of course not. I knew Jim was lying about that as soon as he said it. He was always going to be in debt because he loved betting on the races. He said his job gave him an inside track on predicting which horses were going to run well and which ones weren't. When Jim was on a winning streak, the whole barn knew it. He'd strut around the place like he was on top of the world."

"And when he was losing?"

"We all knew about that, too. He'd be even more short-tempered than usual. Snapping and swearing and calling us all incompetent, no matter how hard we worked. Lately, there've been a whole lot more bad days than good ones, I can tell you that."

Rose considered what he'd said. "Do you think Jim might have gotten himself in trouble with someone he was in debt to?"

"I don't just think so," Nico said. "I know he did."

Peg and Rose shared a look.

Before either could respond, one of the guys by the truck called over to them. "Hey Nico, hurry up! We're doing all your work over here."

He held up his hand. "Just one more minute, and I'll be there."

"Nico, this is important." Peg's fingers flexed at her side. If it came to it, she was prepared to physically hold him in place until he revealed what he'd meant by that. "What kind of trouble was Jim in?"

"There was something I overheard," he said, keeping an eye on the other guys. "At the time I didn't understand, but later it became clear."

"What did?" Rose asked impatiently.

"Martin Shrady stopped by the farm one day to see the yearlings his partnership owned. While everyone was around, he talked about how great they were doing and all the money he expected them to make at the sale. But later, before he left, he and Jim went into the barn together.

"Martin started talking about the Snow Cloud colt. He said he'd paid a lot for him as a weanling, and the only reason Zara King had agreed to spend that much was because he'd guaranteed the colt would be a star as a yearling. Martin had promised her that the colt would make back his purchase price, and more, at the September sale."

"But the colt got hurt and missed the sale," Peg said. "The partners were really upset about it. We already know that."

"No," Nico said. "You don't know. That wasn't all Martin said. He told Jim that Snow Cloud had a bad throat when he was a weanling. Martin figured it was worth the risk because, chances were, he'd outgrow the problem by the time the yearling sale came around."

"Does that happen?" Rose asked.

"Sure, lots of times. But it didn't in this case, and now Martin was really feeling the pressure from Zara. He needed more time for things to come right. He told Jim it would be better for both of them if the colt didn't make it to the sale. Martin said, 'You owe me, Jim. Do this one thing for me and we'll be square.'"

Peg had a sinking feeling in the pit of her stomach. She was afraid she knew what was coming next.

"What did Jim have to do for him?" Rose asked.

"I'm sure you can figure that out," Nico snarled. "Martin picked up a hammer and handed it to Jim. He said, 'Wait until I'm gone, and then just take care of it.' And Jim did just what he was told."

Chapter 25

"That's insane," Rose said. "Please tell me I'm not the only one who thinks so."

They'd left barn 14 and were on their way to the other Six Oaks barn. Peg was letting Hope leap and play at the end of her leash. After the patience she'd shown during the conversation with Nico, the Poodle deserved to have a little fun.

"It's crazy, all right," Peg agreed. "But it's also believable. With the amount of money people have invested in these horses, you can see how they might get desperate when things aren't going their way."

"I suppose," Rose conceded. It wasn't like they hadn't met desperate people before. "What I'd like to know is where Leo fits into all this. Do you think he agreed to go along with Martin's plan, or was he kept in the dark like Zara?"

"Good question." A yearling walked past and Peg reeled Hope back against her hip. The filly didn't even flick an ear in their direction. "Leo is Snow Cloud's breeder, and he put him through a sale when he was a weanling. So he must have been aware of his throat problem."

"In that case, it wouldn't surprise me to learn that Martin made some kind of side deal with him too." Rose was thinking out loud. "Martin and Leo needed Zara's money, so it was in both their best interests to keep her happy. I can see how they might have decided between themselves that there were things she didn't need to know."

Peg growled under her breath. The noise sounded indignant enough to make Rose wonder if something similar had ever happened to her. Peg didn't volunteer anything further, however, and Rose wasn't about to ask.

"Think about it," she continued. "If Zara believes Martin and Leo are trustworthy—and they're her only sources of information about the partnership horses—they can tell her anything they want and there'd be no way for her to find out differently."

"I'm going to agree with you about the throat issue," Peg mused. "Zara clearly didn't know about that. But I suspect that Leo wasn't aware of Martin's transaction with Jim to keep the colt out of the sale. Otherwise, he wouldn't have been so angry at Abel."

"Although, as it turns out, Leo was right to be suspicious," Rose pointed out. "Because the colt doesn't have a stone bruise after all."

"This is like trying to unravel a Rubik's Cube." Hope had her nose to the ground, and Peg allowed the Poodle to lead her over to a patch of grass beside the driveway. "Compared to Thoroughbred sales, dog shows are beginning to seem like a walk in the park."

Rose huffed out a laugh. "What a convenient memory you have. I've watched you get into plenty of trouble at dog shows too."

Peg ignored that comment. They were almost to barn 31. Looking ahead, she could see that her colt was being shown on one of the walking rings. Two men and two women were talking among themselves as they examined him. Manny was holding the colt's shank. He nodded at Peg as she, Rose, and Hope entered the courtyard. Rose took Hope's leash and the two of them went to sit down on the bench.

Bryce was calling cards. Peg headed his way. She was curious about the amount of interest her colt had drawn from shoppers since she'd checked in the day before. The group inspecting her colt circled him once again, blocking her path. Peg was forced to wait before slipping past them.

"I don't know," one of the men was saying to the other, "do you think he's big enough?"

"Plenty big," the other man replied. "And don't forget, he's a yearling. He's not finished growing yet."

"Yes, but some of the others we've looked at were taller."

"Tall doesn't mean fast." One of the women spoke up.

"I like a horse with a long stride," the first man said stubbornly.

Manny caught Peg's eye and made a face. He was probably five foot ten, and Peg's colt made him look small. But some buyers made ridiculous demands. There was nothing sellers could do about that.

"Thank you, we're done." The man dismissed Manny and the colt with a wave of his hand.

Manny led the colt back inside the barn. While the group moved on to their next horse, Peg skirted around them to get to the consignor table. Bryce was standing in his usual spot, directing another looker to a show ring on the far side of the courtyard.

As always, he greeted her with a smile. "Hi, Peg. I'm glad you stopped by."

"Oh? I hope everything is all right."

"Better than that." He fanned the stack of cards in his hand. "Your colt's been popular today. He's been out more than twenty times, all second looks. Plus, his vet records in the repository have been looked at six times. Based on the people who've shown interest here, I'm sure that's only the beginning."

"No scopes yet?"

"No, but it's still early." Bryce wasn't concerned. "He

doesn't sell until tomorrow afternoon. There's still plenty of time."

Peg glanced at the quartet whom she'd watched critique her colt. Now they were moving on to the next barn. "That last group didn't seem to like him much."

Bryce gave a derisive snort. "You heard what they were saying? Don't pay any attention to that."

"Why not?"

"First of all, because there are plenty of people shopping at this sale, and no yearling is going to suit all of them. And second, because sometimes people will insult a horse on purpose because they think hearing it will make a consignor nervous, and then they'll lower the horse's reserve."

Peg frowned. "Does that work?"

"Hardly ever. But it doesn't stop people from trying. Most sellers have a very good idea what their horses are worth, however. And they figure that buyers can either afford them or they can't. Which brings me to my next point."

"There's more?" Peg asked with interest. She felt as though she learned something new every time she stopped by the barn.

"You're at a horse sale," Bryce said. "Of course there's more. At the moment, your colt is one of the more popular yearlings in our consignment."

"So you said."

"That group that just finished looking at him? They probably can't afford to buy him. But they're looking anyway because they're hoping he has a flaw that might cause him to fall into their price range."

"Does he?" Peg inquired.

"Nope."

"Good."

"Yes, that's very good. At least for you. Not so good for them. The man who complained that your colt was small is married to the woman who disagreed with him. I'm guessing that in the interest of marital harmony, he would rather convince his wife that they don't want the yearling, than admit to her that he can't afford him."

"Oh," said Peg, brightening. "I suppose that makes sense, in a weird, manipulative kind of way."

"Welcome to my world," Bryce replied. "Nothing around here is as straightforward as it seems."

Considering what she and Rose had recently been up to, Peg had already learned that.

"Thank you for enlightening me," she said.

"You're welcome. Thank you for entrusting your nice colt to Six Oaks. It's a pleasure to be able to sell a colt that makes people smile every time he walks out of the barn. They don't all do that."

"Yes, I know." Once again, Peg was reminded of the similarities between judging dogs and judging Thorough-breds. They couldn't all be winners. Some didn't even come close.

Lucia was showing a nearly black filly to two men in a nearby ring. Peg had been observing the process out of the corner of her eye. By her count, Lucia had walked the yearling back and forth in front of them at least five times so far. Peg wondered what the men could possibly be look-ing for that they hadn't already been able to see. Maybe they didn't know either.

"After Lucia finishes with her filly," Peg said to Bryce, "would it be all right if I pulled her aside for a minute?"

His gaze skimmed around the courtyard. "I suppose so. We're not too busy right now. I can probably spare her for ten. But don't go far. You never know when another wave of shoppers might appear."

"We won't," Peg promised.

She and Rose sat down on a low stone wall that was outside the border of the courtyard. Hope chose a spot between them. A few minutes later, Bryce sent Lucia over to join them.

"Is everything okay?" she asked anxiously. "Bryce said you wanted to see me."

"Don't worry," Rose said. "We just want to ask you something."

"Oh. Okay." Lucia sat down next to Hope. She tangled her fingers in the Poodle's ears. Hope leaned over and rested her muzzle on Lucia's knee. Peg watched the interaction with a small smile.

"Peg and I talked to Officer Sherlock earlier today."

"That's wonderful. Thank you!" Lucia's face lit up. "What did he say?"

Rose hated having to quash her optimistic response. "I'm afraid it didn't go well. He still considers you a suspect in Jim Grable's death. Maybe even his primary suspect."

"No. That's not right." Lucia spoke fiercely, as if denying Rose's words could make them disappear. "Did you tell him what you saw? Does he know that Jim and I weren't fighting?"

"We did," Peg said. "But Sherlock didn't care. He told us someone had witnessed a previous physical altercation between you and Grable. In his mind, that supported the story of this blowup."

Rose was hoping Lucia would deny the accusation. Instead, the young woman slumped in her seat. She didn't say a word.

"It's true, isn't it?" Rose asked gently. "You can tell us."

"Why?" Lucia's head snapped up. "So you can decide I'm guilty too?"

"No, so that we'll have a better of what we're up against. You need to tell us what happened."

Lucia's lips set in a grim line. "I'm sure you can guess."

"Tell us anyway," Peg said. "It will be much harder for us to help you if we don't know everything."

"Jim was a big man. He had long arms and strong hands." Lucia spat out the words. Rose didn't blame her for being angry. Just listening made her angry on Lucia's behalf.

"There are plenty of times in the barn when people are working in close quarters. Like in a wash stall, or the feed room. Whenever I was in a place that I could be cornered, Jim would manage to show up."

Lucia's voice dropped. "He'd get between me and the door and then he'd laugh. Because he knew there was no way I could stop him from putting his hands on me. One day I'd had enough. I picked up a bag of feed and I swung at his head."

"I hope you broke his nose," Peg said.

"I wish. But those bags weigh a ton. Once I'd grabbed it, I realized there was no way I could lift it that high. Still, I managed to smack him pretty hard in the stomach. At least that was something.

"Jim hadn't been expecting me to come back at him. After I hit him, he lost his balance, fell backward, and landed on his butt. The bag broke open and everything spilled all over. Jim ended up covered in pellets."

"Good for you," Rose said stoutly.

"I thought so. At least for about ten seconds. Which was how long it took for the commotion to bring everyone else who was in the barn running to see what happened. They crowded into the doorway, looked at Jim on the floor with horse feed in his hair, and started laughing."

"Uh-oh," Peg muttered.

"Yeah, that didn't go over well," Lucia said with a grimace. "Jim jumped to his feet and started yelling. He told everyone I was crazy. And that I'd attacked him for no reason. When he started screaming, everyone scattered. They knew I was in trouble, and they didn't want any part of it."

"What did you do?" Peg asked.

"Are you kidding? I ran too. When Jim got to his feet, there was going to be hell to pay. I wasn't going to wait around for all that anger to come down on me."

"Then what happened?" Rose was curious.

"Jim stormed out of the barn, got in his truck, and drove away. As soon as he was gone, I went back to the feed room and cleaned up *everything*. I swept up even the tiniest particles. That room has never been so spotless. It was, like, pristine."

"How much trouble did you get into?" Peg asked.

"None." Lucia frowned. "It was the strangest thing. After lunch, Jim came back to work like nothing had ever happened. He didn't say a word, and nobody else was stupid enough to bring it up either. We all just went on with our day."

"When did that take place?" Peg asked.

"Months ago." Lucia thought back. "Sometime early in the year. I'm surprised anyone even still remembers it."

"Somebody not only remembered, they made a point of reporting it to Officer Sherlock," Rose said. "It sounds to me as though someone who was there the day Jim died—someone whom you might think of as a friend—is doing their best to make you look guilty."

Chapter 26

Bryce called Lucia back to work as a flood of potential buyers showed up all at once. Grooms and handlers hurried to get the yearlings out of their stalls, spruced up, and delivered to the appropriate rings. Bryce directed traffic with a practiced flair that made it look easy.

"Now what?" Rose asked.

"We need to find Abel and ask him if what Nico told us is possible."

"You think he could have been lying to us?" It hadn't occurred to Rose to suspect that. She knew she was less naive than she'd once been. Even so, she still tended to believe most things people said. Life was much less complicated that way.

"I have no idea," Peg replied. "But Abel's the man who would know." She pulled out her phone.

"Why do you have his phone number?"

"I don't, but Abel's a businessman, isn't he? He must be listed somewhere. How many farriers can there be in Lexington?"

It turned out, quite a few. Nevertheless, Peg managed to locate Abel's contact info without too much effort. She stood up and walked away to make the call.

"I guess it's you and me, kid," Rose said to Hope.

The Poodle didn't look impressed.

"Really?" Rose reached down and ran her hand along Hope's back. "I thought we were friends."

That earned her a perfunctory tail wag. Hope's eyes were still fastened on Peg.

"I'll bet if I had peanut butter in my pocket, you'd feel differently," Rose said to the dog.

"Why would you want to have peanut butter in your pocket?" Peg was tucking her phone away as she came walking back. "That seems like a terrible idea."

"Never mind. Did you talk to Abel?"

"I did." Peg reclaimed Hope's lead. "We're meeting him at a bar in Cheapside at five-thirty."

"Cheapside?" Rose stood up and went after Peg and Hope, who were already on the move. "That doesn't sound promising."

"No, it's fine. It's the name of a social area in downtown Lexington. Sometimes they even have live entertainment, though apparently not tonight. Abel picked the place, and I was happy to go along. After all, we want him to be comfortable while we pick his brain."

"And perhaps even slightly tipsy," Rose said.

"That too."

They drove back to the hotel to rest for a bit, and to feed Hope an early dinner. The older dog was worn-out from the long days she'd been spending at the sale. Hope was asleep on the bed when Peg and Rose were ready to leave again. Peg gave her a quick pat and assured her they'd be back soon.

This time, Rose managed to reach the minivan first. She drove them to downtown Lexington, while Peg sat in the passenger seat and offered a minute-by-minute critique of her driving skills. Rose ignored Peg's grumbling. She thought she was doing a fine job. Until she reached their destination and had to circle the block three times before she could find a parking space.

"You know," Peg said, when they were finally out of the minivan, "I could teach you how to parallel park."

"I know how to do it," Rose said irritably. "I just need more practice. Which I'd have if you let me drive more often."

"You drive like a snail," Peg told her as they turned down the alleyway where the tavern was located. "You're the only person I know who slows down approaching a green light."

"Because it might turn yellow."

"Yellow still means go," Peg pointed out.

"It does not—" Rose began, but they'd reached the bar, and she decided to table the argument for another time.

The building in front of them was tall and narrow. It looked as though it was built a hundred years earlier, and recent attempts at upkeep had been sparse. The green paint was faded and peeling in spots; glass in the front windows was smudged and sooty. When Peg grasped the doorknob, it was sticky beneath her fingers. She sighed and soldiered on.

Inside, the bar was dark and noisy. Even this early in the evening, it was already crowded. The vibe wasn't unfriendly, but it looked like the kind of place where everybody already knew everyone else. As Rose and Peg hesitated just inside the door, it felt as though half the room turned in their seats to check them out.

Thankfully Abel, who was seated at a table toward the back, lifted his beer bottle in a salute that caught Peg's eye. She and Rose made their way in his direction. A waitress with a small tray in her hand and a towel over her shoulder, stopped them along the way. Rose ordered a glass of merlot. Peg asked for a pint of Guinness. She also arranged to pick up the tab for the table.

"You made it," Abel said. "Wasn't sure you'd be able to find this place."

"Perhaps that's why you suggested it?" Peg commented as she helped herself to a seat.

Abel shrugged. "Figured if you were serious, you'd show up."

"We're serious about needing to ask you some questions," Rose said.

"You can ask. We'll see if I answer."

"Fair enough." Peg waited as their drinks, along with a bowl of unshelled peanuts, were delivered to the table.

"Marty must like you," Abel said laconically. He helped himself to a handful of nuts. "She doesn't bring snacks to just anybody."

"I told her the bill for the table comes to me," Peg said. "Maybe she thinks I'm a big spender."

"Nah, that's not it." He opened two peanut shells by crushing them in his closed hand, then popped the nuts in his mouth. "You don't see too many ladies come in here and order Guinness. They all seem to be too worried about calories these days. She'd like that about you."

"I'm a likable person," Peg agreed.

"You're also a person who's looking into things that aren't your business. I asked about you after the last time we talked."

"And what were you told?"

"That maybe I should steer clear."

"And yet here you are," Rose said.

"Hey, you offered me a free beer." Abel almost smiled, but not quite. "Maybe more than one. Besides, I've never been one for doing what I'm told."

Rose took a sip of her wine, then asked, "Who advised you not to talk to us?"

"Walter Tausky. You know him?"

"Yes," Peg said. "He's one of the bigwigs at Six Oaks."

"Bigwigs." Abel's chest rumbled. "I like that description. It fits him all right."

"Will you get in trouble if you answer our questions?" Rose asked.

"Probably not." Abel didn't look worried. "It's not my fault if Walter wants to pretend everything's fine and dandy at that farm. Doesn't mean I have to do the same."

"The reason we're not minding our own business," Peg said evenly, "is because Lucia Alvarez asked for our help."

"She did?"

Peg and Rose both nodded.

"The police think she killed Jim Grable," Rose added.

"No way." Abel grunted. "Sure, those two had their problems. But Lucia's a good person. She works hard, too. I can't see her doing something like that."

"We agree," Peg said. "Yesterday, we spoke to you about the Snow Cloud colt's hoof."

Abel straightened in his seat. "I told you I didn't quick that colt."

"We know that. But in the meantime, we've found out that he didn't step on a rock either. Is it possible that the bruise to the sole of his hoof could have been caused by someone hitting it with a hammer?"

"Holy hell," Abel swore.

"Should I take that as a yes?" Peg asked.

He glowered. "Sure, I guess it's possible. But who would want to do a rotten thing like that?"

"Jim Grable," Rose said.

Abel's eyes narrowed as he processed the information. Peg noted that he didn't leap to Jim's defense as he'd done with Lucia. As far as she was concerned, that all but confirmed what Nico had told them.

"Why would Jim do that?" he rasped. "What was in it for him?"

"Martin Shrady agreed to forgive the gambling debt Jim owed him, if Jim fixed it so the colt was unable to go to the sale."

Abel was quick to put two and two together. "What's the matter with Snow Cloud?" he asked.

"Bad throat," Rose told him.

She didn't actually know what that meant, but everyone else acted as though the phrase was self-explanatory so she figured she'd try it out. Rose was pleased to see it must have worked, because Abel nodded in understanding.

"I'm guessing Zara King doesn't know about that," he said. "And she wouldn't be happy if she did."

"Martin convinced her to spend a ton of money on Snow Cloud," Peg told him. "He promised her the colt would make it all back, and more, at this sale."

Abel just shook his head. "Martin's been in the horse business a long time. He should know better than to make a promise like that. Then again, he's always been a greedy bastard. I'd imagine he saw dollar signs and jumped in, figuring he'd worry about any inconvenient details later."

Abel's beer bottle was empty. Though she and Rose had yet to finish their drinks, Peg looked over toward the bar and signaled for another round.

"We heard that Jim was a heavy gambler," Rose said when the new drinks had been delivered. She looked askance at the second, full, glass of wine that Marty set down in front of her.

Abel shrugged again. It seemed to be his go-to move. "Around here, that's nothing unusual. People wouldn't have racehorses if they didn't like to gamble. The whole industry's a giant game of chance, usually with more losers than winners."

"We heard Jim had been doing a lot of losing lately," Peg added.

"Yeah, so?" Abel reached for the new bottle and helped himself to a long swallow.

"We wondered if you knew who else he might have been placing bets with."

Rose picked up a peanut. Abel watched as she spent nearly a minute separating the nut delicately from its shell. When she was done, she gathered the pieces of shell into a neat pile.

"You know, most people just toss those on the floor," he said.

Peg smirked. "Rose isn't like most people."

"I'd say that's true of both you ladies."

Abel was correct about that. Still, Rose wasn't about to let him change the subject. "You haven't answered my question."

"Nope." He leaned back in his chair. "I'm just thinking about it for a minute. You two in a hurry to move along?"

"No," Peg and Rose both answered at the same time.

"That's what I thought." Abel gave them a full smile this time. Maybe the second beer was loosening him up. Peg could only hope.

"Who else?" she asked.

"You know that expression, 'Don't crap where you eat'? Well, Jim didn't subscribe to that. Instead, he went for proximity. He gambled a lot with the guys who worked with him at Six Oaks."

Peg noted his choice of words. "With him?" she specified. "Or *for* him?"

"Interesting you should ask that," Abel said. "Because it was mostly the latter. Jim liked betting with the guys at the yearling division. Because when he came out on the winning side of a wager, he never had to worry about prompt payment. He held their jobs in his hands, and they knew it."

"What a horrible man he was," Rose muttered. The thought called for another sip of wine.

"And when he lost," Abel continued, "Jim could take his time settling his debts for the same reason. Sometimes he didn't pay at all. He'd just tell whoever had beaten him that he was rolling his losses over to the next day's card. He never liked to settle up until after he'd won his money back."

Peg's frown was ferocious. "Yet another example of Jim taking advantage of the imbalance of power his position gave him. It sounds as though Lucia wasn't the only one who had to be careful when he was around."

"You're right," Abel said. "And what made it worse was that Jim got paid plenty. He played the ponies for kicks. And for the pleasure of lording it over everyone when he won."

He paused for more beer. "Most of those guys who worked for him, they really need the money. Some are sending it home to their families in other countries. Others are using it to support their families here. There's no such thing as disposable income when you're hardly making better than minimum wage."

"I don't understand," Rose said. "Why did the grooms bet with Jim at all? Their salary is a sure thing. Why would they take a chance on losing it?"

Abel chuckled. "There isn't a gambler in the world who doesn't think he can beat the house. Losing feels like a temporary problem—because they're always sure they're going to win the next time."

Rose thought back to the previous day, when the farm's sales personnel had been betting in the barn aisle. Manny's reluctance to settle up with Sergio illustrated Abel's point.

"I'm not sure if you're helping us, or confusing the situation even more," Peg said to Abel. "Based on what you've told us, it sounds like half the guys who worked for Jim could have had a reason to wish him dead."

"Hey." Abel held up his hands in a gesture of innocence. "I didn't say anything about being useful to you ladies. I just showed up for the beer."

Peg chuckled. "Rose and I appreciate that you did. But

now we should be on our way. Do you want me to order you another one on our way out?"

"No, two's my limit these days. But thanks for the offer." He grinned as they rose from their seats. "If you feel the need to bribe me with alcohol again in the future, let me know 'cause I'm available. Although I probably don't have a whole lot more to say. Except maybe this: Good luck with your colt tomorrow. I hope he brings every penny he's worth."

"Thank you. I have my fingers crossed."

"Do more than that," Abel said seriously. "Give some real hard thought to the decision you make about his reserve. And bear in mind what I told you before. Ben and Walter have their own agendas. You do what's right for you."

"Thank you for the advice." Peg nodded. "That's exactly what I intend to do."

Chapter 27

Peg and Rose opted for another early night. Peg's colt would be taking his turn through the auction ring the next day, and Peg wanted to be wide-awake and on her toes that took place. The past week had given her a dramatic reminder that anything could, and did, happen in the Thoroughbred world. A smart horse owner was one who was both well-prepared, and wary of all the ways the proceedings could potentially be manipulated.

"Are you ready for breakfast?" Rose asked the next morning, when they were both up and dressed.

"No, thanks. I'm not hungry."

Standing in the doorway between their two rooms, Rose watched as Peg prowled around the small space between her window and door, picking things up, examining them, then putting them down again. Hope, who'd already enjoyed a long walk outside, was observing Peg's nervous energy from her perch on the bed.

Rose frowned. It wasn't like Peg to miss a meal. "Have you lost something? Can I help you look for it?"

Peg stopped walking. "Yes, I think I may have lost my mind. Frankly, I can't imagine why I ever wanted to get mixed up in the Thoroughbred industry in the first place."

"As I recall, it wasn't your choice." When Rose sat

down on the edge of Peg's bed, Hope snuggled up beside her. "Lucky Luna was a gift, remember?"

"Of course I remember that," Peg grumbled. "What I don't know is why I kept her and continued to breed her, rather than selling her on the spot like any reasonable person would have done."

"Maybe because you enjoy the challenge of breeding good animals. You'd already succeeded in Poodles. I'd imagine it seemed like a fine idea to see if you could duplicate that success with Thoroughbreds."

"A *fine* idea." Peg snorted. "This morning it doesn't feel fine at all. This morning I find myself worried about all the things that can possibly go wrong."

"Except that you're not going to let that happen." Rose looped an arm around Hope's neck and stroked the smooth skin of the Poodle's throat. "You've done this before, right?"

"Yes, but on those occasions, I did it from halfway across the country. Selling a horse seemed easier when I was too naive to fully understand how the process works. I suppose it's like never wanting to eat sausage again, once you know how it's made."

Rose chuckled under her breath. "That's a terrible analogy."

Peg clearly didn't think so. Rose tried again. Being supportive was definitely easier when the subject was more compliant.

"Everyone says you have a very nice colt. They all expect you to do well with him. And they're the experts, right? So maybe you should just try to relax and enjoy watching it happen."

"Martin Shrady is supposed to be an expert too. And look what he's been up to. I'd hate to be in Zara King's shoes and have no idea what's going on behind my back."

"Which, luckily, you're not—because you're much too

savvy a person to allow that to happen." Rose stood up. "If we're not going to eat, then let's head over to Keeneland. I can grab something in the café, and you can go check on your colt. I'm sure you'll feel better once you're there keeping a close eye on everything."

For once, Peg elected to leave Hope behind in the hotel room. The Poodle could nap in comfort there, rather than having to traipse all over the Keeneland grounds on what promised to be a hectic and pressure-filled day. Peg made sure the water bowl was full and left a DO NOT DISTURB sign on the door. Hope didn't appear to mind taking a day off. She was already making herself a nest on the bed when Peg locked the door behind her.

"Don't look so glum," Rose said as they walked toward the minivan. "We'll be back in a few hours."

"I know. But I'll miss her in the meantime." Peg unlocked the doors, then peered over at Rose. "Is that your stomach rumbling?"

"I told you I was hungry." Rose slid onto the passenger seat. "You just weren't paying attention."

"Pish. I heard what you said. I just have bigger problems to worry about."

This time they were able to find a parking place near the sales pavilion. Rose went off in search of food, while Peg headed straight to barn 31.

The auction was due to start in a few minutes. As she cut through the sales building, Peg could hear an auctioneer reading the presale announcements from the podium. Many of the briefings cautioned potential buyers about the risk of purchasing a horse at auction. Peg hoped Zara King was listening for future reference.

Business was booming at the Six Oaks barn. Even from a distance, Peg could see that all the walking rings were full, and all the showmen and grooms were hard at work.

Multiple buyers were taking last looks at the consignment's offerings. By the end of the day, all these yearlings would have gone through the sales ring. With luck, most of them would find new homes.

As usual, Bryce was on duty. He gave Peg a wave of acknowledgment as she slipped through the gate into the courtyard. Then he turned to Walter who was standing near the barn and pointed in Peg's direction. Walter quickly put down the three-ring binder he was holding and came striding over.

In contrast to the sea of Six Oaks-branded polo shirts around him, Walter was dressed in a sports jacket and tie. His hair, thinning on top, was carefully combed to cover a freckled bald spot. He smiled at Peg as he approached.

"Today's the big day, Peg," he said, holding out his hand for her to shake. "Are you excited?"

"A little," she replied. "But more than that, I suppose I'm apprehensive."

"Then let me assuage your fears." Walter gestured toward the bench and they both sat down. "I know these sales can seem scary if you're not used to them. It probably feels like everything's moving a million miles an hour?"

"Something like that," Peg said with a nod. Walter had a dulcet voice and a soothing manner. Both attributes had to be a huge asset in his job.

"I can assure you that you have nothing to worry about. Your colt has been popular and had plenty of vetting. So this is the point where you can begin to relax. My job is to make sure everything goes smoothly today. If you want, I can walk you through what will happen from this point on."

"Thank you. I'd appreciate it." Walter had a wonderful way of inspiring confidence. Peg was beginning to feel better already.

He explained that her colt would go through the sales

ring at approximately twelve-thirty. "That's a good time. Middle of the day. Everyone's here. Plenty of people in the pavilion looking for lunch."

"Lunch," Peg echoed faintly. Food was still the last thing on her mind.

"Around half an hour before the colt is due to sell, one of our handlers will take him down to the back walking ring behind the sales pavilion. I'll already be there, with all his information, in case buyers have any last-minute questions. After he circles that ring enough times to give interested parties a good look at him, he'll go inside the pavilion to await his turn in the sales ring. Many sellers prefer to sit in the gallery and wait for their horses there. But you can follow along and watch each of these other steps if you prefer. "

Peg nodded again. She'd make that decision later.

"Now, everything I've just told you is already set up to happen," Walter said in a measured tone. "You don't have to worry about any of that. The only thing you need to do between now and then is make a decision about your reserve. You know how that works, right?"

"Yes," Peg replied. "And I have a number in mind. But I'd like to hear your input too."

After five minutes of discussion, they settled on a number that suited both of them. It was high enough to be agreeable to Walter, who wanted to ensure that the bidding started in a lively manner. And it was low enough to suit Peg, who told Walter that despite what he might have heard from Ben Burrell, Lucky Luna's colt was at the sale to sell.

"How will the auctioneer know what my reserve is?" Peg asked at the end.

"When the horse gets to the back walking ring, I'll go inside to the office and tell them," Walter said. "But before I do that, you and I will revisit this discussion. Because something could happen in the next two hours that might cause you to change your mind."

"Something like what?" Peg asked curiously.

"An additional scope would be the most likely thing. That might give us another buyer to count on."

"Another bidder is always good. But I'm not going to change my number. I've heard about some of the games that are played at these sales, and I have no intention of taking part in any of them."

"Games?"

Walter looked confused. Peg wasn't buying it. She knew there was no way he didn't understand what she meant.

"Yes, games," she said firmly. "Like the ones Martin Shrady is playing with his partnership."

Walter straightened in his seat. His folksy manner disappeared. "Let me be entirely clear. My job is to ensure you receive the best possible advice on how to navigate this sales experience. I am not—and would not be—'playing games' with you. You've had horses at Six Oaks for several years. I'd like to think we've retained your business because you've been satisfied with both the quality of our horsemanship, and with our results at the sales."

"That's true—" Peg began, but Walter was still speaking.

"Furthermore, placing a reserve on a horse before it goes through the ring isn't gamesmanship. It's the way business is done and it's all totally aboveboard. I have no idea what Martin Shrady might have told you. He is, of course, a client of the farm. But that doesn't make us responsible for the things he says and does."

Peg swallowed a sigh. Walter had been doing his best to be helpful. And while she'd intended to advocate for herself, she hadn't meant to insult him. Now she either needed to apologize, or to explain why she'd said what she had. Peg chose the latter option.

"Would you feel differently if I told you that Martin may be implicated in Jim Grable's death?" she asked.

Walter looked shocked. He opened his mouth as if he meant to say something. Then he closed it again without uttering a word.

"It's true," Peg told him.

"How would you know that?"

"My partner and I were asked to look into what happened." Peg decided she was better off leaving those details as vague as possible. "And certain things came to light about the relationship between Martin and Grable."

"Things like what?" Walter's voice was tight.

"Were you aware that Grable liked to gamble on the horses and that he'd run up some rather large debts?"

Walter shrugged. Apparently that wasn't news.

"One of the people he owed money to was Martin Shrady, a man who has problems of his own."

"Martin always seems to have problems," Walter muttered. "He's not someone I would choose to do business with."

"And yet, as you just pointed out, he's a client of your farm."

That earned Peg a small head shake. As though Walter was distancing himself from a problem that wasn't of his making.

"Last November, Martin used a large sum of Zara King's money to buy a pinhook prospect with a throat problem. It was more than she wanted to spend, but Martin did two things to convince her. He neglected to tell her about the bad throat, and he assured her that the colt would be a star at this sale."

"Snow Cloud." Walter frowned.

"Correct. And as this sale drew near, Martin became the one with the problem. He couldn't admit to Zara that he'd lied, so he came up with another solution. He found a way to keep the colt out of the sale."

Walter looked up. "The stone bruise was an accident."

"No," said Peg. "It wasn't."

Walter's shoulders stiffened. He swore vehemently under his breath. Peg understood. She'd felt the same way when she found out. A full minute passed before he spoke again.

"Are you telling me that Jim was responsible for that?"

"Yes. It was how he repaid his debt to Martin."

Walter swore again. For an accountant he had a rather colorful vocabulary.

"You really didn't know about any of this?" Peg asked when he finally ran out of steam.

"Of course not!"

"It took place on your farm." She was tempted to add *right under your nose*, but maybe that would be rubbing it in. "Perhaps now you can understand why I've decided that the Thoroughbred industry is a perilous place for newcomers. Like I said, I'm not looking to play any games."

"Nor am I." Walter was still angry, though his ire didn't appear to be directed at Peg. "These things you're telling me about what went on between Jim and Martin are in no way indicative of how Six Oaks Farm does business. You're sure of your facts?"

"Quite sure," Peg replied.

Walter shot to his feet. "There are people I need to see." He started to turn away, then abruptly looked back. "I'll be at the back walking ring before your colt goes up. Please believe me, you're in good hands. You have absolutely nothing to worry about on that score."

Peg watched him walk away. Before Walter had gone ten feet, he already had his phone out and pressed to his ear. She hadn't begun their conversation intending to reveal any of that, but her big mouth had gotten the better of her.

Peg hoped she hadn't made a huge mistake.

Chapter 28

"I feel much better now," Rose said. She was seated at a table in the Limestone Café with an empty breakfast plate in front of her. She'd just started her second cup of coffee.

Peg slipped into a chair opposite. She'd picked up a mug of tea on her way to the table. Multiple monitors in the room were broadcasting the sale. Plus the auction ring itself was near enough that over the babble of conversation in the café, they could hear the action happening live.

"Good for you," Peg said. "I feel worse."

Rose looked at her across the table. "Maybe you should eat something."

"No, that's not it. I just had a long conversation with Walter Tausky, Six Oaks' COO and director of sales."

"That's good though, right?" Rose looked confused. "I thought you needed to check with someone from Six Oaks about the details of your colt's upcoming sale."

"I did. But what I didn't need to do was blurt out everything we've learned about Martin and his partners, and what went on between him and Jim Grable."

"Oh." Rose considered that. "How did Walter take the news?"

"Angrily."

"I'd be mad, too, in his position, if stuff like that was happening at my farm and I had no idea."

Peg frowned. "He asked if I was sure of what I'd told him."

"I assume you said yes." Rose had never known Peg to be unsure about anything.

"I did. But now I'm having second thoughts. What if Nico wasn't telling us the truth? What if I repeated a horrible accusation about Martin Shrady and it was a lie?"

"What makes you think Nico would lie to us?" Rose asked curiously.

Peg gave her a look. "I shouldn't have to point this out, but considering the circumstances, *somebody* is lying to us."

"Well, sure." Rose would concede that. "But why him?"

"Maybe Nico told us that story to deflect attention away from himself. Or because he thought it would keep him out of trouble." Peg took a sip of tea. It was hot enough to scald her tongue.

Rose wasn't impressed by that logic. "He'd already admitted to helping Jim pilfer stuff from Six Oaks. If the other information was deflecting, it was too little, too late. And Abel's reaction when we told him about it also lends credibility to what Nico said."

"I suppose you're right." Peg relaxed slightly. "I guess I feel a little better."

"It's a start," Rose said. "What would make you feel a lot better?"

"Is that a serious question?"

"Yes. And here's another one. Why are you talking as though you have marbles in your mouth?"

"I burned the tip of my tongue," Peg said. She stuck it out so Rose could see.

"Oh, for Pete's sake." Rose did not want to look at Peg's tongue. Or anyone's tongue, for that matter. She braced both hands on the table, stood up, and left.

Two minutes later, Rose was back. She was holding a baggie filled with ice. "Put this on it. The cold will make it feel better."

"Thank you." Peg did as she was told. "Where did you get ice? And a baggie?"

Rose gestured toward the adjoining room. "From the bar."

"There's a bar open at this hour?" Peg asked. It was morning. Late morning, but still.

"As far as I can tell about Kentucky, there's a bar open at every hour. Now, what's the next thing you need?"

"I want my part of this to be over." Peg waved a hand in the direction of the auction that was happening across the way. "I want my colt to be sold to a wonderful home, so I can stop worrying about the sale and go back to just worrying about who killed Jim Grable."

"Sorry. I'm afraid I can't help you with that."

"Too bad." Peg sighed. "For an old lady, you've turned out to be unexpectedly good at solving problems."

"That's because I'm getting plenty of practice," Rose told her. "For an old lady, you're unexpectedly good at causing them."

Two hours later, Peg got her wish. Lucky Luna's colt went through the Keeneland sales ring and was hammered down for a price that was high enough to pay her equine bills for the year. Peg had a nodding acquaintance with the people who'd purchased him, so she knew he would be in good hands. Mission accomplished on both fronts.

Ben Burrell, who'd turned up in time to watch the proceedings, took Peg and Rose to the bar afterward for a celebratory drink. "To the breeder of a lovely colt," he said, holding his glass of bourbon aloft.

"And to a job well done," Peg replied, doing the same.

She wasn't at all sure Lucky Luna would still be residing at Six Oaks Farm after everything was said and done, but that was a conversation for another time. Right now, she was just pleased to have put one problem behind her. Plus, the bourbon was doing a stellar job of making her tongue feel better.

Ben gulped down his drink with unseemly haste, then hurried away to shepherd his next client through the sales process. Peg and Rose were left standing at the bar by themselves.

Peg wondered if there was something slightly sad about the optics of that: two older women hanging out together, elbows resting on the shiny counter, tumblers in both their hands as though they made a habit of day-drinking. Even the bartender must have felt sorry for them. She brought them an extra large bag of still-warm popcorn, on the house.

"Better now?" Rose inquired. The bourbon had burned its way down her throat and lit a warm fire in her stomach. She was feeling pleasantly light-headed. Peter would probably raise his eyebrows if he could see her. The thought made Rose giggle.

"Much," Peg said. "What's so funny?"

"Us. Standing here, sipping bourbon, like it's something we do every day. I suddenly feel very out of place."

Peg smiled. She was often struck by how restrained much of Rose's life had been. "It's just one shot. If you don't want to finish it, you can pass it over to me."

"No way." Rose cupped her hands around the glass protectively.

"Suit yourself." Peg was feeling pretty mellow herself. "I'm going to stroll up to the barn to say goodbye to my colt and see if there are any loose ends that need to be tied up. Then we can head back to the hotel and pick up Hope."

"Sounds good," Rose said. "I'll meet you at the minivan in twenty minutes."

Peg had exited the pavilion and started up the hill toward the Six Oaks barn when someone fell into step beside her. Martin Shrady. He was tall enough to look her in the eye, and his face wore an irate scowl.

"You have no idea how much you annoy me," he said.

"Oh?" Peg played dumb. "What did I do?"

"You make this look easy."

"I . . . What?" She hadn't expected that answer. "I don't understand."

"This. All of it." Martin waved his arm in the air. The gesture appeared meant to encompass the sales pavilion, the barns, and even the racetrack. "Breeding good Thoroughbreds is hard. Selling them for what they're worth is even harder. I should know. It's what I do for a living."

Peg nodded and kept walking. She was ready for the conversation to be over. But Martin wasn't finished yet.

"Then along comes someone like you, with a single mare that manages to get in foal every year, and deliver a healthy colt that you can sell for real money. The rest of us are here every day, solving problems, working against the odds, and busting our butts to try to break even, while you meander in from Connecticut once a year and make it look effortless. Which it isn't."

"I'm aware of that," Peg said. "I've been very lucky." And luckier still that Martin apparently didn't have any idea what Peg had told Walter about him.

"Beginner's luck," Martin muttered almost to himself. "I've been doing this for nearly thirty years. Where's my luck?"

Peg assumed that was a rhetorical question. "I'm sorry your Snow Cloud colt missed the sale," she said.

His head swung her way. "You heard about that?"

"Yes. I also heard what happened to him."

"Damn stone bruise." Martin frowned. "See what I mean about luck? Lately it feels as though all of mine has been bad."

The path they were on was a busy thoroughfare. Numerous people were traveling in both directions between the barns and the pavilion. The fact that they were nearly surrounded emboldened Peg to say what was on her mind.

"Except it wasn't luck that kept your colt from making it to the sale. Or a stone bruise."

Abruptly Martin stopped walking. "What do you mean?"

"Exactly what I said." Peg halted too. "I know how your colt got injured. I also know that Jim Grable was responsible, and that you're the person who put him up to it."

Martin wheeled around to face her. The look in his eyes was chilling. "I have no idea where you came up with an idea like that," he ground out. "But you are absolutely wrong."

Peg held her ground and remained calm in the face of his anger. "If you like, I can explain why Snow Cloud needed to be kept from the sale. I can also enumerate the reasons why your partnership with Leo and Zara is in deep trouble. But frankly, since you already know all that, I'd rather skip ahead and ask whether, after Grable had done your bidding, you killed him to cover it up."

"Now you're just acting crazy." Martin's outburst caused heads to turn and look at them. He didn't appear to notice.

"I can assure you, I'm not," Peg said mildly. "I am, however, very well informed."

Martin grabbed her arm. He pulled her out of the flow of foot traffic. They still weren't alone by any means. But now they could speak with a modicum of privacy.

"What do you want from me?" he demanded.

"The truth," Peg retorted, though she wasn't sure she'd trust anything he told her.

"All right." Martin scrubbed his hands over his face. "All right. Listen."

Peg remained mute. Clearly she was listening.

"Maybe I did pull a few strings to keep the Snow Cloud colt out of the sale. But I had nothing to do with what happened to Jim after that. *Nothing.* Understand?"

Of course Peg understood. Believing was another matter.

"You'll have to try harder than that to convince me," she said. "I know Grable owed you money. I'm guessing you owed that money to someone else."

"Sure, Jim owed me money," Martin said under his breath. "But after Snow Cloud, we were square. Besides, Jim owed just about everybody. Half the yearling barn was trying to collect from him. Sergio, Ricky, and Manny—who's still in hock to me for a deal on a weanling we did last year. Bastard keeps telling me he's short on cash. Yeah, well, aren't we all? Do you have any idea what this partnership with Leo and Zara is costing me?"

"None whatsoever. And I don't want to know," Peg said firmly. Besides, that was Zara's money Martin had been spending, not his own.

"Good," Martin huffed. "Because I wasn't about to tell you. I'm just saying that we've all got bills to pay. And when one person stops holding up his end, everyone down the line suffers. And right now, everyone that Jim was in debt to is suffering."

"Except you," Peg pointed out. "Because, as you just told me, he settled your debt right before he died."

Martin's eyes narrowed. He stared at Peg with a look of pure malice.

"That's slander," he said. "You'd better not repeat it to anyone."

Or what? Peg wondered. She wasn't about to ask.

Martin leaned in close to make sure she didn't miss a word. "All you need to know is that I didn't kill Jim Grable. I disliked the man intensely, but I had no reason to want him dead."

"If you didn't," Peg said, "who did?"

Martin didn't answer. Instead, he just shook his head, spun around, and stalked away.

Chapter 29

After a quick stop at barn 31, Peg was nearly back to the minivan when her phone rang. She didn't recognize the number, but she'd met many new people over the past few days, so she picked up.

"Is this Peg Turnbull?" a scratchy voice asked.

"Yes, it is." Peg knew that voice; she just couldn't quite place it.

"This here's Tammy Radnor. You know, at the farm?"

"Yes, I know who you are, Tammy. Is everything all right?"

"Not exactly," the woman replied. "That's why I'm calling. I'm thinking you should come over here."

Peg stopped walking. "Why? Is something wrong with Lucky Luna?"

"Your mare's okay. So's her baby. This is another thing. I don't want to talk about it on the phone. Do you want to meet me, or not?"

"Yes." Peg made a quick decision. "I do. Definitely."

Tammy cackled out a laugh. "Okay. Sounds like you're coming then. I'll be at the broodmare barn. Meet me there in twenty minutes."

The call disconnected. Peg looked up to see Rose watching her. It was a good thing Peg had already reached the minivan. They needed to leave right away. It would take at least twenty minutes just to get to Six Oaks.

"It sounds like we're not going back to the hotel," Rose said as she climbed up into the driver's seat.

"Not yet." Peg eyed the passenger side of the van unhappily. "We need to meet Tammy at Six Oaks and we don't have long to get there. So if you're going to drive, you'd better step on it."

"I can do that," Rose said.

In truth, she couldn't, and they both knew it. Rose's driving was cautious to the point of being near-moribund. She sighed, unfastened her seat belt, and got out of the minivan.

"Much better." Peg flexed her fingers as she slid behind the wheel. "Hang on. I'll fill you in on what you've missed on the way."

"I left you alone for barely any time at all," Rose said when Peg was finished speaking. "And you still managed to get into trouble."

"I didn't start it," Peg pointed out in her own defense. "That was Martin's doing."

"Starting the conversation was Martin's doing. Accusing him of killing Jim Grable was all you."

"Yes, and it worked. Because Martin admitted to everything Nico had told us."

"But not to killing Jim."

"No, not to that." Peg slid a glance across the front of the van. "Like Abel, Martin said Jim owed lots of people money. He mentioned a few of the guys whom we've met by name, including Manny and Sergio. Martin also said that Manny still owes him money from a horse deal a year ago."

"Sergio and Manny are both working at the sale," Rose mused. "That must increase their earning power."

"You would think. But money seems to flow through all

these guys' hands like water. It's as if everyone around here is in debt to someone—and just waiting for their next big score to set them right."

"That's a perilous way to live," Rose said. "But here's a question. Would you kill someone who owed you money?"

Peg considered that for a minute. "Not on purpose," she decided finally. "Because then I wouldn't get paid. But I could see it happening if someone was angry enough." The gates to Six Oaks were coming up. Peg slowed down and turned in. "Let's go see what Tammy has to tell us."

They found Tammy waiting for them outside the brood-mare barn. She was standing in the sun, watching the mares and foals graze in a nearby field. Hearing their approach, Tammy turned and shaded her eyes as she watched the minivan drive up and park.

She didn't come forward to greet them. Instead, she waited in place for Peg and Rose to get out and come to her. Tammy's long gray braid was hanging forward over her shoulder. She flipped it back, then crossed her arms over her chest. The expression on her face was grim.

Rose glanced over at Peg, who shook her head slightly. This wasn't the welcome either of them had been expecting.

"I hope we didn't keep you waiting," Peg said.

"Nope. I had to be here anyway. It's my job."

Rose tried out a smile. It wasn't reciprocated. "You told Peg you wanted to talk to us?"

"Yeah." Tammy nodded. "Mostly to Peg. But it's okay that you're here too. Let's go inside the barn. More comfortable in there."

It was a beautiful day. The temperature was warm, but not hot. A light breeze ruffled their hair. It was hard to see why they'd be more comfortable inside. But Tammy was already walking away, assuming that Rose and Peg would follow. Which they dutifully did.

Lucky Luna's shedrow barn was right in front of them.

Tammy led them past it to a smaller barn off to one side. This one had a wide center aisle with a row of stalls on each side. The barn's double front doors were partially open. Its back doors were closed, throwing the interior space into gloomy shadow.

"For the weanlings," Tammy said, before Peg could ask. All the deeply bedded stalls were unoccupied now. Presumably their inhabitants were turned out somewhere. "Come on this way."

Rose hesitated. She'd never been inside a barn before, and she saw no reason to change that now. "Where are we going?"

"Somewhere we can talk in private." Tammy waved a hand impatiently.

Peg and Rose shared a look, then followed again. Once they were out of the sun, the air became much cooler. Rose shivered as they entered the darkened building. A cross-beamed ceiling rose high above them. She wondered if there were bats up there.

Everything around them was quiet and still. The empty stalls gave the place a deserted air. This was Tammy's home turf, but the unfamiliar surroundings made Rose uncomfortable. Here, she felt like an interloper who didn't belong.

Peg must have been thinking the same thing because she took two more steps, then planted her feet. "That's far enough. Whatever you have to tell us, you can do it here."

Tammy finally stopped. She turned to face them. "I heard your colt sold well earlier," she said to Peg.

"He did. I was very pleased."

"Good. Now that your business is done here, it's time for the two of you to go home."

"We're not finished," Rose said. "I made a promise to Lucia that I'd do my best to help her, and I intend to keep my word."

Tammy scowled. "That girl was foolish to ever get you

involved in the first place. What went on here is none of your business. This is Kentucky. We take care of our own."

"That's not what it sounded like to me," Peg said. "Who was looking out for Lucia when Jim Grable was harassing her?"

Tammy aimed a hard stare her way. "In the end, Jim got what he deserved, didn't he?"

Peg refused to back down. "Is that your way of telling us that you were responsible for his death?"

"Hell no," Tammy spat out. "But don't think I didn't consider it more than once over the years. You think Lucia was the first girl Jim hit on? Not even close. I wish I'd had the guts to brain that jackass with a hammer a long time ago."

Rose gulped. No one ever stood up to Peg like that. Now both women were glaring at each other. They looked like they were about to come to blows.

Peg had the size advantage, but Tammy was every bit as tough as the horses she took care of. Rose hoped she wasn't going to have to step between them, because there was no way that would end well.

"The fact that everyone knew Jim Grable was an awful man doesn't help Lucia," she said in a level voice. "Officer Sherlock still considers her the chief suspect in his death."

"Well, he's wrong," Tammy snapped.

"If you have proof of that, you should give it to him," Peg shot right back. "And if you don't have proof, then you need to get out of our way. Rose and I already have some of the answers we need, and we're close to figuring out the rest."

In a sudden flash of inspiration, Peg realized what she'd overlooked earlier. There were numerous employees on the farm who were in need of the money Jim owed them. But only one of them had good reason to be desperate. Because only one was in debt to someone else who was also frantic to be repaid.

Martin had told Peg that Manny still owed him money—and that was the key. Martin was a man whose financial situation was dire. A man so determined to protect his reputation that he'd stoop to laming a horse rather than admit that he was in over his head. If Martin had been willing to go that far to hold together his partnership, how much more pressure might he have brought to bear on Manny, who'd been in debt to him for a year?

"Peg? Are you all right?"

Roused abruptly from her thoughts, Peg realized that Rose was staring at her oddly. Tammy looked similarly perplexed. Peg didn't care. Because she finally knew who was to blame for Jim Grable's death.

"Listen," she said, grabbing Rose's arm. "There were so many things happening at once that we allowed ourselves to be distracted by all the background noise. But in the end, it was simple. Jim didn't die because of sexual harassment, or petty theft, or even the terrible thing he did to the Snow Cloud colt. He died because—"

Peg flinched as a hinge suddenly screeched. A door in the darkened wall beside them drew open, and Manny stepped out to join them. Dressed in dark jeans and his Six Oaks shirt, he blended seamlessly into the shadows. He glanced at Peg and Rose only briefly before his gaze landed on Tammy.

"I told you this wasn't going to work," Manny growled. "These two are too stubborn for their own good. They're not going to stop until someone makes them stop."

Peg saw Rose's eyes widen. She'd managed to figure things out, but there'd been no time to clue Rose in. There was nothing Peg could do about that now. Rose was a step behind, but she'd have to catch up quickly.

Peg had to admit that Manny didn't make the most obvious suspect. He'd been quietly in the background of most of their equine encounters since they'd arrived in Kentucky. Manny was polite and personable, always quick with a smile or a nod. He handled the young horses, even the fractious ones, with an air of unruffled finesse.

But none of those admirable attributes were evident in the person standing before them now. Manny wasn't smiling. His hands were curled into fists at his sides. His agitation was apparent in the way he was bouncing up and down on the balls of his feet.

"I thought you were at the sale," Peg said, keeping her tone affable. Manny looked ready to pounce. De-escalation seemed like a very good idea.

"I was," he replied. "And I will be again. After."

"After what?" Rose heard the wobble in her voice. She hoped no one else did.

"After I'm sure we understand each other."

"Go ahead," Peg invited calmly. "Tell us what we need to know."

Rose never understood how Peg managed to remain so calm when everything was going sideways around them. What she did know, however, was how to use Peg's equanimity to her advantage. It only took a single step for Rose to slip behind the much taller woman. Half-hidden, she slid her phone out of her pocket, then tapped the screen twice. Now it was set to record. Quickly she tucked the device away.

"Jim's death was an accident," Manny stated.

"I'm afraid the evidence doesn't support that," Peg said.

"No one has been found responsible," he insisted. "And no one will."

"Again, I disagree. The police *will* arrest someone because that's what they need to do. If they're unable to figure out who the true guilty party is, they'll arrest Lucia for the crime."

"Lucia didn't kill Jim," Manny said.

"I'm aware of that." Peg glanced at Rose who was edging out from behind her. "I know who did murder him."

"It wasn't murder. It was an accident."

Peg nodded, encouraging him to keep talking. "Tell me what happened."

Manny shook his head, then grimaced, as though even the memory of the event hurt. "Jim owed me. He kept promising to pay up, but he never did. He just kept putting me off."

"Jim was using his position as your boss to take advantage of you," Rose said.

"Yes," Manny agreed readily. "But I needed that money. Bad."

"Because Martin was pressuring you to pay back the money you owed him." Peg helped the story along.

Rose glanced over in surprise. She'd heard about that earlier, but clearly she hadn't yet connected the dots. Peg couldn't pause to explain. Instead, she kept her gaze trained on Manny. Now that he was talking, she couldn't afford to let him stop.

"Martin." Manny blew out a frustrated breath. "He's good at making promises too. And like Jim, not so good at delivering. Martin and I bought a weanling together. He said he could use his connections to turn it over quickly in a private sale. But that didn't happen, and then the bills started adding up. Board, vet, farrier, it was always something."

"In my generation, we refer to a man like Martin as a smooth talker," Peg told him.

A ghost of a smile played across Manny's face. "That's exactly it. That guy'll say anything to make a sale. I should have known better than to listen. He let the money ride for a while, but not anymore. This new partnership is sucking him dry. Martin didn't care how I got the money. He said I had to pay. Or else."

Peg almost smiled herself. That threat had a familiar ring.

"Or else what?" Rose asked in the silence that followed. Seriously? Was she the only one who was curious what the warning meant?

"Martin said if I didn't pay up, he'd see that I lost my job here, and then ensure that no other farm would hire me. I knew he meant it too. Martin has connections everywhere. He could make it happen with a couple of phone calls."

"When you heard that, you must have gone to Jim and demanded he pay you what he owed," Peg prompted.

"Of course I did." Manny's eyes flashed angrily. "What choice did I have? I have a good job at Six Oaks. I need the money I make here. *My family* needs the money I make here. Jim had to give me what was mine."

"But Jim didn't care about any of that," Tammy said. It was several minutes since she'd spoken, but she'd been listening. "That was Jim all over. If there was something he didn't want to do, he'd just dig in his heels and smile because he knew there was nothing you could do to make him. I can't count the number of times I wanted to wipe that stupid grin off that man's face."

"We got into an argument," Manny said. "Yelling, maybe a little shoving. Both of us lost our tempers. I guess I took a swing at him. I just wanted to teach him a lesson, you know? Jim just laughed at me. Then he turned his back and walked away."

Peg could picture the scene. Manny's slim, wiry physique would have been no match for Jim's brawny strength. Jim had held the upper hand in every way that mattered. He wouldn't have felt threatened by Manny. It wasn't bad enough that he'd refused to honor his debt, Jim had also humiliated Manny in the process.

"There was a hammer sitting on a ledge nearby," Manny

said. "I must have picked it up because next thing I knew, it was in my hand. I never meant to hurt Jim. I only wanted to threaten him. I just wanted my money back."

He opened his mouth and let out a soft wail. "I never meant for Jim to die. All I want is for none of this to have ever happened. I just want everything to go back the way it was."

Chapter 30

For a minute, nobody said a thing. Manny's confession, and the emotion with which he'd uttered the words, had shocked them all into silence.

Then Rose turned to Tammy. She still had questions. "How do you fit into this?"

"I'm just here to help out. Manny wasn't sure you'd come if he called. Or that you'd listen to what he had to say. Manny's a good guy and y'all know what I think of Jim. Manny didn't deserve for any of this to happen."

Yes and no, Rose thought. Manny might be a victim too, but he was far from blameless in this scenario. He'd gambled—both on the races and the deal with Martin—with money he couldn't afford to lose. And, intentionally or not, Jim had died because of his actions.

"So you had nothing to do with Jim's death?"

"Nope. I wasn't even around when it happened. Like you, I just heard about it later."

"So, like us," Peg said to Tammy, "you don't know whether the story Manny told us is true or not."

Manny looked up. He'd been scrubbing his face with the hem of his shirt, and his eyes were still rimmed with red. "It's true. Why would I tell you that if it wasn't?"

"Because you want us to believe Jim's death was an accident. Because you want us to do what Tammy suggested earlier: Go home and forget about what happened here."

"Yes," he said. "It's time for both of you to leave Kentucky."

Privately, Peg agreed with him. But she wasn't going to lie about what she and Rose would need to do in the meantime. She glanced at Rose to see if she was thinking the same thing. For some reason the woman was looking down at her phone. Peg wondered what that was about. Surely this conversation was more important than anything she could see there.

"We're leaving soon," she said to Manny. "But before we do, Rose and I are going to have to tell Officer Sherlock what you've told us."

"No," he replied firmly. "That's not going to happen."

"Yes, it is." Rose looked up to agree with Peg. "There's nothing you can do to stop us."

The corner of Manny's mouth lifted in a sneer. "That's where you're wrong. Because I've seen the way you interact with your horses. I know how you feel about them. Now consider the fact that their safety depends on the goodwill of the workers at this farm. Horses get hurt all the time. Perhaps you're already aware of how easily accidents can happen?"

"Manny!" Tammy gasped, horrified. "You don't mean that."

"I wish I didn't, but I have no choice. I have to look out for myself and my family." He leveled a hard stare at Peg. "If you ever tell anyone what you know, I'll make sure you're very sorry you ever got involved."

Peg swallowed heavily. Rose grabbed her hand and squeezed it. Now what? Once they left the farm, there'd be no way to ensure that Manny didn't carry out his threat. Peg considered their options. Maybe she should call Officer Sherlock right now—

The thought vanished as Peg caught a sudden movement out of the corner of her eye. It was Tammy and she didn't look happy.

"What the hell's the matter with you?" the woman yelled as she smacked Manny on the back of his head with the flat of her hand. Peg and Rose both heard the sound of a hollow thunk. "Are you crazy?"

"Oww!" Manny howled and ducked away. "I thought you were going to help me. What did you do that for?"

Tammy rounded on him, her hands fisted on her hips. "Because my helping you doesn't extend to listening to you threaten to harm any animal on this farm. You're in enough trouble already! Saying stuff like that only makes things worse. Now you sit down and shut up."

Tammy gave Manny a hard shove. He went stumbling backward, and the backs of his knees connected with a bale of straw sitting outside a stall. When his legs folded beneath him, Manny sat down gracelessly on top of it.

"Stay there," she said sternly, pointing a finger in his face, "while these ladies and I figure out what we're going to do."

Unexpectedly Peg found herself biting back a laugh.

"Thank you." Rose looked dumbfounded. "I think?"

"You're welcome," Tammy snapped. Then she turned to Peg. "Rose told me you have experience in this sort of thing. So what do we do next?"

Rose would have answered "pray," so it was a good thing Tammy hadn't asked for her opinion. Hopefully Peg would have a better idea.

"Our experience has been with catching criminals, not with what comes after that," Peg said. "But it seems to me that the first thing Manny needs to do is get himself a lawyer. Then the two of them should go to the police station so Manny can turn himself in."

"That sounds like a terrible idea," Manny muttered.

"No." Peg turned to face him. "The terrible idea was

picking up that hammer and using it on Jim. I'm not going to mince words, Manny. You're in a lot of trouble. But a good lawyer can probably find mitigating circumstances. Or make a case that what happened was an accident. Given the disparity between your size and Jim's, maybe you acted in self-defense."

"Yeah, that's true." He brightened briefly, then his head dropped again. "Who am I kidding? I don't have any money to hire a lawyer."

"You leave that to me," Tammy said. "We'll figure something out. There probably isn't a single person on the farm who isn't happy to see Jim gone. I bet lots of them would chip in something. And I don't want to hear another word about you doing something stupid to Peg's horses."

"No, ma'am," Manny mumbled.

Rose knew she shouldn't feel sorry for him. Nevertheless, she did. "You have until tomorrow morning to do what Peg advised," she said.

He glanced up. "Then what happens?"

Peg and Tammy both looked like they were wondering too.

"Peg and I are heading home. But before we leave town, we'll stop at the police station." Rose held up her phone. "Everything you said earlier? It's all on here. If Officer Sherlock has already heard your side of the story, we won't say a thing. If not, I'll play the recording for him and you'll be in even bigger trouble than you are now."

"Don't you worry about that," Tammy growled. "Manny's going to step up and do what he needs to. I'll make sure of it."

"Don't let us down," Peg said, and Rose nodded.

Tammy held up her hand and spit on her palm. Then she offered it to Peg to shake. Peg hesitated for a moment. Then she spit too. The two women clasped hands firmly and shook on it.

"What the heck?" Manny said.

"That's a spit shake," Tammy told him. "It means neither one of us can break our word. So don't you even think about making a liar out of me."

"No, ma'am," Manny said again, looking chastened.

"Don't ask me how right now, but you're going to get through this. Understand?"

When Manny nodded, Tammy lifted her gaze back to Peg and Rose. "All right. You can go now. I'm going to get to work on finding Manny a lawyer. Could be Walter can help out with that."

"Walter Tausky?" Peg asked, surprised.

"Yup," Tammy confirmed. "Or Cousin Walter as we call him in the family. He's got more education than anyone else I know. Probably some pretty good connections too. I'll put him to work on Manny's behalf."

"Will he be willing to help?" Rose asked.

"Willing?" Tammy cackled. "I don't intend to ask about that. I'll start by calling his mama. After I get done talking to her, he won't have a choice."

Peg smiled. "Tammy, you're a woman after my own heart."

"You know it," Tammy agreed. "And the same goes for both of you. Unless you're an idiot, you don't get to be our age without learning how to take care of business. So you ladies can head on home. You've done all you can do here."

Peg and Rose walked out of the shadowy barn, leaving Manny and Tammy behind. It felt good to step outside into the brightly lit yard.

Rose hadn't realized how close she'd been to shivering until the afternoon sun infused her body with warmth and she felt her shoulders relax. Rose walked straight to the minivan and climbed into the passenger seat. For once, she was happy to let Peg drive.

"Do you think Tammy will keep her word?" she asked, once they were on their way.

"After a spit shake?" Peg chuckled under her breath. "I hope so. Tammy seemed determined to do the right thing. I doubt she'd start dragging family members into this unless she was serious."

"*Cousin Walter,*" Rose said with a smirk. "I thought the notion that everyone in Kentucky was related to everyone else was a joke."

"Well apparently, the joke's on us. Which turns out to be a good thing." Peg looked over at Rose. "Were you telling the truth back there? Did you really record what Manny said?"

"I think so. I tried to, anyway. But the phone was in my pocket for most of the time, so I don't know how clear the recording will be. It may be too garbled to understand. I'm hoping we don't have to use it."

"Me, too." They'd reached the iron gates at the farm's entrance. Peg slowed the minivan, waiting for them to open.

"What do you think are the chances Manny will turn himself in?" Rose asked.

Peg considered before replying. "Left to his own devices, probably no better than fifty-fifty. But with Tammy's support, I'd say his odds improve dramatically. And if she succeeds in getting Walter on board—and from what we know of Tammy, I suspect she will—I think we can feel reasonably safe in anticipating a good outcome."

Rose leaned her head back against the seat and closed her eyes. All at once, she felt unbearably tired. "I guess we'll find out tomorrow," she said.

As things turned out, they didn't have to wait that long. Both Tammy and the Six Oaks Farm PR team must have been hard at work that afternoon. The early evening news made an oblique reference to Jim Grable's death, saying that new details had come to light from several people connected to the farm. The brief story finished by saying that the Versailles police had closed their investigation into the accident.

Peg and Rose had paused in their packing to listen to the report. They'd barely had time to absorb the information before there was a knock on Rose's door. When she went to answer it, Hope hopped off the bed and bounded across the room to go with her. Hope's tail was already wagging when Rose drew the door open to see Lucia standing outside.

She was dressed in the Six Oaks uniform and looked as though she'd had a long day. But a radiant smile lit up her face. "Did you hear the news?" she asked eagerly.

"We did, just now." Peg came around the corner from her room to join them. "Come in and sit down. Let's talk about it."

"I can't stay long." Lucia leaned down to give Hope a quick pat. "I've just come from Keeneland, and I'm on my way back to the farm. Things will be crazy busy everywhere until the sale ends. But Walter pulled me aside to tell me that someone had confessed to killing Jim. So it's finally over." She bounced happily in place. "That means I'm off the hook for good."

"I'm so pleased for you," Rose said. "That must be a big relief."

"*Huge,*" Lucia replied, looking back and forth between Rose and Peg. "Walter wouldn't say anything else about it. But I'm guessing that the two of you know a lot more. You do, don't you?"

"Maybe," Peg admitted. She didn't want to say anything that might impact plans Walter might be making on Manny's behalf.

"I knew it!" Lucia sounded jubilant. She looked at Rose. "I was sure this had to be your doing."

"Peg and I worked together," Rose said. "We both wanted to help you, and we're glad it worked out." Lucia would find out soon enough that it was one of her co-workers who'd been responsible for Jim's death. But Rose didn't need to break the news to her now.

"I can't thank you enough." Lucia stepped forward to wrap her arms around Rose's neck. Suddenly she looked as though she might be on the verge of tears. "I was in so much trouble. I didn't know what to do. Or which way to turn. And then you came along . . ." She paused for a heavy gulp. "This is a big deal to me. You've given me back my life."

Lucia released Rose and turned to Peg, who was standing there with her hands on her hips. "You don't look like the hugging type."

"I'm not. But in your case, I'll make an exception."

Peg held out her arms and Lucia walked into them. "Thank you for everything," she said softly. "I'll never forget what the two of you did for me."

"We were happy to be able to help," Rose said. She was feeling a little misty herself. "I'm glad you have nothing more to worry about."

"It might be even better than that." Lucia stepped back and split her gaze between them. "When I talked to Walter, he mentioned the opening in the yearling manager position. He thinks I should apply for the job. I mean, I'm not a shoo-in or anything, but maybe it could happen."

"You should definitely apply," Rose said. "I bet your chances are better than you think."

"As it happens, I'll be speaking with Walter myself in a week or two," Peg said. "If Six Oaks wants to retain my business, they'll need to do some work to rebuild my trust. I'll tell them they can start by strongly considering you for the position." She paused for a wicked grin. "Maybe that will light a fire under them."

"Let's hope." Lucia crossed her fingers and headed for the door.

"One more thing before you go," Rose said. "Maybe it didn't feel that way, but Tammy Radnor was always on your side. So you be sure to take good care of her. Tammy was a big help to us when it came to getting everything settled."

Lucia nodded solemnly. "I suspect you ladies didn't need much help, but I'll remember what you said. I appreciate your kindness, and hopefully I'll have the chance to pay it forward."

Lucia had just left when Peg's phone buzzed. She walked over to the bureau and picked it up. When she read the text that had come in, Peg had to laugh.

"What is it?" Rose asked.

Peg showed her the message. It was from Tammy. **All good here. Now go home.**

"I'll second that advice," Rose said.

Chapter 31

Early the next morning, they headed home. Peg let Rose drive for most of the way so she could stretch on the back seat with Hope in her lap, and her arms curled around the Poodle's neck. Considering how slowly the scenery outside the van was passing, Peg was just as happy not to be able to see the speedometer from where she sat.

They finally switched places for the last leg of the long journey. Even so, it was nearly midnight by the time Peg dropped Rose off in front of the compact, ranch-style home she and Peter shared in Stamford. All the house's outside lights were on. Most of the interior rooms were lit too.

Rose smiled when she saw that, pleased that Peter had waited up for her. She and Peg had only been gone a week, but it felt like much longer. Between the dog shows, the horse sale, and tracking down Jim's Grable's killer, they'd packed a lot into seven days.

But oh my, it felt good to be home.

Peter had the door open before Rose even reached the front steps. She dropped her suitcase on the stoop and went straight into her husband's arms. He gathered her close and held on.

That was all Rose needed. She rested her head against Peter's shoulder, closed her eyes, and sighed. Secure and cherished, she felt as though she could stay there forever.

Peter allowed her two minutes. Then he pulled back fractionally and said, "Good trip?"

"Busy trip," she murmured.

Peter chuckled. "Considering you were with Peg, I would expect nothing less. Did she sell her horse?"

"Ummm," Rose said.

"I'll take that as a yes. Did anything else interesting happen?"

Rose opened one eye. "Hope taught me how to talk Poodle. That was interesting."

"I'll bet." Peter sounded bemused by that information. "So . . . there wasn't any other excitement? No crooks to chase? No murders to solve?"

Of course he'd had to ask. Not that it was Peter's fault. Time spent with Peg aroused similar suspicions in everyone.

As Rose lifted her head to reply, Marmalade came strolling out onto the step. The kitten twined herself around their legs, as if she was binding them together. Rose liked that thought.

"About that . . ." she said.

"Really?" Peter looked as though he didn't know whether to laugh again or groan.

"I'm afraid so. You know Peg."

"Peg's not the only one I know. It appears you've learned how to stir up trouble too."

He had a point.

"Maybe I'm making up for lost time," Rose mused. "After all those quiet years in the convent, maybe this is my chance to go a little wild."

Wild, Peter thought. Not his Rose. Not in this lifetime. But he enjoyed the fact that she thought so.

He rested his chin on the top of her head. "I've missed you, Rose."

She felt her heart flutter. Her husband was so very dear to her. "I missed you too. Maybe we should go inside and celebrate."

"I like the sound of that." Peter stepped back and slid an arm around her waist. "What are we celebrating?"

Rose exhaled slowly. She realized she wanted to celebrate everything—from how lucky she was to have found this man, to how much she loved the life they were building together. It was more than she'd ever dared to hope for. But right this moment, that felt like too much to express all at once. So Rose went for something easier.

"Homecomings," she said.

Peg lived in a refurbished, hundred-year-old farmhouse on a quiet lane in backcountry Greenwich. No street lamps lit her way home, and her minivan was the only vehicle on the road. Peg kept a wary eye out for the deer and wild turkeys that were often active at night.

She was tired. Bone tired. Dog show trips didn't used to take this much out of her. Then again, this hadn't been just another dog show trip. In addition to the shows, she'd had the Keeneland sale and Lucia's plea for help to deal with. She and Rose had been busy nearly every minute of every day.

Now Peg couldn't wait to get home and fall asleep in her own bed. She was sure Hope felt the same way.

"You do, don't you?" Peg asked, glancing over.

For the short trip from Stamford, Hope was sitting up front in what Peg had come to think of as "Rose's seat." Now a canine sixth sense alerted her to the fact that the trip was almost over. Hope stood up and pressed her nose against the window. Her feet began to dance in place.

"That's what I thought," Peg replied to herself. Living with three rather chatty Poodles, she was accustomed to having to articulate both sides of a conversation. Her distinctive roofline with a chimney at each end came into view. "One more minute and we'll be home."

Peg had been in frequent contact with her dog sitter while she was away. The woman knew when Peg and

Hope were expected back. She'd left earlier in the evening, but there were lights on in the house. Peg could see her other two Standard Poodles, Coral and Joker, when their heads popped up in the front windows.

Both Poodles recognized the minivan. Both immediately began to bounce up and down. Hope gave a sharp bark. An answering symphony of howls came from within the house. Peg smiled at the sound. There was nothing better than an enthusiastic welcome.

She pulled into the garage, grabbed her suitcase, and ran around to let Hope out of the van. A short set of stairs led from the garage up to the main floor of the house. When Peg opened the door, Joker and Coral were on the landing above waiting for them.

Hope flew up the staircase in two graceful leaps. Peg was only a step behind. She dropped to the floor and opened her arms. The next five minutes were a frenzy of pink tongues, warm noses, and wagging tails.

"I know," Peg crooned. She pulled all three Poodles close, then hugged them to her and buried her face in their hair. "It was a long time for me to be gone. But I'm back now. And it's *so* good to see you."

Eventually Peg extricated herself from the canine scrum. Surrounded by a Poodle honor guard, she went to the kitchen and glanced at the note the dog sitter had left on the counter. Her dogs were fine. She'd worry about everything else in the morning.

While the Poodles went outside for a last run, Peg put on her pajamas and brushed her teeth. Then she called the trio back in, locked the door, and turned off the lights. The three dogs galloped ahead to her bedroom. By the time Peg got there, they'd already commandeered all the best spots on her queen-sized bed.

"Make room, you lot," she grumbled happily as she slid beneath the covers. "I've had a very long day."

Hope waited until Peg was comfortable, then inched closer until their bodies were aligned from head to hip. The Poodle's nose rested on Peg's shoulder. Her warm breath tickled Peg's neck.

Peg sighed contentedly. As far as she was concerned, life didn't get any better than this. She was home.

"That was quite a trip," Rose said, several days later. She and Peg were sitting across from each other at the butcher-block table in Peg's sunny kitchen.

The three Poodles were asleep on the floor around them. Peg was drinking Earl Grey tea. Rose had a cup of coffee. Both women had a wedge of mocha cake on a plate in front of them.

"Have you heard from anyone in Kentucky?" she asked. "Walter? Ben? Tammy?"

"Not a word. I'd imagine they're all trying to pretend that nothing ever happened."

"Like Las Vegas." Rose smirked. "What happens there, stays there."

"Precisely." Peg slipped a piece of cake into her mouth. "I plan to have a conversation with Walter eventually. Depending on how it goes, I may start researching new farms for Lucky Luna and her foal."

Rose nodded. She wasn't surprised.

"I might need to go back to Kentucky and check out a few places in person."

"Next time, fly," Rose advised. "You can go there and back in a single day."

"What?" Peg smiled. "You're not coming with me?"

"No, thank you. Once was enough for me. Still, though . . ."

"Yes?" Peg prompted.

"I enjoyed our trip. Even with everything that went wrong, we still had fun, didn't we?"

"We did."

"And I'm glad we were able to help Lucia. Face it, Peg. You and I make a good team."

"I never said we didn't," Peg huffed.

Rose's brow lifted. She reached into her pocket and pulled out her phone. "That's what you say now. Shall I play the recording that proves differently?"

"Pish." Peg eyed the device suspiciously. "There's nothing on there. You're bluffing, aren't you?"

Rose laughed and snatched away the phone before Peg could grab it. Then she helped herself to another piece of cake.

"I'll never tell," she said.